The
UNEXPECTED
CHAMPION

Books by Mary Connealy

From Bethany House Publishers

THE KINCAID BRIDES
Out of Control
In Too Deep
Over the Edge

TROUBLE IN TEXAS
Swept Away
Fired Up
Stuck Together

WILD AT HEART
Tried and True
Now and Forever
Fire and Ice

THE CIMARRON LEGACY
No Way Up
Long Time Gone
Too Far Down

HIGH SIERRA SWEETHEARTS
The Accidental Guardian
The Reluctant Warrior
The Unexpected Champion

The Boden Birthright: A CIMARRON LEGACY *Novella*
Meeting Her Match: A MATCH MADE IN TEXAS *Novella*
Runaway Bride: A KINCAID BRIDES *and* TROUBLE IN
TEXAS *Novella* (With This Ring? *Collection*)
The Tangled Ties That Bind: A KINCAID BRIDES *No-
vella* (Hearts Entwined *Collection*)

The
UNEXPECTED
CHAMPION

MARY
CONNEALY

BETHANYHOUSE
a division of Baker Publishing Group
Minneapolis, Minnesota

© 2019 by Mary Connealy

Published by Bethany House Publishers
11400 Hampshire Avenue South
Bloomington, Minnesota 55438
www.bethanyhouse.com

Bethany House Publishers is a division of
Baker Publishing Group, Grand Rapids, Michigan

Printed in the United States of America

Library of Congress Cataloging-in-Publication Data
Names: Connealy, Mary, author.
Title: The unexpected champion / Mary Connealy.
Description: Minneapolis, Minnesota : Bethany House Publishers, a division of
    Baker Publishing Group, [2019] | Series: High sierra sweethearts ; book 3
Identifiers: LCCN 2018034286 | ISBN 9780764219313 (trade paper) | ISBN
    9781493417209 (e-book) | ISBN 9780764233180 (cloth)
Subjects: | GSAFD: Christian fiction. | Love stories.
Classification: LCC PS3603.O544 U54 2019 | DDC 813/.6—dc23
LC record available at https://lccn.loc.gov/2018034286

Scripture quotations are from the King James Version of the Bible.

Cover design by Studio Gearbox
Cover photography by Steve Gardner, PixelWorks Studios, Inc.

Author is represented by Natasha Kern Literary Agency.

19 20 21 22 23 24 25   7 6 5 4 3 2 1

The Unexpected Champion
is dedicated to my unborn grandbaby.
I haven't met her yet,
but I already know she is beautiful
and smart and dearly loved.

CHAPTER

1

JUNE 1868

Dismal, Nevada—never had a town been named so right.

The sheriff's office and barbershop were in the same building because the sheriff and the barber were the same man. Penny Scott suspected the man made more money at his barbering.

"Trace has been in there a long time." Penny looked through a window, a small one built with an eye toward saving money on glass. She watched Trace Riley tell their story to the sheriff while the sheriff lathered up a man's face.

Trace was her brother's wife's sister's husband, but honestly they all lived fairly close. Going strictly by geography, she was claiming Trace as a brother.

"I don't know who's getting a shave." John McCall watched through the dirty window and ran his hand over his face as if wondering about going next in the barber's chair. He was a tidy man, a city slicker in a black suit and a flat-topped black Stetson. Dark blond hair and blue eyes.

"But it isn't right for the sheriff to question a witness in front of someone."

"You know the law?" Penny thought of all she didn't know about this man. It was high time he answered some questions.

She'd met him over Raddo's dead body.

Penny hadn't shot the outlaw, but she'd been running toward Raddo Landauer with her gun drawn, and she'd witnessed the whole thing. She felt the weight of being willing to kill a man.

Raddo had shot Cam and Penny's brother. Now he had three bullet holes in him.

Her brother Cam had pulled one trigger. Cam's wife, Gwen, had also shot him. Raddo was threatening to kill her and the two children.

And John McCall had supplied the third gunshot when he'd seen Raddo ready to shoot Gwen. The first time Penny had laid eyes on McCall, he'd been standing there with a smoking gun.

Trace had come along after the gun smoke had cleared, and he'd ridden to town with them because he knew the sheriff. He was the only one of the three of them who'd come to Dismal since the sheriff had arrived. And Trace believed Raddo had killed his pa years ago. Trace had brought in two men last fall to Carson City, one dead and both partners of Raddo. If Raddo had been alive, Trace would've taken him there, because Dismal's sheriff might not be up to housing prisoners. Unless there was a jail cell tucked in the back room of the barbershop. But with Raddo dead, none of them saw any reason to ride one mile farther than necessary.

John McCall, who'd told them he was a Pinkerton agent, had come as one of the shooters. Penny had come as a witness.

Gwen and Cam had stayed home because Gwen couldn't stop shaking, Cam was frantic to hold on to her, and the children were beside themselves.

Trace Riley was anxious to get back to his wife, Deb, who was Gwen's sister. He talked to the sheriff to vouch for the attacks on all of them all through the winter. Well, no attacks on John, as he'd shown up just today.

Trace came out of the barbershop and part-time sheriff's office. "Sheriff Walters has a lot of questions about what happened today. I told him you two could answer them." Trace hadn't really seen anything. He'd come galloping in like mad at the sound of gunfire.

Penny took a step toward the building, but then John caught her arm. "Let's wait until after the haircut."

"He's done with you, then?" Penny asked Trace.

"Yep, I'm heading back to your place." Bringing along a man the sheriff knew and trusted was a mighty good idea when a group rides into town with a man draped over a saddle, a man with three gunshot wounds and a whole passel of teeth marks from a wolf. "Sheriff Walters doesn't seem to be planning to lock any of us up, and he told me I could go if you'd stay."

"Be glad to," McCall said, not sounding all that glad. He probably didn't like shooting a man much. Penny sure hoped he didn't like it.

"I'll ride the body over to the undertaker. Then I'm heading out."

Trace went off with the body.

Penny looked at John McCall. "Let's go find a quiet place to talk."

McCall arched a brow but came along, as if the empty

dirt street of Dismal wasn't quiet enough right where they were standing.

Dismal had two strips of businesses that faced each other like a couple of gunfighters at high noon. The dirt main street was just wide enough for two buckboards to pass by going opposite directions. Probably fifteen buildings in all, one ramshackle store after another, bare wood, hand-painted signs if the owner was ambitious . . . and plenty weren't. Half of them stood empty. Some had space between them, while most shared a wall.

There were a few houses scattered here and there in the wide plain, set slap in the middle of mountains, woods, rocks, and a long stretch of wilderness.

There was wealth to be had a day's ride from here. In cattle, in timber cut from the dense forests, even in tourism because of the beauty of nearby Lake Tahoe. Add in the heavily traveled California Trail that ran along the north side of the lake and there was plenty of money to be made. There was also the Comstock Lode that'd turned hardworking miners into millionaires.

Yep, there was wealth to be had, but somehow Dismal managed to avoid it. Apparently, ambitious folks rode a day away and didn't come back.

Penny tapped her foot impatiently. She needed to get somewhere so she could yell in private. It would be easy to find a quiet spot. The whole town was a quiet spot. Of course, it wouldn't be quiet once she got there.

"I want to know exactly who you are, mister." Penny walked away fast from the sheriff's office. Just as well she put some space between her and the law. In case this came to fists. She didn't want the sheriff mad at her in the event she was within a few minutes of committing a crime. McCall struck her as the type not to go and punch a woman, so who knew how tough she might be able to get?

He kept up with no trouble. He was a long-legged galoot. Good enough looking, but she spent most of her life surrounded by men, so few of them impressed her much—especially when it came to looks. She'd learned long ago a pretty face didn't make up for a foul character. And how could this child-stealing varmint be anything but?

"Where'd you get the blamed fool notion you've got any right to my nephew?" Penny had to admit they'd been busy, yet why had no one demanded some answers?

She heard thundering hooves and turned to see Trace gallop off at top speed on his fleet-footed black stallion. He'd gotten shut of their prisoner, or what was left of him after he'd been chawed on by a wolf, then shot to death three times.

That left her alone with this low-down coyote.

Penny decided they'd come far enough. Past all but two empty storefronts at the far edge of town. She stopped between the last buildings and turned to face him, arms crossed.

"We're going to clear this up right now. You will never take my nephew."

"Your nephew is the grandson of the people who hired me to find him and bring him home. They have a solid claim on the boy."

"I know the Chiltons. I lived with Abe and Delia for two years, since before Ronnie was born. The Chiltons—"

A gun cocked with an ugly metallic click in the darkened alley between the stores. A second gun jacked a bullet into the barrel. A third. Penny whirled to face three masked gunmen.

The one in the center said, "Not a word out of either of you."

Penny gasped and stumbled back a step right into McCall. He slid an arm around her and pulled her back, getting one shoulder in front of her.

"Freeze." The middle outlaw extended his gun. "I only need one of you alive."

McCall stopped. Penny felt him tense with frustration that he hadn't put himself fully between her and those guns.

"We don't have much money," McCall said. "Take it all, we won't—"

"Shut up!" The gunman cut McCall off. The man was wearing a heavy coat, thin leather gloves. His face was covered with a red bandanna, with a hat pulled low over eyes that glowed black.

"I have questions, and if I get the answers I want, no harm will come to you. Don't fight me. I'll shoot one of you dead and wound the other. One is all I need to get my answers, and you'll talk better if you're bleedin'."

They stood frozen, waiting. Penny hoped for an opening to run or draw her gun and attack. She always carried her pistol in the bag she wore slung over her head and under her arm, dangling below her right hand. But it was her left side that McCall shielded. No possible chance to get her gun drawn in time to shoot three cold-eyed men.

"Ask your questions. We'll tell you whatever you want to know, just don't harm the woman." McCall the hero. He was lucky she was too cautious to move, or she'd've swatted him.

His voice was as smooth as water over a stone, too. Calm and cool. Like he'd had so many guns aimed at him that he didn't take much notice anymore.

The cool was fake, though. She felt his coiled muscles, knew he was looking for an opening. And, like her, he was well aware that these men weren't about to give them one.

"Walk toward the alley. Side by side, slow, and get outta the street."

No ideas sprang to her mind to save her and McCall, so when he stepped forward, she stayed with him.

The alley swallowed them up. The men, much closer now, wore different colored bandannas, different hats and coats, yet they were three of a kind.

When they were out of the line of sight of anyone on the street, one man said, "Turn around and put your hands behind your backs."

McCall turned first, and his eyes met hers, his jaw rigid. He glanced at the boardwalk just a step away from the alley entrance. He wanted her to make a run for it. He'd block her, and there could be no doubt these outlaws would shoot.

McCall was offering to die for her.

The big gallant idiot.

She stepped aside and took another pace forward out of blocking distance. She wasn't about to save herself at the cost of his life.

McCall glared, but there was more to it. His brow furrowed. Worry, maybe even grief. He didn't expect this to end well. And judging by the steady hands on those guns, and the short, clear demands, she knew they were dealing with a salty bunch.

Penny suspected he had the right of it, but even if she'd dove away and run, in this mostly deserted town with no witnesses at hand, these men would've grabbed her and dragged her back. Done their worst.

She wasn't going to let McCall die for her, but it'd be even worse if he died for nothing.

Turning, she put her hands behind her as they'd ordered. A man stepped up. Her hands were wrenched hard. The outlaw enjoyed causing pain. Her stomach twisted with fear from what might come next.

Penny was a woman who'd followed her brother into frontier forts. She'd seen every way evil could show itself in the Wild West. She knew just how ugly this could be.

A rope wound tight around her wrists, cutting into her flesh. A sideways glance showed another man doing the same to McCall.

Her brown eyes met McCall's. His were light blue, but right now they darkened, and she saw him thinking, planning, still coiled.

She stayed ready should a chance come to run or fight back.

Hard hands grabbed her shoulders and spun her around. A dull thud beside her drew her eyes over her shoulder. Before she could look for the source of that sound, she was hoisted over a man's shoulder, and the man strode toward the back of the alley.

Lifting her head as high as she could, she saw McCall collapsing to the ground. One of the outlaws holstered his gun, which he must've used as a club. As he grabbed McCall's feet, the other picked him up by the shoulders. They weren't men who were brave enough, or stupid enough, to trust mere ropes to hold a man as strong as McCall.

She was whipped around and tossed on her back in a wagon. The outlaw was quick to gag her, flip her onto her stomach, and tie her bound hands to the side of the wagon. The ropes were already cutting into her wrists, and now with her arms wrenched to the side, every moment made the pain worse.

John landed hard right beside her. Even though he was unconscious, he was gagged and secured by his bound hands just as she was.

Facedown in the wagon box, she couldn't see much. But then something big was thrown over her, blocking out the sun. A tarp or a large blanket. The wagon lurched forward. Hoofbeats fell in beside the wagon. Already at the edge of town, they were leaving it behind fast.

Their horses were hitched in front of the sheriff's office. How long before Sheriff Walters noticed? How long before someone even suspected that Penny and McCall had been very smoothly kidnapped? Trace had gone back to her brother Cam's house and would tell everyone that Penny would be a while coming. They might not even start to worry until dark, and by then these men could get themselves well hidden.

Three men, deadly aim, a few seconds' time. It worked so well that she knew they'd done it all before. She was now in the clutches of three very skilled kidnappers with no way to escape and not much hope they'd make a mistake that gave her a chance.

Except they'd made one. They'd left her bag draped over her neck. Her hands were tied so tightly that she didn't think she could reach her gun, not now. She'd try, but there was no room to even wiggle. Still, she'd be ready, watching and waiting.

And she'd be listening, too. Maybe she could figure out what in the world was going on.

CHAPTER
2

The creaking woke him.

John's head throbbed, his thoughts all muddled. One thing he did remember was not to move. Not so much as a twitch. Assessing danger before letting anyone know he was conscious was second nature to him, something learned in the war.

Because he was bouncing along and lying facedown on something hard, his brain moved slowly. It was dark. Was he inside something or had night fallen? He had no idea how much time had passed. It'd been midafternoon when Riley had ridden away and left him in Dismal with Miss Scott.

Penny Scott! Those men!

He snapped wide awake—and still didn't move. He figured out why he was addled. That low-down coyote in that alley had slammed his six-gun into John's head. Three men with their guns out and aimed. Impossible odds, except he'd given Miss Scott a chance, and she hadn't taken it.

Now his hands were tied and his mouth gagged. He was being driven along, probably tossed in the back of a wagon.

That was where the creaking came from. He could hear the wheels rumbling along.

The man who'd taken them said he had questions. Which reminded John he was supposed to answer the sheriff's questions. Had Sheriff Walters missed them? Was he searching?

John worked the gag out of his mouth. It was hard to move, and he didn't want to draw attention to himself, but he had to know about Miss Scott. She was a feisty little thing and none too happy about John coming for her nephew. She wore trousers, and—of all the scandalous things—she had even worn them to town. Snapping brown eyes and brown hair streaked with glitters of sunlight and streaks of cinnamon in two dangling braids that seemed to shout that she considered tending her hair a nuisance. There was little feminine about her manner. Even so, she was pretty enough. It was hard to see under the Stetson and the scowl, but John had noticed.

Though she was an odd character, that didn't stop his protective instincts from roaring to life. Why hadn't she run when he'd given her the chance?

The bad part was, he knew why. He'd offered to shield her from a bullet, and she'd declined to let him die for her. He respected that, but at the same time it made him half-crazed with worry. Where was she? What might men like these do to a woman? What might they have done already while he'd lain here uselessly?

Fighting to keep his breathing even, as if he were still out cold, he listened for her but heard nothing, sensed nothing. Maybe she lay unconscious right beside him. He eased his right foot to the side and felt the edge of the wagon box. He moved his hands a bit and could tell they were bound to the wagon, wrenched sideways and bound painfully tight. He ached in his wrists, elbows, and shoulders. Not to mention his head.

Inching to his left, hoping the men who'd kidnapped them weren't watching too closely, he pressed against something solid but soft.

"McCall?" Her voice was more a breath than a sound. Wherever the three men were, at least one of them was driving this wagon, which meant an outlaw was only a few feet away from them.

"Shhh . . . yes." And that was all they said. But he felt her ease against him, shoulder to shoulder.

The way she moved close told him she was afraid, and yet the rigid muscles of her arm said she was ready to fight. Since he was both of those things too, he could only respect her for it.

As they rode on, John became aware of more details. He heard the clopping hooves of two horses pulling the wagon. The occasional slap of the reins sounded like the driver was sitting centered just past and a couple of feet higher than John's head, which meant the other two men were somewhere else.

Listening, he located both of them riding along on the left side of the wagon, up close to the driver.

Time went on. Suddenly he woke up, and that was the first he realized he'd passed out again. No idea for how long a time. The pain in his head was less, still there but not so overwhelming.

A man's voice had stirred him.

"That went smooth." One of the riders said it. He made no attempt to whisper, and that meant no one was around. They hadn't driven to another town, then.

"Yep, it was like pickin' off a pair of three-legged elk. They never stood a chance."

John ignored the insult and waited, straining to listen. Miss Scott was right against him, her right shoulder against his left. He nudged her, and she made a move that told him she knew he was awake again.

Nothing more passed between them, though he could sense Miss Scott listening to their captors as closely as he was. Any information they learned might be the one detail that saved their lives. John heard the wind blowing past and decided from the clean, steady sound of it, and the scent of dust overlaying the wood of the wagon bed and the musty smell of the tarp, that they weren't in the forest.

He felt warmer on the left-hand side. Sunlight. He had no idea how long he'd been unconscious or how far they'd gone. Considering that the day was wearing down before they'd left Dismal, that meant they were headed north with the sun low in the sky to the west. Dismal was a rugged town and a long distance from anywhere.

Heading north led to Carson City, and beyond that the little town of Ringo, and on past that, Virginia City and the Comstock Lode. John had learned the lay of the land while he waited for the trail to open this spring. He'd spent a long time traveling to get to little Ronnie Scott, to fetch him home to his grandparents. A good chunk of that time he'd been stranded in Virginia City.

Carson City was the state's capital. There was law there. If that was where they were headed, help would be close at hand, and John might find a chance to get them to safety.

The heat of the sun lessened. They'd entered a stretch that blocked the sun, which probably meant it was wooded.

Something scratched the edge of the wagon as they rolled on. Was it a branch? Were they on a narrow trail? The branches scraped again, on both sides this time.

The hoofbeats to the left of the wagon were gone. The trail must be too tight for them to ride abreast.

The scratching stopped for a few paces, and then the wagon creaked to a halt. As much as John wanted this ride to be over, because he saw no way to escape until it was, now that they'd stopped, his stomach twisted with dread as he considered the danger they faced.

John risked a few more words to Miss Scott. "I'm knocked out."

He felt her head rest against his shoulder, and she nodded.

He waited. Thanks to his years as a Pinkerton agent, and his service during the Civil War, he knew too much. He knew just how cruel people could be to one another. He'd heard someone once call it "man's inhumanity to man," and it was the pure truth.

And these outlaws seemed like the type to do their worst.

The blanket was thrown off.

Penny saw the deep woods and dusky sunlight filtering through oak and pine.

Rough hands grabbed her, untied her hands from the wagon edge but left her bound, and dragged her out. Her face scraped along the wood, because with her hands bound she couldn't protect herself. They stood her up. She fought for balance and stumbled until she hit the end of the wagon box. She wobbled, but she remained upright. They were in a clearing, surrounded by forest. Scrub pines and weeds pushed up between rocks.

John was thrown out of the wagon and hit the ground. He landed hard, and his head bounced. If he hadn't been playing possum, they might've let him stand. Now she had to wonder if he was faking unconsciousness, or if he was really knocked out . . . again. He'd come around in the wagon, then blacked out and come awake. She saw blood dried on the back of his head and gritted her teeth to keep from crying out in dismay at the ugly wound.

"Make sure the man's out," a man whispered from nearby. Out of sight in the woods somewhere.

The man nearest her grabbed John's hair and lifted his head. Blood trickled from a cut above one eyebrow. It bled freely, not like the blackened blood on the back of his head, so it was probably new.

He had been knocked out. His neck was completely limp, and she didn't see even a twitch of his eyes. Bright flowing crimson was the only color in his ashen face. No man could pretend this well.

The man dropped John's head, and it hit hard again. He didn't even groan.

"Cover her eyes," Whisper Man said.

One of the men whipped out his kerchief and blindfolded her. Despite this dire mess, Penny felt a surge of hope.

The men in the alley had worn masks, and they still did. Now there was a fourth man, and he didn't want to be seen, either. It was a sign that they might be planning to let them go.

She flexed her wrists as she'd done many times on the drive here. She'd found just a bit of room. If her hands were free, if she could rip off the blindfold and grab the pistol from her bag—they'd never searched it—she might beat them. She had a six-shooter—six bullets and only four men. Unlike before, she didn't have a gun pointed right at her head, or at least she hadn't before the kerchief had gone on, and why would they start pointing now?

The men had no way of knowing how fast she was or how accurate. She just needed a chance.

"Saw you bring Raddo in." Whisper Man startled her.

She'd wondered if the Chiltons were involved, but Raddo? He'd had partners last fall, but since those two men had gone—one by a bullet, one to jail—there'd been no sign of anyone helping him.

"Yes." She needed to think. What was this man's purpose? What might she say that would give him whatever he needed? She'd spent a lot of time with tough men, and some mighty tough women at those forts, too. And she knew about hiding weakness, hiding hurt and suspicion and even happiness. She'd never played it, but Cam, her brother, had told her she'd make a heck of a poker player.

She had to be very careful to give Whisper Man no notion she knew his identity, and so far that was simple because it was true.

Still whispering, the newcomer asked, "What did he say before he died?"

"Nothing. He came in shooting, we shot back."

Silence stretched between them.

"Did your man here talk to him?"

"No, the same as me, we heard gunfire and came running. We opened up as soon as we had a shot." Her voice trembled, and she let it. Let the man think she was a fragile little woman, upset over a shooting. In truth, she was upset. As that thought swept through her, she trembled harder, and her throat closed. She'd use all this emotion to distract the man from more questions.

"No one talked to him?" Whisper Man asked. "He left nothing behind?"

Penny fell silent, trying to think what to say. Someone shoved her hard. She cried out in pain as she staggered into the sharp tailgate of the wagon, and she nearly fell.

"No, I'm not refusing to talk. I'm just trying to think. He didn't even have a horse, not that we saw. No saddlebags, nothing in his pockets." She had a vision of that tattoo. What had it said? *Luth.* She remembered that. Something about . . . a jewel?

She swept her mind back to fear and admitted nothing. While the blindfold covered much of her face, she did her best to show no expression, even one they couldn't see.

"We never spoke to him." She wanted to demand to know why, but maybe she already knew. This man who was so careful to keep himself a secret might just think Raddo had mentioned him.

Instead, she said, "P-Please don't hurt us." Her voice broke, and that was all phony. Penny wasn't a woman to cry when she was in trouble. She was a lot more likely to make a fist or grab a gun.

She sure hoped she didn't have to conjure any tears.

"Sit her in the wagon box for a spell," Whisper Man snapped. "I don't like her answers, and I may need to ask my questions a little harder. We'll see what her man has to say when he wakes up—a little pain for his woman might make him talk."

Someone grabbed her with two hands on her waist and threw her into the wagon. She landed on her back. Her hands, twisted as they were from being bound behind her, scraped and made her back arch, and her head hit with a crack. She cried out in pain, something she'd've normally bit back, but not for these coyotes. She wanted them to think of her as helpless. And sure not as a woman who had a gun hidden in the leather bag draped around her neck and shoulder.

"He's out," Whisper Man said. "She's tied up. We need to make some plans." She heard footsteps walking away, crackling on twigs and rustling over last fall's leaves.

She rolled to the side, doing her best to get the pressure off her arms and back. The sound of retreating footsteps sounded like four men. The three who'd kidnapped her and Whisper Man.

Silence made her hope she was alone.

Struggling with the blindfold, she rubbed the side of her face against the rough wagon floor, then stopped. Maybe she didn't want to see anyone? It went against the grain not to fight, not to try and loosen her bonds and regain her sight.

But maybe, by letting them be in control, she had a chance to live. It didn't suit her at all. This might be her only chance to get away. But how would she carry off an unconscious man? She couldn't escape and leave McCall behind.

Because her nature was too strong, she scraped off the blindfold, then fought to free her hands. She began enlarging the wiggle room she'd spent the whole drive working on.

As she worked, she prayed.

She had a mighty God. And she'd never needed Him more than right now.

CHAPTER

3

John got his hands free and peeked over the edge of the wagon just as Penny sat up, untied, gun in her hand. Their eyes met, then hers slid to his bleeding forehead and all the color drained from her face. She must really be upset about this. He didn't have time to calm her down, so he lifted her out of the wagon.

He didn't mean to be heroic, he just wanted quiet.

He set her on her feet, grabbed her hand, and they slipped into the woods in the opposite direction of where he'd seen those outlaws step out of sight.

No doubt so that the whispering fool could talk out loud. Well, they had just badly underestimated their prisoners.

John led the way, moving fast. Miss Scott was absolutely silent. John was doing his best and his best was decent, but if he hadn't held her hand, he would have glanced back to see if she was there.

Every second counted. Every step they took put space between them and the kidnappers. John hadn't passed out when he was on the ground, so he had a glimpse of the fourth man's legs, and he suspected that alone would buy him a death sentence.

Miss Scott tugged on his hand. He looked back to see her pointing for some reason. She changed to leading and went off at a right angle from the way they'd been going. He couldn't yell at her, nor get in a wrestling match about who went first, so he followed instead. It took him five minutes before he realized they were on a trail.

It was so thin it only became a trail when a man added a powerful imagination. Overgrown with grass, with branches stretched clean across it. It must've been a trail for a mighty short deer, because limbs slapped at them down to about knee-high.

Mainly imitating Miss Scott, he did his best to stay low, every slapping limb making a sound. He watched for twigs and carefully didn't kick any stones that could go tumbling.

Minutes passed, not enough of them, and a shout sounded from the wagon. They'd been discovered missing.

Every survival instinct John owned came roaring to life. Miss Scott kept up the same pace, though he noticed she had her gun out again. He wanted to take over leading and run like mad. But she didn't even speed up. If anything, she was more silent . . . except what was more silent than silent?

John didn't think there were footprints visible on this grassy trail. At least not to his eye, and he'd had a little experience with tracking in the war.

Not a lot, but enough . . . he hoped.

He noticed that dusk was settling in. Good. Better to hide in the dark.

They moved on. John wasn't even sure which direction

they were headed. On and on they went, dodging limbs, fighting for silence.

The trail twisted and curved. It went up, then around, then back down again. John had no idea where they were. He thought they'd come north from Dismal, but he wasn't at all sure.

A gun fired behind them. John kept moving.

"Found our trail," Miss Scott hissed, sounding furious.

The gunshot was an alert. The men had split up, and now one man was telling them all to come running.

"Gunshot's a ways off. We've gained some space." She was breathing hard, yet her pace didn't slacken. John didn't know how long he could keep running—he'd never tested himself. But a gunman on your trail would push you past all your limits.

A very female squeak from ahead was his only warning. Miss Scott vanished. John had no chance to stop. He went over the gully edge, tumbling, sliding, trying to protect his head from further injury. For a second he fell clean, no contact with the earth at all, and then he hit an outcropping.

He caught sight of Miss Scott below, saw her skidding along, then suddenly she was on her feet and running, almost straight down . . . well no, but a real sharp descent. Still, better than what they'd been falling down. John gathered himself for the instant he reached the slightly less steep section. Sure enough, he hit it and went head over heels. His head was already wounded, and he felt every bump. Then he struck a large root jutting out of the slope. It stopped him with the force of hitting a brick wall. For a second.

But that second let him get his balance and he lost hold of the root, this time with his feet under him. Going at full speed was stupid and reckless, but he saw no way to stop and honestly no point. They had to be making a racket, and those men would be coming soon.

But maybe the men behind them wouldn't risk jumping over a cliff.

And that was the last coherent thought John could muster. He ran like he had a grizzly on his tail. Below, he saw the woods thicken. The slope was finally ending. He braced himself to slam into an oncoming tree. He missed the first one, and the land leveled. He dodged three more trees and forced his speed down until a low branch hit him like a clothesline against the face.

His feet flipped forward while his body stayed behind. He landed on the dirt with a thud that knocked a grunt out of him.

He seemed to be alive still. He jumped to his feet, thinking to find Miss Scott, just in time to be slugged in the stomach. He tried to see the men—they must be here. They must be attacking.

Then he noticed it, lying at his feet. A pistol. If he wasn't mistaken, it was Miss Scott's pistol. She'd lost it, and it'd gotten behind her somehow . . . and went straight into his belly. He picked it up, then saw her.

She'd lost her hat too, and her braids were unbound. A quick look behind him showed no hat for her, but his wasn't too far off and would be visible from the top of the cliff, so he grabbed it. He didn't want to leave a trail so clear. He saw nothing else, and she was on her feet and moving. He walked after her.

They'd taken his pistol but not his holster, so he put her gun away and turned to find Miss Scott rushing into the woods.

She looked back. Took such a long look at his face that he wondered what she was staring at. Then she saw the gun and visibly relaxed.

Shaking her head as if to clear her muddled thoughts, she said, "Keep moving."

Turning, she vanished into the woods. He had to admit she was right. This was no time to rest. He went after her, hoping they got out of sight and the dust settled before those men came.

<hr />

"I'm not waiting one second longer." Cam Scott slapped his leg and launched himself toward the door.

Cam grabbed his hat off a peg in his raw, floorless cabin. He snarled over his shoulder at Trace Riley, "I can't believe you just rode off and left my sister with a stranger!"

Everyone at the table started talking at once. Cam's wife, Gwen, with two youngsters. Deb, Trace's wife and Gwen's sister. Adam and Utah, Trace's hired men. They'd all come over to Cam's house to help him build his cabin and had been waiting for Penny to return ever since.

"He's a Pinkerton agent." Trace was out the door on Cam's heels.

"You left Penny based on nothing but the word of a stranger who'd already shot someone right in front of my eyes."

"He shot Raddo, and so did you, and so did Gwen. That makes him our friend." Trace was right behind him.

Utah came fast.

Trace yelled, "Adam, stay and guard the place. Hide Raddo's horse and bury his saddlebags. I don't want anyone who comes looking for Raddo or that horse and money to see it unless we're all here."

They'd had to backtrail Raddo to find his stakeout. But McCall had pointed out where he'd first seen Raddo slinking along. Raddo's behavior had drawn the detective's notice and gotten him involved. Cam'd found a fine animal and saddlebags loaded with enough gold coins to make Raddo a rich man. And he'd struck none of them as rich.

A mystery.

One Cam didn't have time to solve right now. He looked down at a fistful of gold coins and wondered about them. They were twenty-dollar double eagles, and he hadn't seen many of them in his life. They were heavy and stamped with a picture of the head of the Statue of Liberty. He'd passed them around, and Utah'd seen them before, but no one else had. And sure not a stack of them like this.

"Cam, take my horse. He's fastest," Adam hollered after them.

"Thanks," Cam called back to Adam, then added, "Hey, if a gunslinging stranger comes along, just go right ahead and hand over Deb to him. I'd as soon my wife not leave, but he can have Trace's."

"I told you he had paper work," Trace snapped. "Add to that, I rode the whole way there with him. He's an honest man, I'd swear to it. A city slicker, though. I wouldn't've left him there, but I figured Penny could get him home. And the sheriff is a slow-talkin' man. He was fixing to keep us there for a long spell, and I'd already told my part three times. I knew about Raddo chasing after us, but I wasn't even there when he was shot. I was all out of things to say. I wanted to get back here and get to work. You'd have left her, too."

Cam didn't answer that because he didn't want to admit Trace might be right. John McCall had been here for a spell after Raddo was shot, and Cam had never for a minute considered the man wasn't who he said he was.

Cam had taken only a passing notice of Trace coming home alone. They'd talked about it, and Cam had trusted that Penny would come along in an hour. When the hour stretched to two, Cam started glancing up from where he was building on Penny's cabin. He'd picked a spot to work where he could see all down the trail. They'd been gathered for afternoon coffee when the third hour passed and Cam snapped.

"I can't believe I've been dawdling all this time. If I could reach it, I'd kick my own backside." Cam broke into a run for the corral.

Trace said, "I'm sure he's not the cause of whatever trouble they're in."

"So, you admit they're in trouble?" Cam vaulted over the poles of the corral fence, grabbed a lasso, and dropped a loop over Adam's horse. He was saddling it almost before the rope tightened around the horse's neck.

"They'd be here by now if they weren't." Trace sounded grim as he slapped leather on his black stallion.

Utah was a step behind, but he was better at just about everything than the rest of them, so he rode out on the trail toward Dismal at the same time they did.

Deb, Gwen, and the children stood at the door, all of them looking worried.

"I don't like things upsetting Gwen, Trace. Considering Raddo tried to kill her today, she offered her life to save the children, and she ended up shooting him, I'd say she's had more than enough. And now here I am riding off and leaving her."

"But you're not leaving her alone. Adam's a top hand."

"No, not alone, but I'm sure not there to protect her. Just like I wasn't there to protect my sister." Cam slammed the side of his fist into the pommel of his saddle, then kicked the horse into a trot and led the way down the wooded trail. They came out into the broad valley where Cam had claimed a homestead, then turned and, three abreast, set out galloping toward town, hours away on a fast horse.

Adam's horse was the fastest critter Cam had ever seen. Utah's was plenty fast too, and Trace's wild-born mustang was one speedy animal. While they couldn't run at top speed the whole way, all three men were riding horses with plenty of stamina.

"I'm not waiting for you." Cam didn't even spur the horse. Instead he bent low over its neck and pressed with his knees. The horse knew he was asking for speed and gave it to him. This beast surely loved to run.

He left Trace and Utah in the dust and tormented himself with thoughts of just how lost one woman could get in a wilderness this vast.

⁘⸙⸙⁘

Another trail popped up in front of her, this one even smaller than the one up at the top of the cliff. She took it.

Finally it felt safe to talk. The woods closed around them. No openings, not even overhead, where they could be visible by the men if they found that cliff.

"Falling over a cliff was the luckiest thing that could've happened to us."

A strange noise from behind swung her around to see that McCall had walked into a tree branch. "It was not. I can name ten things luckier than that."

He was a mess. Maybe they'd come upon some water and he could wash some of the blood off of him.

"Now we're ahead. And we came on this trail headed downhill."

"We're walking uphill and sideways as much as downhill."

The man really should just listen. He was no hand at wilderness travel. "It's mostly downhill, I can tell. Especially that cliff—that was a big ol' step down."

"Can't argue with you there."

"And you found my gun. I appreciate it. I'll take it back as soon as we find a place to hole up. I'd better recheck the load. A fall like that might shake things up. But there's no time for that now."

"I've got an Army Colt like this one. I checked the shots and repacked a couple of them while I've been walking. It's ready to fire."

Well, the man knew guns at least. Still, she wanted to check it herself. "Let's hope we don't need it, but if we do, I've got my bag. It near to strangled me a couple of times when we went over the cliff. I'm glad I didn't lose it. I've got bullets and powder to reload."

"The only reason we'd need to reload is if we get in a shootout. Let's try and avoid that."

"This is our chance to plan." Penny kept her eyes sharp. "I want to find water."

"You're thirsty?"

Penny skidded to a stop and turned to face him. "I wasn't until you mentioned it. Anyhow, that's not why I want a stream." She started off again. "A stream will run through the lowlands between mountains. I'm hoping we find one and can follow it up or downstream, keepin' our feet in the water. That'll put an end to our trail."

"And then?" McCall sounded funny. Almost like he wished he were leading. Except of course he had no idea where to go. Neither did she, but she knew terrain. She could read signs as well as her brother Cam, better honestly, but she didn't like reminding him of that. It pinched his manly feelings. As it probably would with McCall. And she didn't want any manly feelings to add up to stupid.

"We're almost out of daylight," she said. "I don't want to chance walking in the dark if I don't have to. We'd have to inch along. We might walk right off another cliff that makes the last one seem like a wide and well-traveled road."

"So, find water, then walk to quit leaving tracks, then a hideout before dark, then what?"

"Then what? As if that's not enough to do in the last half hour of dusk. Wait, do you hear that?"

"Water. It's a trickle, but it's close."

"Yep." Her relief was huge. "When we do all we need to do before dark, and it's plenty considering dark is almost upon us, we need to figure out where in the world we are and how to get back home."

She considered herself an optimist, but honestly sometimes it was exhausting to be so blasted chipper.

"I was hoping," McCall said, "somehow you kept track, or were you knocked out, too?"

"No, they spared me that." It made her feel like she'd failed, like he was branding her a greenhorn for not being able to see through a tarp. Since she knew better, she ignored it, yet it wasn't that easy. "But under that tarp for hours, I wasn't even sure which direction we were going for a long while after we left town."

"North, I think." The mostly unconscious man she'd been riding with had an opinion. "I felt heat on my left. Sunlight."

"I reckon you're right, but while you were knocked cold as a snowcapped mountain, we didn't go straight in one direction. Nope, no idea in the world, and these mountains are a mighty big place. I'm not worried about it, much. I can live off the land, hunt, and find trails traveled by men, maybe a town."

She thought of Trace Riley, who'd been stranded out here as a half-grown boy. He'd been so lost he couldn't find a town. Penny didn't think that'd happen to her, though the trees blocked her vision of all but a few jagged peaks. The sun was mostly set, but there was enough of it that she knew which way was west. As those peaks loomed high overhead, almost laughing down at her, she admitted—privately—to having some doubts.

Honestly she thought of herself as a woman who always looked at the bright side, but right now it was taking all her gumption to do so.

Where were they? Where had they been driven? If she could find the stream and wade along it for a few miles, pick the right spot to step out, then there'd be no trail left to follow.

And then she'd figure out where they were.

The water poured out of a stone ahead of them. Not a stream but more like a spring that fell one hundred feet or so. John came up beside her, and together they gazed down over the gushing water.

"Yep, if we can just figure out how to get about one hundred feet straight down, we'll be set."

Miss Scott punched him in the shoulder. He didn't even blame her.

"We can get a drink at least." John needed it badly. He cupped water in his hands and drank deeply. It was so cold it made his teeth hurt, but it felt good going down. "I wish we had a canteen."

"While you're at it, wish for a couple of horses, and why not wish for a cavalry unit and to be flown on angel wings right back to Cam's place?"

The woman had a practical bent and apparently an inability to keep her mouth shut.

"That way." She pointed straight into what looked like

an impenetrable forest. So far, she'd done a real poor job of leading them on this little trek in the woods, considering the cliff, but walking in water to cover their tracks was an idea with merit. Maybe they should find a way to get down there.

She seemed to be beating her way through the woods this time. No trail. Not even a pathetic, mostly invisible one. He hadn't appreciated those before now.

Crawling over felled trees, shoving through brambles of undergrowth, every step took time and effort. Then she dropped about a foot. He grabbed her and dragged her back.

She turned, still firmly in his clutches, and arched a brow. "What are you doing?"

"I'm saving you from falling over another cliff."

Miss Scott gave one shoulder a bit of a shrug, followed by a tilt of her head. "Thank you. I do appreciate that. But I wasn't falling. There are rocks here almost wide enough to look like a stairway. We can get down to where this water joins that stream."

She pointed down. He came forward so they were side by side and saw it. A steep, rough little stretch, but with good layers of rock jutting out like an unfriendly staircase. "Are you sure we should go down there? This is like a crack in the earth." He looked into the dark hole. Though it wasn't actually a hole, not really. It was wide enough that he could see a sizable stream. Other springs trickled and cascaded here and there to make the water into a true creek.

"That stream down there is flowing to somewhere. I think we can follow it, at least for a while. Let me go."

He hadn't really noticed he was still hanging on to her. He released his grip, and she turned and went on down.

Calling softly after her, John said, "I'm torn between following right on your heels in case you need me to grab you again, or hanging back. I might fall off this stairway of yours and sweep you right off the mountainside."

"Go ahead and wait." She said it almost as if she didn't trust him not to fall. That was just plain insulting . . . even if there was a smidgen of truth to it.

He waited a few moments, then down he went. She was right—it was honestly the simplest traveling of this whole misadventure. No cliff. No invisible trail. No tarp. No whack on the head.

They made short work of descending into the huge crack in the earth, and when they got down it was perfect—except night had truly fallen in the shadowed canyon. A stream about twenty paces wide glistened and tumbled. It was flanked by flat, sandy banks, and walls rose on both sides to a dizzying height.

The stream wasn't deep, and if it got deep, the shoreline was wide enough for them to walk on. Assuming the shoreline didn't vanish right about the same time this trickling creek turned fifty feet deep.

She reached the bottom and gave him one backward glance, as if to say she would come back and save him if necessary. Insulting again, but still, he appreciated that. It bolstered his spirits.

Before he reached the bottom, she set out walking right down the middle of the stream.

"Hold up." He wasn't bolstered enough to keep walking. "We've been busy running for our lives. But my head hurts. Let me bathe these lumps I've gathered and see if the wounds need bandaging." John drank his fill, then splashed water onto his face and scrubbed. Dried blood darkened his finger-tips. Gingerly, he touched a lump on the crown of his head that was the size of a chicken egg from where that low-down varmint hit him with the butt of his gun. Another smaller gash cut across his forehead above his right eye. He'd landed face-first. He'd been faking unconsciousness, and even if he hadn't been faking it, his hands tied behind his back would have prevented him from breaking his fall.

He regretted the new cut on his head, but he'd seen a bit while he lay there, and it might help them get even with the men who'd done this.

John washed again and again, and still his hands were blackened by blood and dirt. He started to feel a little sorry for Miss Scott. "I must look awful. It's a wonder you didn't run from me as fast as you did those bad men."

"You look better now." When she finished taking a drink of water, she pulled a kerchief off her neck, soaked it, and pressed it to the back of his head. "That's a bad bump."

"I noticed." He found his own kerchief in his back pocket and pressed it against his forehead with his left hand while he went on washing with his right.

"McCall," Miss Scott said, "I'm long past judging a man by anything but his character. You're a good-lookin' fella, though with a couple of wicked blows, you look pretty dread-ful. You've held up well in this mountain run we're on, but it doesn't change that you're here to kidnap a child."

John bent to bathe the blood out of his hair.

Miss Scott left off pressing the rag to the wicked lump on his head and wrung it out. "The reason I mention your looks is because I don't care a whit what you look like. What bothers me is you coming for my nephew."

"The boy's grandparents want to care for their orphaned grandchild. That doesn't make them bad people." Though John knew them more than a little, and what he knew wasn't encouraging.

"Those low-down Chiltons hated Abe and did everything in their power to make his life a misery. And they never said a kind word about their only grandson, Ronnie. So why did they send you out here to take him back to them? He's in better hands out here with Cam, and we're not going to stand by and let you kidnap him."

"It's not kidnapping to take a child home to his grandparents when his parents are dead. And it's not kidnapping to come right up to you and clearly state my intent. Kidnapping is what these outlaws did to us. Surely a woman so wise to the ways of the West can see the difference."

"The main difference is that one is a whack to the head, another to the heart. In the end, someone's still taken away against their will."

Since John had some misgivings of his own about taking little Ronnie, he decided not to pursue the point. He had even deeper misgivings about a lone man transporting a toddler across the country. He could just imagine the crying.

"If the Chiltons think they've got a claim on those children, then they need to talk to the law, talk to a judge, and do it right. Don't send a man out to grab him."

"They didn't send me for the children, they sent me for the child. They make no claim on your niece."

"You mean they heard the folks caring for two small children had died, and knowing there were two, they only showed interest in one?" Miss Scott's crankiness turned to fury. "Were you supposed to find a home for Maddie Sue? Or did they want you to just abandon a three-year-old girl in the wilderness with people they thought weren't fit to care for their grandson?"

John didn't answer because he could only remember the Chiltons' cold insistence that if he brought the girl back, she'd be his to deal with. They had no interest in her.

"You've got a decent character that I can see, judging by how you helped me escape those men, and by the way you offered your life to save mine. There's no finer thing. But you have to know this is wrong."

John straightened, and she pressed the cloth to his head again. Their eyes met. Shadowed by the night, her eyes caught starlight. Her skin was washed blue. Every feature on her face—her cheekbones, nose, brow, and those eyes and lips—were displayed in their sweet curves and fine bones.

With no hat and her hair tangled, she looked like a magical creature. Brave and smart. Beautiful as an angel, and mad as the devil. His eyes dropped to her lips. Full and pretty and sassy.

He'd never before been this close to a woman like Penny Scott. A woman in boots and trousers who knew the frontier, who truly was closer to an untamed creature than a civilized, proper woman.

How could a man not find her fascinating?

She didn't move, and he sure didn't tell her to.

It went on far too long before the cry of an owl, the whisper of the breeze, and the rustling of branches from far overhead broke the trance. He stepped away and her fingertips, cold from the cloth, slid down his face and his neck, then dropped to her side.

He cleared his throat and said quickly, "This plan to quit

leaving tracks made sense up on that trail, but down here, with these banks hanging high over our heads and the stream just beginning from springs out of solid rock, there's nowhere else we can walk, so if they follow us this far they'll pick the same direction."

Miss Scott sighed. "You're right. But we still don't want them to know where we break off. How long do you think we should walk? Should we try and get out of this canyon? Or look for a sheltered place down here?"

She was consulting him. It was a proud moment. "The stars are out now, let's keep pushing. And if a place to stay pops up, we'll rest awhile."

"It's a decent night, not too cold, but the water must be runoff from the snowcaps. It's nearly as cold as ice. I've got some beef jerky in my bag here." She fished it out and handed him a couple of pieces. "But no blanket, certainly no dry clothes. I can't hunt, the noise would give us away. We'll be none too comfortable."

She kicked into the icy water and began wading knee-deep. "Watch for a bank that has a stony surface. We'll need to get out of this water now and then, or our feet will freeze."

He couldn't help but notice her lovely figure right in front of him, despite those outrageous trousers she had on. A man had to be very careful of his mind wandering off, thinking thoughts he ought not to ponder. Instead, he thought about whether to take up their talk of Ronnie again but decided to opt for peace, at least for a time. What became of that little boy needed to be settled, and yet John had accepted money to complete the job.

But he wouldn't steal a child away except to protect that child. "Since I've met you, you've threatened to shoot me, you're wearing disreputable clothes, and you're traipsing through the wilderness alone with a man you only met today."

And he'd decided to keep his mouth shut, hadn't he? And yet here he was, yammering. "I'm not sure Ronnie is safe with you."

Even in the dark, with her a few paces ahead, he saw her shoulders square. He'd bet her chin just jutted out and her eyes flashed fire.

Well, at least he was getting to know her.

Trying not to dig himself any deeper into trouble, John said, "I can see you care about him, but I'll bet the Chiltons haven't been shot at in years."

Tossing her head, Miss Scott kept walking. Again he decided to shut up and eat his evening meal . . . and his midday meal . . . breakfast too, maybe. He could barely remember back that far.

"If you really love that little boy"—this was not shutting up—"are you sure you're behaving in a way that's best for him? It's a wild, dangerous land. And the Chiltons are in a position to give him safety, decent food, and clothes. They can send him to good schools and guide him toward a well-paying job. If you really love him, shouldn't you want those things for him? Or, are you letting your feelings override what's best for the boy?"

She stopped and stormed right back at him. "I know the Chiltons. Do you?"

"I met them, and they've done business with the Pinkertons a few times. Many times. They are investigating fools, honestly. Especially that Florence. Always wants someone checked out." John didn't mention that he and his fellow agents drew straws to decide who would go see the Chiltons. John had lost.

"I know she was worse than cruel to Delia."

"Really?" John thought they should probably keep moving. He came up beside her. The stream was wide, and anyway his feet were too cold to just stand here soaking them. He caught her arm, turning her around, and they went back to walking, this time side by side. "Cruel? What did she do?"

"I lived with them for two years, and in that time, the Chiltons barely saw Delia. And when they did it was always ugly. They hated my brother. They wanted her to leave him."

"Well, she married outside her level of society. It's not fair or even wise for parents to be cruel to their daughter for that, not if they want to know their grandchildren. But it's understandable."

"When Ronnie was born they acted like he was beneath them because of who his father was. I wonder why they want him now? They may have changed their minds, but I'll never believe they can treat that little boy with any kindness or love. No matter the danger out here, no matter the hardship, he is better off with people who love him. Money, comfort, education, opportunity, none of that is worth much if he doesn't have love."

"He's their only living family, and they've realized their mistakes. They learned of Delia's death, along with her husband's, and knew their grandson was alone in the world. Of course they sent someone to get him."

Shaking her head, Miss Scott looked skeptical. "It took them too long to decide they loved him. They did nothing but make his life harder as a baby."

"I thought you said they weren't around much."

"Oh, they weren't, but they found a way to punish Abe . . . hoping it would bring Delia running home. The Chiltons would cause trouble, tell lies, spread money around, and before you know it, Abe would be fired. He was a good man, hardworking, honest, decent. And he and Delia loved each other. Add to that, with so many men gone to war, he could have had his pick of jobs. Once we figured out why he kept getting fired, he worked for a few people real privately, shoveling out barns at night and the like, honest work, but it didn't pay well. I managed to find work in a general store and mostly supported the whole family. The Chiltons didn't notice me enough to realize I was working, or they'd've ruined that, too.

"Heading west was mostly done to escape their control. If anyone's responsible for Delia's death, beyond the murderous vermin who did it, it's the Chiltons. They set us on that trail."

Silence lingered between them. The water was chilling his feet, and the sweet breeze felt cold because of it. John didn't want to admit he had serious concerns about the Chiltons, so he changed the subject.

"You know, a stroll in the moonlight might almost be considered romantic."

She surprised him by grinning. "This *would* be the kind of romance I'd get."

"Nothing wrong with it."

"Except for the ice water."

"Yep, that puts a damper on things, I'm sure."

"Damper's right." She kicked one foot through the water and laughed, then punched him in the shoulder, hard. Must be her idea of a friendly gesture—or at least it suited him to count it as one—if punching could be friendly.

"And except for the lumps on your head," she added.

"My brain is pounding like it wants to get out and go live in someone else's skull."

"And except for the armed gunmen."

"Now, that's not fair. No one's shot at us for at least an hour. Maybe two—or three even."

She smiled over that—he was definitely cheering her up. "True enough. It's romantic, then, except you're trying to steal my nephew. And you're a city boy, who I'm probably going to have to drag out of these mountains, probably carry you on my back before we're done, and since you look heavy, that might end up killing us both."

"Yes, except for that."

She stopped, every muscle at attention. "You hear that, McCall? The water's louder ahead. Either a stretch of white water or a waterfall. We'd better get out of this stream before we fall over something even meaner than that cliff."

Sure enough, with Miss Scott back in the lead, they came upon a waterfall and a rugged trail alongside it that led downward.

As they descended, the temperature dropped. Feeling the cold, desperation took hold of him, and he studied the terrain ahead. "Look at that." It was near pitch-dark, but a blacker-than-black circle, tucked half behind the falls, caught his eye. "If it's dry in there, let's hole up awhile."

She came back to his side and saw what he was pointing at. "Stepping out of that water helped me realize how cold my feet are. I'm ready for more jerky, and a few hours of sleep would make the going easier."

Should they build a fire and maybe take their clothes and boots off to dry them? That would be the smart thing.

He shook his head at the idea. Nope. Such a suggestion

would be downright improper and might just cause her to punch him even harder.

———❦———

Cam peered ahead of them. "It's hard to tell for certain in the dark, but that looks like Penny's horse over there." Cam reined in his own horse toward the livery, feeling the tension in his shoulders relax a bit. "Riding all this way without meeting them had me half out of my mind thinking of all that could've happened. At least we know they're still here in Dismal."

Cam dismounted, lashed his horse to the hitching post, and strode inside the livery, with Trace and Utah after him. There was a hostler just coming out of a stall, carrying the hammer a man used to shoe a horse.

"Help you fellas?" He was a stout man, with forearms corded with muscles. A fire flickered in the forge, and the man was covered by a leather apron tied around his neck. His face was blackened with soot, and what little hair he had wrapped around his head and left the top bald.

He sounded friendly, but he had shrewd eyes that slid between the three men and his grip tightened on his hammer. A man who'd had trouble before.

"We're looking for a man and woman who were riding those horses out in your corral."

"I have two horses brought in a few hours ago by the sheriff. The folks riding them were a man and woman like you said, but they disappeared."

"Disappeared?" Cam shook his head, the tension he'd just let go flaring back to life. "You mean, like, in front of your eyes?"

The hostler barked out a laugh. "Nope. The sheriff was waiting for them to come in and answer some questions, and they never came. That's it. The sheriff waited a long while, figuring they'd taken off to eat, then he got impatient and went hunting them. They searched every building in town, and they're not here, but no one saw them leave."

"Without their horses? Do you honestly believe they walked out of town?"

The man shrugged a shoulder. "If'n they did, not a man in town seen 'em go. But go they did. Must've, 'cuz they're sure enough gone."

Cam glanced at Trace. "Did McCall have it planned from the time he headed out to my place? Or did he see we weren't giving up Ronnie and grabbed Penny, hoping I'd hand over the youngster to get my sister back?" Cam spun on his heel. "Or maybe there's some connection to Raddo. I've got to talk to the sheriff."

"Here now, someone's gotta pay to board these horses. I'm claimin' them for mine if you don't."

Cam whirled around, yelling, "My sister is missing! I don't—"

Trace threw himself between Cam and the hostler. "We don't have time for this."

"I'll handle it, Cam," Utah said. "You and Trace go."

Trace turned Cam around forcefully.

"Sorry," Cam muttered, not loud enough for the hostler to hear. "I know I'm acting like a madman. I'm just—my head is going crazy with all the things that could've happened to her. That could be happening to her right now."

Sweat had broken out on his forehead, and his stomach twisted thinking of a woman at the mercy of a stranger.

"Let's go. McCall was a greenhorn. If he's taken her, he'll be easy to catch."

"If he wasn't pretending to be unskilled, so we wouldn't be expecting much from him."

"Remember your sister. If anyone can leave a trail, it's her. And if McCall's got her, all he needs to do is give her a chance, and she'll escape."

That was the most encouraging thing so far. "It's true. If Penny gets free in the woods no one can catch her, no one can pick up her trail. She's had to learn a lot of skills in a mighty hard school thanks to us growing up in the mountains of Pennsylvania, then me dragging her around to frontier army posts."

Feeling more hopeful, Cam picked up his pace as he headed for the sheriff's office, grimly determined to get some answers, and get them fast, because he had a sister to find and a kidnapper to haul to jail and see hanged.

Penny made the decision that they could light a fire. The cave was deep and twisted around and had an opening near the back of it that wasn't far from the entrance they'd come in but was still a second way out. Both ways were tucked around the waterfall. She liked that.

The back entrance led straight into the water and was half-blocked by a huge muskrat nest. She was so cold she didn't think she'd be able to get a lick of sleep without a fire. She figured it was safe to build one. If the smoke escaped, the waterfall would conceal it, and they needed rest.

And that was true even if they hadn't shed those outlaws.

Rather than consult McCall, which usually just slowed her down, she got to work on a fire.

She gathered an armload of branches, reeds, and leaves off the muskrat nest.

"Can I help?"

Giving him orders was the best part of this mess. "I'm building a fire. Bring me the driest branches you can find, and I'll get it lit."

He went to work while she unhooked her bag. Matches, jerky, a gun. The basics of survival.

Kneeling on the hard rock, she soon had the flames licking through leaves she'd crumbled nearly to dust. When the fire ate into the reeds and branches, she piled on every bit of kindling she'd collected.

McCall came back with his arms full. A little more of this and she might start expecting common sense from him.

She built the fire bigger, but not huge because she was worried the cave might fill with smoke. Then she rolled off her knees to sit and tug at her boots. "My feet are freezing. Our boots will dry overnight and—" she wasn't taking anything else off, so—"if we sleep with our feet stretched out close to the fire, our clothes will dry overnight, or at least get good and warm."

"It's going to be miserable."

She couldn't have gotten kidnapped with a man who looked on the bright side of things?

"No blankets. Just cold, hard stone." He sounded purely depressed about it.

"It beats being dead."

He sat and went to tugging off his own boots. In the firelight, he looked like a wreck. He had on a black city suit with one sleeve ripped badly at the shoulder and a white shirt darkened with dried blood. His head was bare and his

50

short dark blond hair mussed. His black boots weren't in the normal western style, and they'd been shining earlier. Now as he tugged them off, the firelight revealed the leather was worn and sagging with wetness.

She handed him jerky. It was all she had, and it was only from a lifetime habit of being prepared for trouble that she had that. After eating her ration and filling her belly the rest of the way with the fresh water, she lay down on the cold, hard ground, pondering all she knew of mountains. It didn't seem like near enough.

Where in the world were they?

"We lost 'em, boss."

Luther Payne needed to shoot somebody, but these three men were the only help he had.

"Get back out there and find their trail."

All three hesitated, and they usually jumped when he gave an order.

"They fell over a cliff," Dudd Schroeder, one of his three hired guns, said. "And we can't find a way down, not in the dark. I decided we should come back and report to you."

"Fell over a cliff?" Luth thought that sounded hopeful. All his problems might be solved. "Did they survive the fall?"

"It's too dark to see to the bottom or to pick our way down. We'll try it if you say so, but our chances of making it down in the dark are slim. Best to wait for daylight."

Luth knew it was true. He also knew he needed those two to answer questions. But did they know anything? The woman seemed to mean it when she started whimpering about Raddo not carrying anything.

Where had he left the evidence? Luth had no doubt it was somewhere, but maybe Raddo had been too smart for his own good. Maybe he'd hidden it so well no one would ever find it.

Luth had no problem pulling a trigger, but he knew better than to go shooting his own men like a headlong fool just out of a mean temper.

"I'm going home. I've been out too long now, considering those two disappeared and questions might be asked about an alibi. No reason they should look to me, but I want to make it real easy for them to never consider doing that."

Luth went to his horse, already saddled and ready to go. "Start searching first thing in the morning. Don't come back until you find them. Or their bodies. But don't let yourself be seen following them."

⁂

"This wilderness is huge." McCall sat on the floor of their hideout cave, his wet legs extended toward the fire.

"You don't miss much, do you, McCall?" She had to give him credit, though. He didn't do any whining.

"I'm so sick of this, I'd like to—"

Not much whining anyway, and since she'd found a gift for ignoring him—and she actually agreed with him—it didn't bother her overly.

"I was awake the whole trip." It was baffling how lost she was. "Yes, the trip took hours and we wound around, but I think we headed mostly east, then north. To get home we should head south and west, right? Simple."

"I'm starving."

She sat up and faced him. "Listen, it doesn't do one lick of good for you to complain."

"Sure, it does some good. It keeps me from running around in circles screaming."

"Look, McCall, your whining is—"

"Stop calling me that."

"What? A whiner?"

"No, I don't mind that. I deserve it. I'm annoying myself even more than you."

"I kinda doubt that."

"Stop calling me McCall."

She met his eyes and arched a brow at him. "It's your name, right?"

"Call me John."

"Nope. That's too friendly. I'm not feeling all that friendly."

"You're my best friend in the world."

Somehow, she doubted that. "Because I helped us fall over a cliff? Because I'm feeding you? Because I have yet to punch you when you start fussing?"

"Well, all of those, honestly. Except you have punched me a couple of times." He rubbed his shoulder.

She laughed. "Now that I think of it, you're becoming a good friend, too. Not best. I reckon Cam is my best friend, and I'm partial to his wife, Gwen, and her sister, Deb. Besides Trace, Deb's husband."

"That's all family. You can't count family."

"I like Trace's hired men more than you."

"Two of them." John nodded with what looked like complete satisfaction. "I'm third, then. I can live with that."

She laughed again. She had to admit Trace's hired men had never made her laugh. "Okay, you can call me Penny. As for getting out of this wilderness, all I can figure is that coming down the waterfall took us miles away from any settlement. We can't pick a direction until we get out of the canyon, and we are headed north, not south. We just walked into the belly of a wild land, and there's no easy way out."

"Have you heard of the Donner Party?"

"I don't think it'll come to that. Maybe if we're still out here come winter. And you seem like the gentlemanly type, so you'd probably let me be the cannibal and you be the food."

"There's your sunny outlook again. I've noticed you're an optimist."

"Yep, that's me. Always the bright side."

"Good, then you'll see the bright side when I give you some bad news."

There was an extended silence.

Penny leaned forward, so he knew he had her attention.

"What bad news is that?"

He paused because they'd been getting along really well and he hated to end it, and he was probably going to.

"That stream we hiked in, that waterfall we climbed down, that cliff we fell over . . ."

"Are you just repeating the steps of our journey? I don't see why when we were both there."

"No, I'm just mentioning them because they're all going to be mighty big obstacles."

"But we're past them now. Of course, there may be more trouble ahead, but—"

"The thing is, I'm mentioning them now because . . . because they're going to be even harder tomorrow, going up-stream, climbing up a waterfall, going up a cliff, because we have to go back."

He leaned back against the rock. Might as well get comfortable while he waited for the explosion.

CHAPTER

6

"Go back?" Penny exploded to her feet.

"Hush, you could give away our hiding place." The lunk-head didn't even stand up. In fact, he seemed to be making himself comfortable.

"And there you go making my point." She did drop her voice, and she moved so she leaned against the tunnel wall across from him. If someone came bursting in, guns blazing, they'd see the lunkhead first.

"We are *hiding* right now from armed men who seemed to have a mighty powerful itch to do us harm. And it all has to do with that filthy murderer who's been plaguing us all winter. Considering how relentless Raddo was, and how ruthless Whisper Man acted wanting to know if Raddo told us anything, there's a better'n good chance that when we got away from them, they didn't just shrug their shoulders and go on home. Those men are still hunting."

"I think we probably lost them." He sounded like he was fighting not to laugh at her.

She clenched a fist and considered doing something that'd make him get real serious, real fast.

"Men who didn't turn a hair when they knocked you over the head. Men who—"

"Men"—John cut her off and sat up straight. For the first time she saw the fire in his eyes—"who need to be stopped."

He'd been acting cool, but he was furious. "Men who are kidnappers for hire, connected to Raddo, a vicious murderer. Men willing to do murder themselves. Men who attacked a Pinkerton agent and think they can get away with it. They are not going to. Not while I'm alive."

"Which you won't be," Penny said, pointing out the obvious, "if you walk up on an armed man."

"Well, that's why I'm lucky to have you. You can help me sneak."

That bought him a few seconds of silence while she tried to figure out what he meant by that, considering she was hollering at him right now . . . well, hollering with her voice real quiet, but she was sure he felt the yelling. The fire crackled, embers glowing as red as a lake of fire. She hoped he could see she matched him for fury. Which made her mention, "Right this minute you shouldn't be feeling all that lucky."

She sure hoped he heard the threat in her words. She saw him glance at her hand, clenched into a fist. And at that bag she'd never been separated from, that held their food, her weapon, honestly way more things than a woman needed to survive in the wild for a good long while . . . unless you got peppered with lead, of course.

"It's simple, Penny. I'm going after those men."

"Let's go to a town, report this to the sheriff, and round up a gun for you."

"I've got my hideout gun in my boot."

"A real gun, not that peashooter. Then we'll find my brother and tell him what happened, then go after the kidnappers with a posse." Now she sounded like she was afraid. Which she was, but she didn't like admitting that to anyone, man, woman, or child . . . especially *this* man.

"You go ahead and find a town and a sheriff and a posse if you want, but first thing in the morning, *I'm* going back."

"I want them too, McCall. I no more intend to let this stand than you do. I just don't want to go after them outgunned and outnumbered. Four armed men to two people with two guns between them—one of those guns little more than a toy." Although Penny could rain trouble right down on those men, she reckoned.

This greenhorn was calling her a coward, and it stung. But it kicked in all her stubbornness to refuse to let him insult her into doing something as stupid as tracking down those varmints and showin' them a little frontier justice. She felt a yearning to do just that, but she kept her mouth clamped shut until she was sure she could control what came out of it.

When she had a hold on herself, she asked, "Do you know how to read a sign?"

"Read a sign? You mean like the one printed over the sheriff's office in Dismal that says *Barber Shop and Jail*?"

He was just teasing her. She hoped.

"No, read signs, like follow a man's trail through forests and over mountains. You know we walked down that stream to hide our trail, well, that's what I mean by signs. I was doing my best to leave no sign of which way we went."

He heaved an impatient sigh. "If I see a footprint, I can tell which end is the toe, so I know which way a man is going."

"But in the woods, you have to notice if a twig is snapped off, then see if the break is raw or weathered, so you know if someone passed through recently. And know if the twig was broken, or the grass bent over, by a man or an elk or a grizzly bear—there ain't always footprints, just signs that someone has passed through. You have to listen to the birds to see if they suddenly go silent. It means something is disturbing them—and don't forget that sometimes the thing that is disturbing them is you, so you need to judge that. You have to smell. The forest is full of smells. Some of them belong, almost all of them belong for a fact. So, you eliminate anything that's supposed to be there, which you know if you've had experience in the forest, and pick up on the scent of a man or horse. You have to—"

"All right." He waved both hands at her like he was shooing her away. "I know I'm no good at it, Penny. That's why I said I was lucky to have you. But if you're not going to help, I'll bet I can find my way back to where we escaped. I don't have to read signs to follow this stream backward to where we came down the side of that waterfall. From there I can find that little trail, find that cliff we went rolling down, climb up it, and I'll bet at the top of it, I'll find the hoofprints of shod horses. I'll be able to tell if four riders hunted us together or split up. I can follow that to where we were held captive. Maybe the wagon will even be there, and if it's not, someone had to drive it away. It's not that easy to hide wagon tracks."

"It's not that hard, either." Penny crossed her arms, hornet mad thinking about those low-down hombres who'd plucked her up and carried her off with no more regard than they'd show a gunnysack full of taters.

He glared at her. "So no, if I see a busted-off twig, there's a good chance I'm not going to know if those men did the busting, you did it, or a grizzly, but I'm thinking those men chasing us were racing around, and they weren't being all that sly. I'll bet they left plenty of good tracks. And," he added, "I'm figuring they've given up on the search by now."

"Don't gamble your life on that."

"I'll be watchful in case they're still around. I'll just be sniffing up a storm thanks to your warning, though the men picked me up and tossed me on the ground and I didn't notice any particular smell. But I'll use my nose as well as my eyes and ears. When I find where we were held, I'll pick out their leader and follow him as best as I can."

His voice rose with each word. "If I lose him, I'll find him again. It's how I make my living, and I'm good at my job."

"Quiet," Penny hissed and looked down the tunnel that led to whoever might be out there.

"You can go on home." He surged to his feet, closed the distance between them, and jabbed one finger at her chest. His voice dropped to a cold whisper. "But I'm not going to leave this to a sheriff who might think his jurisdiction is the edge of town. So yes, in the morning, I'm going back."

"Then I reckon I'm going back, too."

His jabbing finger dropped. He straightened away from her and his brows rose in surprise. "Really, you'll go with me?"

"Might as well. The one thing I haven't mentioned about this is . . . well, I haven't wanted to think about it."

"What's that?"

"What my brother will be going through right now. He's a man to protect what's his. When I don't show up at his place, he's going to come looking, and he'll come hard. He'll find those men and the wagon tracks, though it might take time.

But then, Trace Riley is with him, the man who saved the children from that wagon train Raddo and his outlaw gang massacred. Riley is the best I've ever seen in these mountains, and my brother and I are both good, so that's saying something. He'll be coming, too. Maybe more than just those two. I hate knowing how Cam is feeling right now from worrying about me."

"Should we head back now? It's dark, but if we go slow—"

"Thanks, I appreciate that. But no, we wait until it's daylight. I could make it, probably, but let's give those men who kidnapped us a chance to calm down and holster their guns. But, in the morning, we move fast. Get some sleep, John. I'm not waiting for you tomorrow."

She thought he might start yelling again. Instead he smiled, and those teeth shone like the sunrise. She went to the opposite side of the fire, as far from him as she could get, extended her wet feet toward the fire, and took her own advice.

CHAPTER

7

Penny hissed.

John crouched low and froze. He'd learned that mighty fast. Of course, she'd pounded it into him all morning.

He listened. He looked. He did it all without moving. She'd almost clobbered him for turning his head earlier, when they were hiding from what turned out to be a deer.

The wilderness wasn't his strong suit. But for the love of Mike, the woman was inching along. He could've walked all the way back to Philadelphia by now.

Still, if he annoyed her and she clobbered him, he couldn't hit back because he didn't believe in hitting a woman.

So he froze, just as he'd been trained.

He didn't see anything, didn't hear anything. Even Penny wasn't visible. She'd slid behind a tree, and in these dense woods, that put her out of his sight, too. Bad enough he couldn't see whatever made her hiss, but he couldn't even see her.

He hoped he was hiding properly from whatever she was hissing about.

Then she jerked on his pant leg, and he jumped and yelped like a wounded hound. She must've crawled on her belly because he hadn't seen her coming. She jerked her head, which meant for him to get moving.

He was getting great at communicating with her without words. In fact, he preferred it when she didn't talk. When she did, she usually had something to say that he didn't want to hear, so this suited him just fine.

They'd been hours on the trail. He couldn't see the sky most of the time, but it had to be past midday, and they'd started at first light. They'd come upstream to the base of the waterfall, climbed the rocks alongside it, and walked back to that cliff. Once there, it hadn't been hard to get to the top.

Not running for your life made everything easier.

At the top of the cliff things had gotten slow. Penny had seen tracks, and she'd gone to inching along. All John could do was be quiet.

And now he'd embarrassed himself by jumping and squeaking like a frog on a hot rock. A cowardly frog on a hot rock.

"This is it. They're gone." Penny talked right out loud, like she had no worries about the outlaws being close at hand.

"How can you be sure?"

She arched one brow in a way that John had never been able to do. He envied her mobile eyebrow.

After too long a silence, she said, "I've circled the wagon site twice. I found tracks, three heading one way, one another. You saw them, didn't you?"

John tried to think of an answer that didn't make him

sound like a complete failure. And he tried even harder to ignore the warmth creeping up his cheeks. He was blushing, and he wished that cliff was handy so he could toss himself over it again.

"No, I didn't see them." He sounded defensive, and that embarrassed him even more. He dug in and said with absolute confidence, "If I'd been in charge of finding tracks, I'm sure I would have. But I've been leaving all of it to you and just following along and being quiet when you tell me to."

Penny shook her head and looked so disappointed in him he was half afraid he was going to get his fingers whacked by a ruler.

Penny turned to a tight opening in the trees. "Wagon tracks right here." Crouching, she pointed to a pair of surprisingly subtle indentations. "See them?"

John did indeed see them. And he saw more. Behind a scrub pine. He reached through the prickly needles that lined a trail so narrow John couldn't believe they got a wagon through. He lifted up a tangled mess. "They left a rope behind."

"That's the one I got off my wrists." Penny absently rubbed her wrists as if she was just now untied. "I remember tossing it when we lit out. They didn't find it and take it with them. So now I know for sure we're in the right place, though I was confident before."

"Did a single rider go off alone?"

"Yep, but I've had a fine idea, McCall. One I think you'll agree to, even though you don't seem overly worried about facing down an armed man alone."

John crossed his arms and waited.

"We could go to town and fetch our horses. That's not

too cowardly for you, is it?" She did a good job of sounding reasonable and nice and even a little like a delicate female who'd like to ride rather than walk for miles. It was a pathetically false effort—but he appreciated that she attempted it.

"The three men rode away in a group, but judging by these wagon tracks"—she pointed to a farther area of ground that looked pretty bare to John, though there might be a few broken twigs among the rocks and grass—"they didn't go back to town. They lit out in a new direction. I want to follow the trail that goes back to Dismal. We can fetch our horses, stock up on supplies, then ride after this coyote armed and loaded, ready for the long trek ahead of us."

She gave him a pat on the shoulder as if encouraging him and continued in her falsely sincere voice, "Won't that be better?"

On the one hand, having a horse was necessary, and he admitted he hadn't thought of it last night when he was giving his high-minded speech about bringing down a criminal.

"We saw three men in that alley and a fourth out here and have been assuming that's all of them." John studied the wagon tracks. "I hope they didn't have someone else there in Dismal to hide our horses, steal them maybe. It'd be a better way to cover their tracks, but a horse thief would've had to walk right into the center of town and hope no one saw. And they seemed determined to conceal their faces. Let's go to town."

She heaved a sigh of relief and set out down the tight trail. The trees were so dense John didn't think he could get off the trail if he wanted to. They canopied overhead and cast shadows as if it was near twilight, even though it was the middle of the afternoon.

They'd been walking about an hour when a distant rumble caught John's attention. Thunder, but he couldn't see overhead to check clouds, or even feel if the wind was picking up. The forest was a natural windbreak.

"Rain will wash out the tracks." Penny picked up speed. John considered that he could only somewhat see . . . mostly in his imagination . . . the trail now. If it rained and washed away the tracks before they got to town and returned with their horses, they'd never catch up with those men.

No, he would catch them. Rain was just going to make it much harder.

The thunder picked up. A flash was bright enough to light up their heavily shadowed walk. "It's coming in fast." Penny moved almost at a run now. And the trail was rough, with brush that seemed to reach for John's legs and grab at him.

Finally, they got to a wider clearing, and the clouds looming overhead were nearly black. The first spit of rain peppered John's face.

Penny pointed up to where the clouds seemed to reach solidly all the way down to the treetops. "It's raining hard."

A bolt of lightning split the sky. Less than a second later, it was followed by a crack of thunder.

"Don't trees draw lightning?" John had worked on a ship during the war, and he knew about storms at sea. Mountains, well, he didn't know as much.

"They sure enough do." Penny pivoted and headed at a right angle to the direction they'd been going. "Head for that downed tree over there."

She didn't even look back to see if he followed her. She just headed there herself at a jog. And of course he went after her. He'd've followed exactly what she did without her saying a word.

"Let's get under it if we can, that'll protect us from the rain. At least it might protect us from lightning—or any trees that are struck."

The wind picked up. The spitting rain hit like little needles. In the distance, the sky was shrouded with more pouring rain. A loud crack of thunder split the gray curtain, followed by a blaze of lightning.

John realized he was outrunning Penny. He slowed, caught her hand, and dragged her toward the fallen trunk. It had landed on some boulders, forming a cave.

There came a thunderbolt so loud, so close, it hit his ears like a blow. The ground shook. Then another burst of lightning flashed right on top of the sound. Glancing back, he saw the bright finger of jagged fire strike a tree and blow it apart. Burning embers blasted in all directions. John felt a slash of pain. He looked to see his arm was on fire—the one he was using to drag Penny along. He slapped at it, without letting her go.

Thunder roared again. John stumbled from the impact of the sound but kept his feet and ran on. He hit the trunk just as the sky opened up and the rain became a deluge.

Penny shouted, "Look there. Down low. Crawl in."

John towed Penny under the massive trunk. "Get in there." John dragged Penny to her knees and shoved her past him into the little space. She was scrambling faster than he could push her. He stopped, ready to block the small entrance with his own body to protect her.

Another lightning bolt hit close enough that John staggered. He looked up, then even higher up.

A burning tree was toppling right for him.

"Get in here." Penny jerked him toward her. He practically fell into the small space. He dropped to his belly, surprised and relieved that he fit.

"Plenty of room," Penny shouted over the rolling thunder. The tree crashed to the ground, the limbs lashing at John's legs as he pushed in deeper.

He knocked into Penny, and the two of them tumbled to the back of the small shelter. The falling tree now blocked the entrance well enough that no rain got through.

John was a few seconds gathering his wits, then he shifted away from Penny and spun to look at the branches of the huge tree. Some were blackened, but the rain must have doused the fire. The ceiling of their little den was only high enough to allow him onto his hands and knees.

"We're not completely blocked in." He turned around and sat down with his back to the opening. The little space they were in was about four feet high at the entrance, and just about that wide and deep. "We'll let the rain pass and then get back on our way to town." John drew up his knees and rested his forearms on them.

"The trail is gone. Long gone. We're going to have the worst kind of work cut out for ourselves finding those varmints."

They sat, catching their breath, and their silence only made the violent storm louder. The thunder rolled, the lightning crashed. Wind whipped and howled. Sheets of rain pounded the earth. But they were out of the weather. They were safe. For now, anyway.

"Have you got any more beef jerky in that magic bag of yours?"

Penny seemed to relax. She'd been so alert. So eager to

snap orders at him all morning. Maybe resting for a spell suited her.

She dug in the bag and extended two pieces of jerky to him, and he was glad they didn't have to deal with debilitating hunger on top of everything else. Penny ran a hand through her hair. It'd been in a braid when they'd started the day, but now it was as wild as the weather. Her fingers ran into snarls, so she gave up on her hair.

He chewed, and in the dimness, there was a sense of peace. They couldn't get away from each other, and they couldn't get back to work saving themselves. For once there wasn't anything to bicker about.

John wondered how such a pretty, messy woman had found her way to the frontier, but then pioneers came from everywhere.

"I don't have much savvy in the woods," John said easily. "But I've been a Pinkerton agent from the time I was twenty. Not counting the years spent in the war."

She leaned against the side of the crevice. "Come over here, so you're farther from the opening."

He scooted closer, their knees brushing, as there just wasn't room enough for him to leave her any space.

"A lot of men born and raised in the city learned tough lessons about scavenging and following tracks during the war, and I did some, but I spent most of it on a ship."

Penny looked over at him. She finished what she was chewing and swallowed. "Cam spent the whole war fighting, and I've heard a lot of stories from him and other men at the forts I lived in following my brother around. But I've never given much thought to ships. Were you . . . wasn't there a siege around Vicksburg somewhere?"

"I wasn't at Vicksburg, but I was involved with the Anaconda Plan, and Vicksburg was a part of that."

Penny frowned comically. "Anaconda? Never heard of that. Is it a Southern city? Chattanooga, Chickamauga, Anaconda?"

"Nope, good guess. It's a huge snake. I think they're from South America. I'd never heard the word before, either. The anaconda kills its prey by slowly choking it to death."

Penny winced.

"General Scott's plan was to do that to the Southern states. I think he hoped to avoid a shooting war because he had Southern sympathies. Some called it Scott's Great Snake, but the real name was the Anaconda Plan."

"Scott's Great Snake?" Penny smiled as if she thought he was teasing her.

John nodded. "The North's navy set out to control every port in the South, cut the Confederacy in half up the Mississippi, and stop any shipping traffic."

The thunder rolled outside, and the rain poured. A lightning bolt hit hard, close to them, again. There was nothing out there that suggested to a man he oughta get back to walking.

"General Scott was the commanding general of the army for a while, though not during the Civil War, he was past his prime by then. We called him Old Fuss and Feathers, but he was a great man. He was from the South, but he believed in the Union and chose to side with the North."

Penny shook her head. "And his plan was to blockade every southern port?"

"Yep, what an uproar. A lot of generals wanted to march for Richmond, Virginia, the capital of the Confederacy, and put an end to the war. But Old Fuss and Feathers knew the

South would fight, and fight hard. He had no stomach for Americans shooting Americans. He hoped his Anaconda Plan would stop the war without years of bloodshed."

"I've never heard that before. I wonder if Cam knows that."

Penny was listening to every word. It made John feel tall and strong. Admired. He hadn't had many women admire him—of course, he'd been busy with the war and being a detective, which kept him on the move. Still, there was a good chance that this proud feeling added up to his being pathetic.

Penny tilted her head. "All right, so you spent the war on a ship. You didn't see much action, then?"

Now it sounded like she considered him the littlest bit of a coward. He wanted to launch into tales of blockade runners and battles at sea and slipping onto Confederate shores to gather information or cause havoc. But that felt pathetic, too.

"I saw plenty of action," he simply said. "And then I got back to Philadelphia after the war and signed back on with the Pinkertons, and I've been working at that ever since."

"And got yourself sent out here to kidnap a child."

John glared at her.

She smiled back, looking not one speck afraid of him. And he'd been told he was fierce.

"So, how'd you spend the war years?"

Penny told him more about living with Delia and Abe. Virtually supporting them because Abe could never hold a job. Penny blamed all that on the Chiltons, but John had to wonder. Was Abe a persecuted man? Or was he an idler who lived off his sister's hard work? Maybe the Chiltons were right to be worried about their grandson. John had only met

Cameron Scott for about an hour while they'd dealt with loading Raddo over a saddle. And he was the one with little Ronnie in his home . . . a home that wasn't built yet. John wasn't sure what was in Ronnie's best interests or what he believed about the Chiltons, Cam, or Penny. He needed to stay around and see how the child was treated.

But before that, he had an outlaw to hunt and hang.

"When Cam headed west with the army, I went along. He was an officer and the pay was good, and with all the menfolk coming home from war, jobs were scarce. So, Cam stayed in the army. I was living with Abe and Delia in an attic with one tiny bedroom—it was all we could afford. It was so crowded, I decided to go with Cam. We both sent money back home, and Cam had been paid out from the war enough that Abe and Delia could save up and, with the money we sent, make plans to head west with a wagon train."

"So, you weren't involved in that wagon train massacre?"

"No, we only found Ronnie and Maddie Sue at the tail end of last autumn. Deb and Gwen are sisters who were traveling with Abe and Delia. They saved the children from the massacre, and Trace saved them from the wilderness. Since then Trace and Deb have gotten married. Cam and Gwen too, and the children have come to think of Gwen as their mother. And of course, Gwen's marriage to Cam makes Deb their legal aunt, so now they have two aunts to love them. My brothers' children. It makes my guts churn to think of how close we came to losing them in that massacre."

"There's no doubt Cam is Maddie Sue's father, but Ronnie's a different matter. Those children may treat Gwen and Cam like parents, but they've got no closer relationship to Ronnie than the Chiltons. In fact, legally his grandparents are closer, and they want him. They've got a strong case that he should be with them."

"The Chiltons hated Abe, and they were always nasty to Delia, trying to get her to leave her marriage and come home. How is Ronnie supposed to live with people that treated his parents so poorly?"

"I'm listening to your side, Penny, but the Chiltons are well-to-do people who are willing to raise their grandson in fine style. Add to that, they've gone to great effort and spent considerable money to find him and offer him a home. We may need to see a judge about who gets to take care of that little boy."

"Ronnie thinks of us as his family. We've all been living at Trace's house through the winter, and he's come to belong with us. It'd be cruel to tear him away from us and travel across the country, just him and you, to make him live with strangers who'll raise him to believe his parents were bad people."

"Like I said, I'm listening to your side. And I'm not going to grab him and run. I'm not that big a fool. I know none of you would sit still for it. Whatever happens, we'll decide it between us with all sides agreeing on what's best."

Penny jerked her chin in agreement, and John wondered why she conceded so quickly. As if maybe she knew that never in this lifetime would she agree to let Ronnie go, so it was all settled.

She went on. "We claimed three homesteads between Cam, Gwen, and me, and we are just now building on our claims. Cam's gonna raise horses and cattle. I've got my own claim, and I'll run cattle on my place, too."

"By yourself?" John couldn't quite picture it. "A woman homesteading alone?"

That wasn't right.

"That's right. And I'm looking forward to it. I've been answering to a boss for too long. First back in Philadelphia and then in jobs attached to the forts. Now I'm gonna work for myself. I've been breathing easier ever since I staked my claim last fall."

John couldn't hold back a smile.

"There wasn't a thing funny about what I just said." She studied his unfortunately handsome face, wondering what he was up to now.

"Since I've met you . . . has it only been two days?" McCall leaned his head back to rest it against the tree trunk. "I've been in a shootout and killed a man."

He gave himself a little shake and rubbed one hand over his mouth, looking distressed. There were a few seconds of silence before he went on. "I've been kidnapped and knocked out cold by a man who I suspect intended to kill me. We ran for our lives and fell over a cliff while dodging gunfire. And now we're hiding from a lightning storm under a dead tree like a couple of mushrooms."

He glanced over at Penny. "That's only been since I got here. For you, Raddo chased you all winter, burned down Trace's house, and ended up dying in a shootout. What kind of life have you led that this madness makes you breathe easier?"

And then she smiled, too. "I didn't even mention wading through snow up to my horse's chest to get to Trace's or living in one bunkhouse with nine people. Or Cam getting his leg caught in a bear trap. But I'll stick with what I said. I like this life. I like bossing myself."

"The army must be tough." He smiled wider, then he chuckled.

She felt laughter bubble up then escape in an embarrassing giggle. The bane of her existence.

McCall laughed full out. "That is an extremely feminine sound. You must hate it, but it's pretty."

She choked down the stupid giggle, and the heat in her cheeks felt like she was blushing, drat it. Good thing they were in a dimly lit hole in the ground.

At last she felt able to speak. "The army is tough, but mostly it was just bossy. I wasn't actually in the army, but I was working for them, and they all know how to give a well-placed order, my brother included. I learned to swallow all my fine opinions and do as I was told because that was the job I was hired for. But the freedom of being my own boss is a wonderful thing."

She sat forward, wanting to put it into words, so he could see why she'd choose the mayhem of her life in Nevada.

"The day we rode away from the fort, it was as if I had a tightly wound spring inside me, like a clock wound all the way up. I didn't even know it was there until I felt it uncoil. Tick by tick, the farther we rode. Cam and I talked about the amazing sense of freedom, like we were birds escaping a cage." She breathed in deeply of the air she'd chosen for herself.

He leaned back so his shoulder rested against the tumble of brush that made a back wall out of their shelter, and listened, really listened in a way few men did to a woman.

"It's been hard. *Easier* was the wrong word. There's nothing *easy* about freedom. You have to strive. You have to make a plan and stick to it. There was nothing easy about finding out Abe was dead." That ended any desire she had to laugh. "And Delia. She was the finest woman. Smart and kind and truly devoted to my brother, and so in love with Maddie Sue and her own little son. No, not easy."

"I am sorry you lost your brother. I am the youngest in a big family. There were thirteen of us in all."

"Thirteen!" Penny gasped. "My goodness."

"My father lost his first wife after she had eight children. When he remarried, he had five more. I'm the last, and a straggler by seven years to the next youngest. My oldest brothers and sisters were grown and spread far and wide before I was born. I've got three sisters and two brothers I've never met. Most of them went west, and the West seems to swallow a person up. I had two brothers killed in the war. Losing them leaves this gaping hole in your life and nothing can fill it." He shook his head. "It's a loss you live with forever. I forget how much it hurts, sometimes for days at a time. And then it'll hit me again."

"And when it does," Penny asked, "do you feel guilty? As if you've abandoned them?"

"As if they weren't important or I don't love them enough?" McCall reached forward with his left hand, his right propped on the wall, and touched her upper arm. The offer of comfort warmed her beyond just a simple touch.

"But no one can hold that great a sorrow forever. Even knowing that, it feels like I've betrayed my brother by not thinking of him for days."

McCall eased her forward into a hug. She leaned against him. She rested her cheek against his strong shoulder and felt his press against her hair. The support, the simple decency of it, was as wonderful as that first sense she'd had of freedom.

She'd had so little support like this from a man outside her family. She'd always worked hard. She had a family to provide for, a ranch to save for and plan on. There'd been no time for men.

The embrace became more than comfort, more than warmth. Her arms crept around his neck, and the feel of him brought with it a sense of being fully alive, wonderfully strong, overflowing with hope for the future.

And being a woman.

She honestly hadn't spent too much time thinking of that in her busy life. But now she came alive in a way she'd never known. Raising her head, she looked him in the eye. He seemed to be waiting for something. And then he lowered his head and kissed her.

Her brain stuttered, tripped, and fell. Her first kiss. She'd had no idea a kiss felt so . . . so . . . Words failed her as her brain gave up on everything but feeling.

He lifted away, their eyes met. But she wanted him back for another kiss, his arms offering their strength.

A crack of thunder hit so loud, so close, that she jumped and smacked her head on the tree.

A needed dose of reality. She tried pulling away, yet it wasn't as smoothly done as it should have been, because he had to help her unwind her arms from around his neck.

And she couldn't help but sneak in a couple more quick kisses. And he did the same.

At last she moved away and aimed her back at him. Finally able to think clearly again, she turned to look straight into his eyes. "What in the world are we doing?"

McCall shrugged, looked a little sheepish, and said, "We were—"

She slapped her hand over his mouth. "Don't say it."

Then she snatched her hand back, both upset and embarrassed by the warmth of her palm where it'd touched his lips.

The message had been delivered, though. He didn't answer her half-witted question but instead shifted to look between the tree branches that covered the front of their little cave. The topmost branches of that fallen tree were reaching inside. The rain came down like a curtain, so hard and fast that there was no sensible way to leave . . . which Penny considered doing anyway. A nice, long, miserable walk in the rain might be just what she needed. Then another blaze of lightning followed by a crack of thunder cleared her mind of that.

McCall looked straight out. There was no reason on earth to stare at the pouring rain and yet he paid it strict attention, and she could only be grateful.

It was a long time before the rain slowed, a long time more before it stopped.

"It's going to be a swamp out there," McCall finally said. Those were the first words spoken by either of them, possibly for as long as an hour.

Penny was usually a good judge of the passing of time, but right now she couldn't decide if the rain had poured down forever, or if it just seemed like forever because she wanted to get away from this cozy den.

"Let's go." McCall looked over his shoulder at her. "I have no idea where."

"And there'll be not one single hoofprint to help us find our way back to Dismal." Penny thought she could find her way on down the tight trail the wagon had been on, but with the cloud cover, the winding trail, the way she'd been hauled out here with a blindfold on . . . She thought she was right about what direction they'd headed out of town. She hoped she was right.

"Nor will there be a single hint of a trail for us to follow to catch our kidnappers." John sounded fierce and determined. And frustrated to a fare-thee-well.

Speaking with confidence she didn't really feel, she said, "I can find our way back to that trail where we followed the wagon. We'll start there and find our way back to town. It'll be simple."

***

It was complicated.

"Why don't these animals ever go to town?"

Penny looked back at McCall. They'd been following deer trails that led nowhere . . . for days.

She'd quit kissing him after that first time—or maybe it was more honest to call it the first five times—but there'd only been that one episode. She'd stopped thinking he was a city-born weakling on day two.

And she'd caught on to his jokes about the hardship on day three. He was a strong man who'd keep going as long as it took. He knew how to keep her going and lift her spirits by making jokes at his expense. And he was a full partner in all the work.

It was now day four and never once had he goaded her about getting them hopelessly lost. But today was the end of that. She'd found a trail. A real, for sure, trail. Not one used only by mountain goats. She smiled. "Look at that."

"Shod hooves, even I recognize those," McCall said. "I'd started to wonder if we were alone in the world. I've known for a long time the wilderness is vast, but I've never really realized it before this. Which way?"

Penny fought down the urge to punch McCall in the nose because, drat it, she didn't know which way. They'd found another stream and stuck with it, Penny reasoning that waterways often led to settlements. But it meandered into and out of deep woods, through one narrow valley or mountain gap after another. Sometimes the shores were wide and easily followed. Sometimes they were steep and treacherous, with waterfalls and white water churning over rocks. They had to veer far away from the water to find a path they could walk, then find the stream again and go back to following it.

Her stomach rumbled, and she ignored it and hoped John couldn't hear it. They'd been days with only the most meager food. Working hard, hiking, climbing, pushing on. She'd been skinny already, but after days of this, she'd probably lost ten pounds.

"If we pick the wrong direction, we might end up lost again. I feel like the right answer is life and death." She gave him an uncertain smile.

John rested a hand on her shoulder. "You're just saying that because you're excited. We'll go that way." He pointed right. "The freshest hooves are going that way. It has to lead somewhere. That rider is going between two places. We'll end up at one of them."

Penny nodded, then pointed up to the mountain peaks. "That's west." Then she pointed north. "My guess is, that leads to Carson City. If we go left it might lead to Dismal, and this trail connects the two. Dismal is closer to home, but those outlaws might've gone back there, and I don't trust the law to protect us. Let's go to Carson City."

As if she knew that's where it went. Optimist for sure. "We'll go wherever this goes, and in the end, we'll be somewhere."

"We're somewhere now."

That didn't deserve a proper response. "Let's go somewhere else."

CHAPTER

8

"You're Penny Scott?" Sheriff Walters seemed overly excited to see them.

"This isn't Carson City," John whispered into the back of Penny's head.

She didn't punch him, and that probably oughta earn her a medal. No, this wasn't Carson City. They'd ended up back in Dismal, and Penny had no idea why she'd been so turned around or where they'd been.

When they got to the familiar town, Penny had led them straight to the sheriff. She thought it showed a lot of restraint on her part. McCall wanted to eat first. But she insisted they report their kidnapping to the lawman.

"You're John McCall?" the sheriff asked.

"Yes, I am." McCall sounded perky, like maybe the sheriff knew him by reputation. Maybe he thought he was famous. "And we'd like to report a—"

"You're under arrest." The sheriff whipped out a six-shooter from under his barber apron and aimed it right at McCall's heart. "Get your hands in the air."

Probably not the kind of famous he'd hoped for.

McCall asked very calmly, while raising his hands, "Are you arresting her, too?"

"Why would I do a stupid thing like that? She's the victim. Now start moving."

"Can I ask what you're arresting him for?" Penny fell in step beside them. McCall marched along with his hands in the air. He was a little red-faced. Penny considered that it might be anger, but more likely he was feeling mighty embarrassed by this. He probably noticed that she was fighting a grin.

"Kidnapping, assault, and possible murder."

"Who is he supposed to have kidnapped, assaulted, and murdered?"

"It's you. He done all that to you."

"Uh . . . I think you can drop the murder charge. And he didn't kidnap or assault me."

"There's those what say he did."

"I was there. Surely my statement would count heavily in his favor."

"I've known victims that've been too afraid to face the villain that harmed 'em."

"Afraid of him?" Penny pointed at McCall with her thumb. "Not one speck."

McCall, walking along at her side, took a second to narrow his eyes and glare at her.

"I've even known a couple of gals who ended up liking the villain what harmed 'em. You might be denying the crime out of that sort of confusion. I understand if you're addled, miss."

"Do I seem addled to you?"

"I'd never be so rude to say it, but since you're defending a man who kidnapped you, I have to wonder."

Dismal, Nevada, was a quiet little place.

Population: one sheriff too many.

Penny walked along, long-legged, relaxed—sure, she could be relaxed. No apron-wearing, mustache-trimming lawman had a gun aimed at her back. John wondered if the sheriff would give him a shave and a haircut. He'd spent days in the wilderness, and he was a mess.

John would've started arguing with Penny, to get her to take this more seriously, if he didn't think the sheriff might decide to shoot him just to protect her from her confusion.

"We were both kidnapped, Sheriff." Penny at least seemed to be trying to clear this up. He could see she was fighting back a smile, fighting real hard. "That's the crime he was going to report before you drew your gun."

"So, you admit there was a kidnapping."

"No. I mean yes. Yes, there was definitely a kidnapping, and assault, though he, Mr. McCall here, was the one who was mainly assaulted."

"He looks fine to me. If he didn't take you, who did?"

"Four men. Tough, armed gunmen. They grabbed us right off the streets of Dismal, as fast and slick as I've ever seen men move."

"Where are they now?" Sheriff Walters asked.

"We escaped."

"These gunmen just let you slip through their fingers? That doesn't sound all that slick."

"We escaped days ago. They took us a long way into the

woods, and we were a while making our way back to civilization."

They reached the jail. John got the door since he was leading this little parade. Once inside, the sheriff said, "Keep moving right into that cell."

"No, don't lock him up." Penny sounded purely annoyed. "You can't accuse him of a crime committed against me if the only witness you have—me—denies there was a crime."

"Turn around."

John obeyed, very slowly . . . making no sudden moves. He lowered his hands as he faced the lawman.

Penny came close to his side and rested one hand on his arm. He appreciated her support and patted her hand.

"I did not kidnap her, Sheriff." He did his very best to sound reasonable, responsible, and noncriminal. "I am a Pinkerton agent and have been for years. I can send a telegram back east. My employer will vouch for me. He'll tell you—"

"Shut up, McCall."

The gun didn't waver.

Silence settled over the room. Sheriff Walters's cold eyes shifted from John to Penny and back. "You seem to have formed some kind of . . . of bond during the week you were missing."

"Bond?" John had no idea what the man meant by that.

"Yes, during the week the two of you were alone together, somewhere private."

"Has it been a week?" John looked at Penny.

"I'd say more like five days."

A plump woman entered the sheriff's office at that moment. A skinny youngster, probably fifteen or so, came in with her. Behind the boy came two girls, ten years old maybe.

John wasn't around kids much, so their ages were anyone's guess. The girls dressed alike and were so close in looks and size they had to be twins. Behind them came a boy another stairstep younger. And then an older girl came in with a baby still in diapers in one arm and her hand holding a small boy who didn't look school age yet. All seven of them had ice blue eyes that matched the sheriff's.

The woman gasped when she saw John and Penny. John didn't know what he looked like, but Penny's hair resembled a muskrat's nest, and he'd recently seen one so he was a fair judge.

"Are you the woman who was kidnapped?"

"Well, yes. But not by—"

The woman threw herself into Penny's arms.

A cloud of dust puffed out of Penny's clothes. Penny raised her hands, much as John had just a few minutes before. Surrendering to a power more fearsome than a gun.

Salt water.

The woman wept deep, wrenching tears. "You poor, poor dear."

The sheriff looked worried, but not enough to lower the gun.

Finally, tears spent, the woman drew back, grabbed a kerchief out of her sleeve, and dabbed her eyes. She darted a glance at John—he saw murderous anger—then her gaze skidded to her children. The woman's voice dropped, as if her children, standing two steps away, suddenly couldn't hear her.

She said to Penny, "Was it . . . was he . . . did he . . . oh, poor child. Poor ruined girl. The nightmare of it. The lost chance, the shattered life, no possible happy future."

John had to give her that. Penny didn't look one bit happy.

"You must be so upset, so terrified. Was he . . ." Now the voice dropped to a whisper, yet John could still hear her and so could everyone else. But he was glad because the woman was acting furiously mad, and he was fascinated by any clue she'd give to what in the world was going on in her churned-up mind.

"You've been . . . been . . . my dear. To be trapped in the clutches of such a ravening beast." The woman smacked John right across the face with the back of her hand. He put his hand up to his jaw. The woman had a wallop.

"If by 'ruined,'" Penny said, wincing as John rubbed his jaw, "you mean I really need clean clothes and a bath—"

"You definitely need that," John said helpfully. "And your hair hasn't seen a comb nor a pin in too long. It puts me in mind of that muskrat nest we used for kindling the first night on the trail."

Penny's eyes narrowed until John planted his feet, ready for the next blow.

"No, no bath or new clothes will solve this. Though I don't doubt you feel utterly soiled. Conrad, I declare this man deserves hanging."

"Did you hear her say I didn't kidnap her?" John wasn't sure just when the woman had joined their little meeting.

"He didn't ruin me, either. I'm fine. Tired and dirty and hungry, but no more so than he is."

"Really?" He looked down at his black pants. His formerly black pants. "I look as bad as you? I bet you wouldn't say that if we had a mirror."

"He has ruined you, Miss Scott. No doubt you've been so bitterly abused you're not capable of rational thought. We have only two possible choices here."

"Two?" John hoped one of them was to eat.

"Yes, you foul man. Hanging would be preferable."

"Not to me."

"And if she won't accuse you and testify against you properly, then the only other possible choice is—" the woman held a dramatic pause worthy of the theater—"she must marry you."

All thoughts of a meal and clean clothes went flying straight out of his head.

His eyes met Penny's. Hers wide with alarm. No, worse than alarm . . . horror. His had to look the same.

"Marry her? Do I look crazy?"

"There ain't enough 'ruin' in this world to make me marry him."

Their voices sounded at once, and it made them both stop.

"Conrad, you're going to have to hang him, then. You can't let them behave as though they did nothing wrong, and do it right in front of your wife and children."

"Mayme Belle, honey, I'm not sure that's a good idea." The cold-eyed sheriff suddenly looked like a slightly disobedient eight-year-old. There was no doubt who wore the pants in this family.

"Yes, it's absolutely the only possible thing you can do. God will demand no less of you than that you hang him and cast her out."

John wondered what exactly was the religion this woman held to, because these rules didn't sound familiar to him. Of course, he was Lutheran, and she might be Methodist. He wasn't up on the differences between the two.

"A woman like her, right here in front of the children."

"Now, just hold on one blasted minute." John was getting mad, but he sure didn't want to sound like a ravening beast.

"Hush." Mayme Belle had a voice she could crack like a whip. "I'll hear no more of that profane language."

"You think *blasted* is the worst language you're gonna hear?" Penny said, sounding impressively dangerous . . . at least to John.

"Why, you're as good as taking pride in the monstrous impropriety that has passed between you and this man." Mayme Belle didn't seem impressed with Penny's dangerousness.

"There was no—"

"It's a disgrace." The sheriff cut her off, throwing in with a will stronger than his own . . . Mayme Belle. "No doubt about it. And she is defending him, too. Claims he didn't kidnap her, when her brother was in saying he did."

"My brother wasn't even there. I was, and I'm saying he didn't—"

"And now she stands there, clinging to him. Of course she would defend him after spending so much time in wild abandon with him. If she wasn't kidnapped then they must've run off together."

Wild abandon?

"I was kidnapped, but we both—"

"Hang him, Conrad."

"I'll go fetch the rope, Pa." The older boy ran out as if he'd done it a hundred times before, and maybe he had. John had heard the family was new to Dismal, but maybe the Walterses had done sheriffing all across the West. A chill rushed down John's spine.

"Nevada is a state now," John said. He sounded so reasonable. Definitely not like a ravening beast of any kind. He wasn't sure what a ravening beast was, but it sounded mighty bad. "A sheriff can't just go around hanging people. There is law now. Judges and juries."

"Ma, a man and woman off alone is no big deal," one of the young twins said. "You and Pa go out into the barn some nights, and I've heard something of a rumpus."

The sheriff gave John a look that was as good as measuring him for a noose. "I'm the justice of the peace, besides being the sheriff."

Mayme Belle piped up, bless her heart. "And I can get a few men from the saloon to act as a jury. We can settle this within the hour."

Methodists weren't that much different from Lutherans. Maybe an Anabaptist, then? He'd heard they were a caution.

"Besides," the sheriff added, "the law is murky on such crimes as this where the woman denies she's been abused."

"The law is not murky." John talked slowly, trying to be calm. There was that boy back with a rope. "The woman denies I abused her because I didn't. That's crystal clear."

"That's an admission the two of you have been living happily together for over a week," Mayme Belle said, sounding triumphant.

"It wasn't a week, and we weren't that happy." That was the wrong thing to say, as it turned out.

CHAPTER

9

⚜

Penny's head was spinning when the sheriff poked McCall hard in the chest with his six-gun to prod out the response, "I do."

It helped to keep things moving to have the sheriff's son standing by McCall's side—best man maybe? The boy kept whacking the noose he held in one hand into the palm of the other.

Mayme Belle was Penny's matron of honor. Penny knew for a plain fact that the woman had not been asked to act as such.

And a whole family full of witnesses. They'd be good ones, because no one could ever forget this mess.

How could the man, in good conscience, perform a wedding ceremony while holding a fire iron? Well, God sure had different rules for these folks than He did for Penny, who was a simple God-fearin' frontierswoman.

Penny didn't say *I do*. Those words were not coming out

of her mouth. She might've growled, and the sheriff-turned-justice-of-the-peace continued on with the ceremony.

Then he did his pronouncing, and Penny stepped out of the jailhouse a married woman.

Her brother galloped into town at that very moment. Miserably late.

"Penny, you're alive!" Cam reined the horse back so hard it reared, and Cam threw himself off before its front feet were back on the ground. He grabbed Penny in his arms. She saw a puff of dust come off her and was surprised. She thought Mayme Belle had gotten all of it.

"I've been so worried." He pulled back, both of his hands on her shoulders. He studied her for a second, then turned and slammed a fist into her new husband's face.

McCall went down hard, flat on his back on the dirt street, arms flung wide to the sides. And he just stayed there, though his eyes were open. Maybe he was just tired and figured as long as he was down there, he could use the rest.

Speaking to God, or maybe just to the sky, McCall said, "This is turning out to be about exactly the kind of marriage I'd've expected had I planned to marry you, Penny."

Cam reached down for McCall and heaved him upward. "I'll teach you to kidnap my sister, you—" He straightened and dropped John back to the ground.

Cam looked at Penny, his eyes wide as a hoot owl's. "Did he say 'marriage'?"

"Yes, marriage," Penny stated in her most practical tone. "The sheriff just forced us to get married. He was going to hang McCall for kidnapping and murdering me."

Cam looked past Penny to the jail, then scratched the back of his neck.

"I guess I'll drag my husband back to my homestead and try to teach him how to raise cattle. He doesn't have much sense when it comes to surviving on the frontier, but he seems to be of at least average wits. I reckon he can learn."

Showing no interest in getting up, McCall said from the ground, "I am picking up your nephew and going home. I live in Philadelphia."

Penny and Cam glared at McCall, who didn't pay them much mind.

"Are you just resting?"

"No, I figure I might as well stay down here. Sure as you're born, Cam is going to have some excuse to punch me again, even though I don't see how the mighty pathfinder here"—he flung one hand at Penny—"who couldn't find her way out of the wilderness, can blame me for any of this."

"No one blames you for the kidnapping, McCall."

"Excluding the sheriff, his wife, seven children, and, apparently, the entire legal system of the state of Nevada."

"Yes, excluding them. But we do blame you for wanting to take Ronnie. In a way, you're really nuthin' but a dirty kidnapper, just like the sheriff and his wife said."

"I could go for some clean clothes, a meal, a bath, and some rest. Any chance of getting any of that in this town . . . without any money?"

"You can't take Ronnie," Cam said. "Promise you won't try and grab him and run, and I'll buy you a meal. Then we'll go back home and discuss this, and we'll help you understand why you can't give that boy to those low-down Chiltons."

"I promise. Didn't I admit what I was here for? I didn't try and sneak around, snatch him, and run. I had no plans to do that."

Cam nodded silently for a little too long, then he reached his hand down. McCall caught it, and Cam yanked him to his feet.

"There's a diner over there." Cam tipped his head at one of the run-down buildings. This one had *EETS* painted on the door. The building was unpainted and weather-worn until it was gray. The word *EETS* was white and looked to've been painted in about two minutes about ten years ago . . . by a man who couldn't spell. Unless it was possible that his name was Eets.

John led the way. Penny fell in beside Cam.

"Now tell me how in tarnation you two ended up married."

"Before we do, let me tell you how we ended up kidnapped by someone who, I think, would've killed us if we hadn't escaped. Someone with a lot of questions about Raddo."

Cam stopped so fast he skidded, then he grabbed Penny's arm so she faced him. "Raddo?"

"Yep. I'll tell you how McCall saved my life."

"She was about to save herself, but I got there first." John hoped being humble endeared him to his new brother-in-law. His jaw hurt enough for one day.

"And how they searched for us." Penny headed for the diner again. Cam let her drag him along. "And we ran over a cliff, and went down a waterfall, and hid in the densest woods I've seen this side of Montana. Then we got caught in the meanest lightning storm I've ever seen and any hope of finding a trail was washed out. We've been trying to find a house or town or any sign of a person ever since. I've never been so lost in my life. I made a fool of myself out there."

"It's a big wilderness." John reached the bottom of a two-step up to the front door of EETS.

He turned to Penny. "You kept us fed and pushed until we found our way out. You saved me just as surely as I saved you. The difference is, you were almost loose from the ropes and would've gotten away fine. But I don't know if I'd've made it out of there without you. You're right, I'm no frontiersman. I might have wandered around out there for the rest of my life. I'm not fit for this life, and I don't want to be. I'm a Pinkerton, and I've no interest in changing careers or being married."

Cam crossed his arms. "Can we get the wedding annulled? We could find out what papers need to be filed and just do that and forget the whole thing."

Penny nodded. "I reckon we could. Not sure how, though. Best to do it quick before anyone finds out about it."

A man emerged from the diner, still chewing. He stopped right in the doorway and stared. Then he said over his shoulder, "This is that couple what run away and lived in sin for months."

"Months?" Penny plunked her fists on her hips.

Mayme Belle was heading down the sorry excuse for a street with her herd of children. She shouted over, "They're married now! Finally done the right thing!"

"They was out all winter, I heered." Another man came up behind the first one. "You two got hitched? Seems like we've been sending out search parties since the spring thaw, ever since your brother reported that this man had kidnapped you, but now you're married so you must've been willing to go off with him."

Someone from inside the diner hollered with a rolling Scottish accent, "Aye, and I'll be reckonin' there's a bairn on the way. Oftentimes that brings the reckless folks around to proper behavin'. Come on in ta EETS. I'll spot you a meal for a weddin' present. Why, we've had half the town out huntin' you."

Penny muttered, "That'd be about six people."

"The lot of us've been takin' shifts. Mighty sorry we couldn't get to it last fall but word just reached us."

"It's only been a week," Cam snarled. "I'm the one who reported it. *Just a week ago.*"

"That's how I heard it, you came in to report soon as the spring thaw let you loose. A week and already she's got a young'un on the way? Not likely. It's high time you two was married. Us folks don't have any use for ones what carry on so without there being some vows. Sheriff Walters fixed you up right and proper, though. Good man."

"Well, nobody outside this tiny town knows we were off alone," Penny said, sounding a little desperate.

"We sent Harold, Dismal's chandler, all the way to Carson City as soon as your brother brought word. Puttin' it in the newspaper, and telegraphing every town in the state."

Penny punched Cam in the shoulder.

"Ouch." He rubbed his arm and looked at John. "The annulment's off."

John hadn't held out much hope for that anyway. He looked at Penny and did a way better job of whispering than Mayme Belle. "I'm going back to Pennsylvania."

"Fine with me, sidewinder. Want me to take a likeness of our baby now and again and mail you a picture?"

His laugh slipped out, and Penny rolled her eyes and grinned for just a second.

"Harold is spreading the word that you're missing." The town crier here just kept giving them unwanted news. "He figured you for dead so they're looking for your body, and he might be swearing out a warrant that'll include bringing you in dead or alive." The man shrugged. "Sorry about that. Harold always was a man to see the dark side of things. There'll be a hoopla about the murder until the truth comes out. Hope you can keep this from the baby. Hard thing for a child to be born in sin like this."

John grimly accepted that when he went back east, he was going to have a trouser-wearing wife in tow. Well, good. She could watch over Ronnie.

They didn't even try to talk about the kidnapping, or their fight for life. The roast venison was too good. Whoever owned this diner couldn't spell, but he could sure as certain cook. Anyway, too many people kept them company to have a talk with Cam.

It was fascinating to hear the made-up details about where John and Penny had been, what they'd done, and how their lives were going to be.

There was a fond wish that the child be a boy.

John ate fast.

"I need to get you two home."

John had bad news for Cam. He wasn't going to anyplace in Nevada and calling it home. He'd've told him so, but he wanted his black eye to heal a little before he made Cam mad.

"The family is frantic. I looked all over, spread the word about your disappearance, and said McCall kidnapped you 'cuz that's the only thing that made some kind of sense. When you didn't follow Trace back, we came riding into town after you. The two of you just vanished with your horses left standing there. The sheriff was mad as a wet she-cat about everyone leaving. We followed the trail of the wagon that carried you off and found where it'd stopped in the woods. I figured John here had some partners."

"I'm an honest man. It doesn't sit right with me to be accused all over Nevada of kidnapping and murder."

"Well, we only met you the day you helped get Raddo, and then within hours you'd disappeared with my sister. And coming for Ronnie the way you did makes you little more than a kidnapper in my mind. It was easy to believe you were up to no good.

"Once we saw all those tracks, including Penny and one other man running for the woods, we started to hope you were working together. We went after you two—led us in circles after you went down that cliff. The three men pursuing you gave up and rode away from there."

"Three men?" John asked.

Penny said, "Not four?"

"Nope. Trace and I split up at that point. I went after you two, and he went back to where the wagon had been to go after that fourth man. I hadn't gotten too far when that rainstorm hit. I'm hoping Trace is at home, and we can find out what he's uncovered."

John stopped in the middle of Main Street. "Did you bring our horses with you?"

Cam shook his head. "No, but I can buy a couple more at the livery."

"I can only imagine the horseflesh available in this town."

"We only need to get horses good enough to get you two home." Cam set out walking toward a shabby barn at the end of the very small town.

"And I don't have any money. I had some with me, but they stole it and took my pistol."

"I have money." Penny patted her trusty bag.

"Those men were sure foolish to not search you better. You've kept us going with all the things they left." He needed to break the news to her. He felt a little guilty leaving her behind, but he didn't see as he had much choice.

"I'll buy the horses," Cam said. "Think of it like a wedding present."

John looked at Cam. The man's face was straight, his eyes serious. But John could've sworn the man was fighting not to laugh.

"I appreciate the horse. Penny, I'm going to need your gun, and some money to buy supplies."

"So you're heading back east right now?" Penny didn't seem overly upset by that assumption.

"No, I'm going to hunt down those men who kidnapped us, arrest them, and investigate them until I can prove they were in cahoots with Raddo."

Penny stopped so short she stumbled. "How will you find them?"

"I'm a Pinkerton agent. Finding people is what I do. I found Ronnie, didn't I? Living miles from the town noted in Deb's letter, and in a house that didn't even exist when the letter was written. I'll find them." And he had an advantage that Whisper Man didn't know about. "When I find them, they'll all hang."

"You have a mean streak I've never noticed before." Penny smiled. "Glad to know it. I think that black eye forming from Cam's fist makes the mean streak seem worse than it is."

"Nope, it's bad. I've just been busy running for my life, then clawing my way out of the darkest woods I've ever seen. No time for being mean until now."

"How will you find him? We were blindfolded, and he even whispered to disguise his voice."

"Because of his questions, we know Whisper Man was involved with Raddo. He was worried Raddo had left behind evidence. Whisper Man had a cold-blooded way about him that tells me he's not afraid to kill. If we hadn't escaped, I doubt we'd have survived the kidnapping."

Penny came up beside him. "Do you think he'll come after us?"

John shook his head hard, twice. "It doesn't matter. I'm not going after him to protect myself. I'm a lawman. I'm not about to witness a crime and ignore it."

"You can't find him in the wilderness."

John went on without reacting to that. "Sheriff Walters may be satisfied that everything is cleared up, but we all know better."

Penny caught hold of his arm.

He talked right over whatever she was going to say. "No group of outlaws is going to kidnap me and assault me and expect to walk away untouched. You add in the rough way they grabbed you, Penny, and kept you tied up. Whisper Man broke the law. What's more, those men with him were hired help. Hiring men to kidnap someone breaks another law. He's a criminal, and he needs to be stopped."

"I'd like to catch the polecat, too. But how?"

Cam said, "We start by asking Trace about the trail he followed after that sidewinder."

"And we have one more advantage." John's jaw formed a single hard line, and satisfaction flared out of eyes that had gone as cold as blue ice.

"What's that?"

"You said we didn't see anything, but that's not true. I pretended to be unconscious because I hoped it would give me an edge. I managed to see a few things. Not his face, though I'm sure he was masked. But his legs, his boots. He was a man dressed in fine, expensive boots, unusual boots, and I know something about it that'll help. We aren't looking for another like Raddo. This is a rich man. There can't be too many of those around."

"We live in the shadow of the Comstock Lode," Cam said. "Every fourth man is a millionaire."

John's shoulders sagged. "That'll slow me down some, but on the other hand we just eliminated three-fourths of all the suspects."

Penny sighed and said, "We do need to go after him, I reckon."

"Not we, Penny. Me. I'm going after him. We'll go on home with Cam and find out from Trace where the other trail led. Then I'll go after this crook. All I need is for you to hand over your gun, your money, and my horse."

Penny looked sideways at Cam. "I feel like we're talking to a bandit."

Cam gave a bark of laughter.

She turned back to John. "I'm going with you."

"I'm going alone."

"I just spent a week with you in the woods. You may be the best all-fired detective in Pinkerton history, but you don't know nuthin' about frontier life."

"Maybe I won't need to know anything. This outlaw lives in a city, I'd say. If Trace got that far, then I'll do the rest."

"And if he didn't, you'll have no choice but to do some trailing. You'll get lost and starve to death. I'm going." Penny turned on the toes of her boots and headed for the livery, faster this time.

"I can find my way."

"You'll die. Not that being a widow wouldn't be handy for me, but I want to get those men, too."

"I reckon I'm coming, too." Cam sounded grumpy.

"No, you're not," John snapped. "You're staying home with your wife and Penny. I'm going alone, and that's final." He glared at Penny. "You swore to obey not one hour ago. Do you remember that?"

"Not really. It's all a blur. I couldn't even believe it was happening. You probably shouldn't get your heart set on me obeying you."

"You took an oath before God, and you're ignoring it?" John heard his voice rising and fought to keep it low.

"I didn't make any oath. If you heard one, then your ears are mighty creative. And I've got a mighty strong suspicion that God wasn't in favor of today. And since I didn't say it, and God doesn't agree with it, I'd say it's not an oath worth worrying about."

Which didn't make the legal paper work go away.

"Well, God wasn't in favor of my being hung, was He?"

Penny didn't answer for what seemed like a long time—way too long. "Probably not." She didn't sound one bit sure. "But marrying me saved your life. Which to me oughta make you the one who's obeying me. I reckon no one in the history of the world has ever written that vow."

"Since these folks in Dismal stand as witness to your ruin"—John shook his head in disbelief—"and they took the ridiculous step of apparently telling people all over the state about it, along with the fact that we've spent the winter together and I'm only marrying you because you are with child—"

Cam started growling and made a fist.

"If you take another swing at me, I'm not going to be so nice about it this time. This is all your fault for accusing me of kidnapping your sister."

To Penny, John said, "Plan on staying at your homestead. Build your cabin if you've a mind to let your brand-new husband ride off without you. I'm going back to Pennsylvania as soon as I've solved this crime. When I have Whisper Man in jail, I'll stop by, and we can talk about Ronnie."

Penny grunted.

"And while we're heading home," Cam said, "I want to hear everything about this." He hesitated for a long moment. "There's . . . uh . . . not . . . not a chance that . . . that there . . . uh . . . might be a b-baby on the way, is there?"

Penny slugged him in the shoulder.

Cam grabbed his arm. "That hurt."

"And I can do worse. Nothing happened between us out there."

Which, John admitted strictly to himself, was not entirely true.

"Just being off together was enough to have the sheriff's wife in a dither."

"Sorry, I just had to ask."

"Oh no, you did not." She punched him again.

Cam looked at John. "She had two brothers and never bothered to pull her punches as a child. You need to be warned."

"Next time you ask a blamed-fool question like that"—Penny swung again but Cam dodged her—"you're going to have a shiner to match John's. Now, let's get home."

She let him avoid the punch, so John decided she was ready to head home. Maybe she was anxious to tell Cam their story.

"We should've waited and told you the whole story after we got home. Now we'll just have to tell it again." Penny reined in her horse, astonished at the neat cabin that stood where a pile of logs was less than a week ago. It wasn't finished, but the walls were up and the roof was framed. "I thought you were searching for me? When did you have time to build a cabin?" She had to admit her feelings were hurt.

"I hunted, Trace hunted, and Utah hunted for a while. We couldn't haul all the little ones along." Cam must've realized how she felt because he wasn't a man to explain himself much, and now he sounded a little desperate. "So, they stayed here. And we couldn't leave Deb and Gwen alone with two babies, so Utah came home, and he and Adam stayed to guard them and built a cabin while they were guarding."

"It makes sense, I reckon," Penny said, giving John a disgusted look. "It just seems like they'd've been a little too worried to carry on so well."

"Besides, someone needed to be here for when John sent a ransom note." Cam jerked his head in McCall's direction. "We thought he might be planning to hold you until we handed over Ronnie."

"You people," McCall snarled as he swung down, "should stop making up crimes I had no intention of committing. I'm an honest man."

"Penny!" Deb ran out of the cabin, Ronnie on her hip.

Deb was the only one who'd seen the men who'd done the killing last fall. Trace had come along the trail to find the massacre and rescue Deb, Gwen, and the little ones. He'd brought them to his home, where Deb had sent word to Cam and Penny. They'd come to fetch the children home and had been trapped for the winter by the deep snow.

Deb had married Trace last fall just before Penny had gotten here, and already there was a baby on the way. She and Trace lived a spell from here, but they'd come over to help build the cabins. Cam and Gwen had married right after the spring thaw. They'd all spent the winter fighting off Raddo's attacks in his efforts to silence the only living witness to his crimes during the massacre, Deb.

Penny narrowed her eyes at her sister-in-law and wondered if those were tears. She'd thought Deb was made of sterner stuff.

"You're alive." Gwen was a few paces behind. Maddie ran along, holding Gwen's hand. The little one laughed and jumped up and down, waving. Gwen, too.

They flung themselves at her until she was almost smothered in hugs. McCall was close enough he put out a hand and kept them from knocking her down.

It was a decent homecoming.

McCall called loud enough to be heard over the din, "I didn't kidnap her. I saved her."

Speaking more normally—no one probably heard him but Penny—he added, "There's a lot more to it, but we can tell the tale later."

"Penny!" Trace came jogging from a corral set up just a few yards away, pulling buckskin gloves off his hands. "I'm glad to see you didn't come to any harm. I've been riding trails all week looking for you." Trace's eyes shifted to McCall.

Penny had never realized just how cold those eyes could be.

"We were kidnapped together. McCall didn't harm me, in fact he saved me."

With a satisfied jerk of his chin, Trace went on. "I found the direction one of the men who was involved took. I came back to get help and go back out."

They were standing by Cam's cabin. He'd chosen a beautiful glen, a broad clearing back in the woods, not far off a wide mountain valley full of lush grass. Before their wedding, Gwen had signed for a homestead right next to Cam's. They shared a property line, and Penny's property was nearby so all the acres amounted to an unbroken piece of land. Cam and Gwen built the cabin so their property lines ran right through the middle of it. They could live on both pieces of property—as was necessary to prove up on a homestead—and still share a home. Penny's cabin would be as close as they could build it and still have it on her own land.

"Did my packs survive my absence?" John asked.

"We were tempted to burn them to a cinder," Deb said. "But we were too busy."

"You carry a lot of baggage," Cam added. "Leave it to a city fella to not know how to travel light."

"Your bags are in the tent on Penny's homestead. We're building her cabin now. Do you have things in there that will help you with your investigation?" Deb said.

"No, well, I do, yes. But that's not what I want in the pack."

"What are you looking for?" Penny asked.

With a heavy sigh, John said, "I haven't changed my clothes for the filthiest week of my life. Well, no, during the war I once spent the night in a swamp, buried up to my neck in slimy bayou mud, hiding from Confederate troops. So that was the worst. But this is plenty bad. I'd like to take a bath and clean up, then see to settling in my wife, Penny, somewhere and get back on the trail."

"What?" Gwen's voice startled the horses.

Penny patted Gwen's arm. "We were trapped into marriage because we were alone in the wilderness for so long. They thought McCall kidnapped me thanks to my brother's big mouth, and when I said he didn't, they thought we'd been in an improper situation for too long. They even hinted that there might be a baby on the way, for the love of Pete. It was either marry him or watch them hang him."

"You're married and—and—and—" Gwen gave Penny's belly an alarmed look.

"I'm married, but the rest isn't true. Good heavens, it was all a mistake." Penny explained about McCall's arrest, the threat of hanging, the presence of a noose at their wedding, and the resulting gossip that had already spread to Carson City and was being telegraphed around the state.

Gwen looked from Penny to McCall and back. "So, you're married? Is that all right with either of you?"

McCall shrugged. "I live in Philadelphia. I hope Penny likes the big city."

Penny snorted. "And I have a homestead in the Sierra Nevada Mountains, and my husband here has little skill for frontier life and no interest in gaining any. So no, it's not all right with either of us, but we can't find a solution. In fact, I tend to forget it even happened. At least as a married couple it's as proper as can be to ride off with McCall here to find and arrest the men who kidnapped us."

"You're not going." McCall headed for the cabin.

"Are you leaving now?"

"No, I'm going to get my pack and clean up before heading out. I've got a job to do. I'll be back to talk about Ronnie once our kidnappers are arrested."

Penny shook her head and said to Gwen, "I wonder how long it'll take to teach him to bust a steer?" She started after McCall.

"You're not going with me," McCall called over his shoulder.

"If you're going, I'm going," Cam hollered from behind Penny.

Penny walked, careful not to catch up to McCall, but all too glad to leave her brother behind. She couldn't wait to see McCall's face when she told him how to hunt and skin an elk.

CHAPTER 12

"I didn't think we'd ever manage to leave Cam behind."
Penny kicked her horse into a trot.

"I should have left you behind." McCall rode along, sullen
and overly quiet.

He was a mighty poor loser.

"Stop fussin'." Penny had little patience for a man who
pouted. "You know good and well you can't find those men
in this wilderness. We could barely find our way back to
Dismal—and you'd've never managed it."

"Dismal about describes it."

"You're not going to be a grouch of a husband, are you?"

"I'm not going to be a husband at all. I live in Pennsylvania
and you live in Nevada." Which wasn't really an answer.

Penny shrugged. "Suits me." In truth it didn't really suit
her. She thought they oughta at least try being married . . . in
the same state. She probably ought to tell him that, but she
decided to wait until right before he left . . . without Ronnie.

"And you know what else, wife?" He snapped out the word.

Penny arched a brow and watched him as they left her family behind, heading for the spot where Trace had lost the trail of the man who'd ridden in alone to question Penny and McCall.

"It sits all wrong with me"—he slashed one arm—"to take you back out into these woods." He pointed at the dense forest all around them. "Where we know dangerous men lie in wait."

He looked at her fully, his jaw clenched, his eyes shining with . . . something. She thought it was worry. Maybe worry for her. But worry buried under grouchiness, so it was hard to tell.

"But I'd never make it without you."

The simple statement said right while she was inhaling made her cough.

He watched her until she got her breathing going along again.

"When we track this man to a town, my talents will be handy, but right now, I need you. I learned out in those woods just how much I don't know. I thought I knew a little about tracking, but now I'm certain I'm nowhere near as good as you. And the sad fact is, I'm no good at all."

Penny sat, stunned. She'd been around a lot of men for the last couple of years, traipsing along with Cam while he served in one frontier fort after another. She knew men had the devil's own time admitting they needed help. Especially in the outdoors. Her brother sure as certain never showed much inclination to ask for a woman's help with what he considered manly skills.

Something softened in her heart for a man who'd proven to be strong in the last week they'd spent together. And one to shoulder every ounce of his own load and as much of hers as she'd allow. Yet here he was admitting to a weakness. This wasn't a kind of man she'd ever known before. And she thought she'd met all kinds. To ask for help struck her as the most confident thing a man could do.

"We'll find the trail and find the men together," she said. "Where the trail's in the country, I'll do the reading, and when we get to a town, well, I've no notion of how to read signs on a busy street. So, you can teach me how that's done."

"Fair enough." He adjusted his gun in its holster. He'd dug money out of his packs, and added to Penny's, it was enough to outfit them with a large stack of supplies.

"What do you make of finding that gold in Raddo's saddle-bags?" McCall asked.

Penny liked being consulted. It was just the worst kind of dirty shame that she was no help. "I've got no notion. He looked like a man down to his last strip of jerky to me. Clothes worn out and no horse, either. Wonder who he robbed?"

"I want to give it some thought."

Which struck Penny as about the politest way she'd ever been told to shut up, so she did . . . since she had nothing to say anyway.

Silence stretched as they picked their way along a trail about as wide as a buckboard. The woods had been driven back just far enough for them to pass riding side by side, but they were a bit too close together for comfort.

The trail was too rough to make good time, and they had a long way to go. The horses were sound, but no sense pushing them and letting them come up lame. The silence gave her plenty of time to think, which she did long enough that her belly twisted into a ball of nerves.

"What are we going to do about being married?" McCall asked.

"I don't know, and I don't want to talk about it."

"We've got days ahead of us on this trail. We've got nothing else to do, so we might as well talk this out." McCall sounded gruff. "How do you feel about actually being married? Do you want to try it? Come back to Philadelphia with me?"

"I lived back east all my life. I like it out here better."

"So, then, you want to stay here on your homestead . . . which I now own. My understanding of the law says all your possessions are now mine."

"That's a stupid law."

"I'd have to agree, but until they change it, that's how it is."

"You can move out here. You can live on my acres. The law says I have to improve the land, which means build a house—which is in progress—and I have to live in that house at least six months out of every year. You're welcome to move in." He wasn't really all that welcome, but she only realized just what it meant for him to move in when the words came out of her mouth.

"I don't care to be a rancher. I'm a Pinkerton agent. So, I'll go home, and you'll stay here. And because we're already married, we'll both have to remain unmarried for the rest of our lives, not counting each other."

The silence stretched again. Penny finally said quietly, "Let's spend these next days searching for our kidnappers, and just get to know each other better. I don't like the idea of being unmarried for the rest of my life . . . unmarried not counting you. I've always thought I'd want a home and family. I've heard of a divorce, but I think a judge needs a better reason than we just didn't mean to get married and we want to undo it. And besides, it's a terrible sin. We can't do that. So, you're my only chance. And—" Penny faltered.

"And what?"

"There was, well, if you . . . uh . . . remember, there was that one k-kiss." Penny felt her gut twist to mention it.

Suddenly McCall reined his horse in. Penny did the same just so she didn't leave him behind. Before she could figure out what he was about, he was on the ground, his hands around her waist, and he pulled her down to stand in front of him.

"I most certainly do remember." McCall lowered his head and kissed her again.

―⤜✤⤛―

Florence Chilton stepped off the stagecoach in Ringo, Nevada, growling.

"You sound," Edmond sniped quietly in her ear, "like a cur hound."

Florence didn't reply, didn't even look at him. She quit growling, though. When had her weak-spined husband gotten the idea he could talk to her like that?

She'd make him pay—oh yes, she surely would—when she'd had some rest and food. No, she'd wait until they had little Cameron back and had settled in San Francisco. She needed a man right now, and Edmond was all she had.

But very soon, she'd crack the whip, and he'd step back into his place in her life.

"We need a good night's sleep." She spoke through gritted teeth. "You see to the bags. I'll get us a room—hopefully without vermin."

Weighed down with the two satchels she never let out of her sight, she headed for a ramshackle two-story building with the words *Bolling's Boardinghouse* painted above the front door.

It looked to be the closest they'd come to a hotel. The boards were unpainted and weathered gray. There was a row of six windows along the second floor, which made it near a mansion by this town's standards. She wondered at people who could live in this squalor.

Florence didn't look back. Edmond would probably handle things with the stagecoach, mainly because it took few brains to watch a man throw down baggage. And they didn't have much. It wasn't easy to carry luggage when a couple was slipping away from creditors in the dark of night.

Add to that, all their true wealth was in Florence's possession. She'd started the journey letting Edmond carry the gold while she carried the lighter but more valuable jewels. Then she'd caught him gambling. Since then, heavy as they were, she'd carried those two bags herself, day and night.

They were finally in Nevada. Now they needed to find out where Trace Riley lived. He was from a town called Dismal, which was the address on the letter Florence had received from Deb Harkness all those months ago.

They'd given up waiting for that Pinkerton agent to come back. Not because he was overly slow—they knew it would be a long journey for him. But because their creditors had run out of patience . . . so Florence had run out of town.

Yes, these two satchels contained enough money to pay what they owed, including their house, mortgaged to the rafters, and bills in all the most fashionable shops in Philadelphia. But to pay their bills would have taken most everything she'd been hoarding all these years, and she had no intention of impoverishing herself.

So, they'd skipped out of town to come after their grandson. A little boy with an inheritance he knew nothing about—from his mother, who'd also known nothing about it. A little boy who, if he was in their care, was worth a fortune.

A fortune that Florence had no intention of seeing go to anyone but herself.

———— ❧ ————

Luther slammed both hands flat on his desk. "They made it back to town?"

"Yes, sir, Mr. Payne. They did." Dudd nodded his head while holding his battered hat with two hands, nervously circling the hat round and round.

Luther had to give it to his hired man. The other two men who'd gone on this ill-advised mission hadn't had the courage to come in and tell about the failed search for those folks who'd brought Raddo's body in.

They'd said Raddo left nothing behind, and Luth was half-inclined to believe them. But Luther knew his brother well. He was as wily as a coyote. Raddo had known coming to Luth for money was dangerous. Years ago, after they'd given up a life of crime, Luth had helped set his little brother up in mining, and warned him he'd do no more.

Then Raddo had wanted more.

What was a little good-natured blackmail between brothers?

Oh yes, somewhere there was evidence, there could be no doubt of it. But Luther was also sure Raddo wouldn't carry the evidence on him, for fear Luth would send someone to retrieve it and silence Raddo for good. Being brothers and thieves and murderers together hadn't bred much trust.

Raddo would leave enough clues behind so someone could find that evidence, if they realized what they had. Did that pair know?

Luth had made Raddo swear to leave the area. And he'd given him enough money to do it in comfort. But of course, Raddo paid no heed. Now he was dead, and Luth hated the thought of secrets, so long buried, surfacing like ghosts escaping from the grave.

And Luth was the one they haunted.

"What do we do, Mr. Payne?"

Luth fumed. Did he dare let it go? He'd been keeping a lot closer track of Raddo than his brother realized, and one of his men had seen him killed and come running with the news in time for them to set up the kidnapping in Dismal. But it had been a huge risk.

And now that pair knew there were questions. His actions might have sent them on a mission to figure out exactly who had kidnapped them and why, and they'd look closer at Raddo while they searched for Luth.

And what about his hired guns?

Luther's gut impulse was to kill all three of them. Getting rid of the witnesses . . . Raddo had learned that from Luth.

But loyal men weren't that easy to find, and Dudd here, and the men with him, were loyal. And besides, Luth could always kill them later. Unlike Raddo, Luth was slow about his killing. And sneaky about it. He'd made sure none of his crimes ever led back to him.

Until this miserable mess.

Had those two seen or heard anything that could be a clue?

Had they found his tracks and come after him? No, they'd be here by now if they had. And he'd heard enough from Raddo to know it wasn't just those two. They came with friends and family.

"For now, I've got some other things for you to do." Luth explained what he wanted. "We'll worry about the pair we kidnapped later."

Dudd nodded and left so quickly, Luth had to wonder if Dudd had feared for his life. That made him a mighty brave man to come and give a full report.

Bravery had its place, but Luth didn't want a man with too much backbone. They were the kind who stabbed you when you weren't looking.

He sat down at his massive oak desk and began to turn over plots and plans in his head.

What evidence had Raddo hidden?

What clues to that evidence had that couple seen?

What was Luth going to do to keep his dynasty from tumbling down on his head?

CHAPTER

13

John pulled away from Penny. "Now we've got another kiss
to remember."

He watched the heat in her dark brown eyes. Not temper—
passion.

Everything about her glowed a shining sable brown save
the golden highlights sunburned into her hair. The doeskin
coat she wore and the slouchy leather hat that looked like
she'd made it herself were brown like her hair and eyes.

She'd twisted her hair into two braids, hanging down
in front. She'd cleaned up from their first adventure in the
woods, then dressed for her own comfort and convenience.

He found he liked that about her. At home in nature. With
little vanity and taking pride only in what true skills she possessed that aided her survival.

A woman with good sense who looked like warmth, felt
like fire.

Oh yes, he surely did remember that kiss.

John looked at her, and she stared right back. And she hadn't insulted him or punched him in quite a while.

"I think we should at least give being married a chance." Those words popped out. He didn't plan them. He didn't mean them. He didn't even know if he wanted to be married to her.

Well, he wanted to kiss her again. And he wanted a few other things that meant he probably should admit he *did* want to be married to her.

If he'd had his druthers he'd've avoided it. But given no choice . . . "Don't we owe it to each other to at least try? We took vows before God—"

"I'm pretty sure I didn't say a word, the sheriff just plowed on over my silence. And I think you said 'I do' when he jabbed you in the belly with his pistol. God was bound to notice we weren't making sincere promises."

"And yet here we stand married. And we'd probably have to take it all the way to the Supreme Court to fight that situation. So—what do you think? I find that I respect you, and obviously I enjoy kissing you and . . . and . . . Do you think we should at least try being married before we put ten states between us and live out our lives alone?"

"T-Try?"

He watched her throat move as she swallowed. Almost against his will, he kissed the spot on her throat he was watching. He'd meant try getting to know each other, try to see if they got along. But when she spoke and that long, graceful throat moved, he'd gotten distracted. He kissed her again. This time on the side of her jaw, and he felt her face pull into a soft smile.

Oh yes, he surely did have something he wanted to try.

She shoved against his chest, and when he didn't move, she stumbled backward. "We have things to do, McCall."

And he had to fight back a smile on that one. They most certainly had some very married things to do. But not yet. They really did need to get to know each other before anything else happened.

"You're right. So right. I've spent the last week at your mercy, Mrs. McCall."

Penny scowled but didn't bother to correct him . . . since he was correct.

"But now we are going to town. I know more about those boots than I let on. I wanted to think it over, consider the possibilities, and I didn't want to debate things with your brother and Trace and all the rest of the family. But I saw flashy boots. Not just new, but shined, calfskin, polished black Hessian boots, with just enough dirt on them to tell me those boots get polished every day."

"A rich man. I think we told you every other man around here is a millionaire because of the Comstock Lode."

John sincerely doubted it. "Those boots weren't by any tinker out here in the mines."

"All the rich types travel to San Francisco several times a year." Then Penny furrowed her brow. "I've heard that when they come to Virginia City, they don't flash their wealth. There are too many outlaws. The richest men build mansions for themselves in San Francisco. They come to Virginia City in the summer and get out before winter hits. Then they spend the cold-weather months dressed in fine feathers and living it up in California. When they're here, they live humbly."

"Well, this man was dressed up—or rather his feet were.

And his connection to Raddo—I have to wonder if he doesn't go back a long way around here. Maybe of a type with Raddo."

"Maybe even an old partner in his outlaw gang." Fire flashed in Penny's eyes.

"He asked us what Raddo said and carried. Now, I'm a suspicious man for a living, but that sounds like a man who fears we know something. And that sounds like Raddo might've been blackmailing him."

John crossed his arms and turned to pace. It helped sometimes to move when ideas where sparking. He stopped and looked thoughtfully at Penny. "I was there when he died. I know he was searched."

"Yes, and what about his horse?" Penny went on. "He had all that money in his saddlebags. Raddo was purely pathetic the one time I saw him, near the end of winter. He was dressed nearly in rags. We didn't think he had a horse, because when he kidnapped Deb, Trace and his cowhands came storming in to rescue her, and Raddo lit out on foot. He didn't have a horse that we saw."

Penny rubbed her hands together. "When he died, he was well set up compared to when we found him in that cave. A good horse, a nice suit of clothes, plenty of money and supplies."

John went back to pacing. "But you found no evidence that would tie Raddo to whoever he was blackmailing?"

"Cam hunted through everything before we took Raddo to the sheriff."

There was an extended silence, broken only by the sound of John pacing, ten strides one way, turn, and ten strides back. Over and over.

Penny asked, "Where would Raddo hide something in such a way it'd be sure to come to light if he died?"

"We call it, 'In the event of my death,'" John said. "And very often the person will leave evidence with a lawyer with instructions to . . . make whatever he's holding public or send it to someone."

With a grimace John found cute enough to stop his pacing for a few seconds, Penny shook her head. "Would such a rough character as Raddo have a lawyer?"

"He could have. But he could also leave the evidence with a friend."

"Raddo wouldn't have a friend he could trust," Penny said with flat certainty.

"Now, Mrs. McCall, have you never heard of honor among thieves?"

Penny snorted. Her wrinkled nose earlier, now a snort. John should not find it all so charming. But mercy, he did.

Grinning, he said, "I happen to agree."

More silence, more pacing.

"Is this how Pinkerton detectives work? Standing around thinking?"

"Thinking often helps. You should try it before you find fault."

She snarled this time. Also cute.

"But I can think and ride at the same time. Let's go."

"I haven't even picked up a trail yet."

John paused a beat. "We need to head to Virginia City."

Penny stopped in the middle of gathering up her reins. "What made you decide that?"

"We've reasoned out that our kidnapper is an old-timer to the area. That says to me Virginia City." John swung up on his horse.

"I think Carson City sprang up at the same time."

"Yes, but Virginia City's the boomtown. It's wilder, more lawless. Carson City, the new state capital, has government, order, probably lots of law. Not where a man with crimes in his past would settle. Let's go to Virginia City and ask some questions."

"A town that's lawless sounds dangerous. I've heard Virginia City is a madhouse."

"Didn't you just come into the country about six months ago, then you got locked in for the winter in a remote cabin? And now you're an expert on Virginia City? You haven't been there, have you?"

Shaking her head, Penny said, "No, but some of the soldiers I knew had. I heard talk. It has as many as twenty thousand people living there amid every kind of vice. For every hard-working miner, and for every mine owner who's gotten rich, there are nearly an equal number of thieves willing to kill you for a few silver nuggets that might be in your pockets." Penny mounted up.

"I came through there on my way out. I'd say that describes it." John set out. He noticed she followed, despite her dire warnings.

"It's a good thing we're married so I can protect you," he said.

"Fine, I'll protect you right back."

John laughed. "I'll take the help."

He wasn't sure if she agreed with him about Virginia City, or if she was just a woman who liked to get going. Whichever it was, she was coming along.

Then he thought of that kiss they'd shared. Having her tag along all the way to Philadelphia was a fine idea.

Cam walked his horse toward the tent near where Penny's cabin was going up. He had a few head of cattle grazing on her grass. He had to force himself not to mutter and fidget. Two things he didn't do. But he was just plain worried about his sister.

Trace had left her with McCall, and Cam had wanted to beat Trace to a pulp. And then Cam had turned around and let her ride out with McCall just like an empty-headed fool.

How long would she be gone? How dangerous was this investigation McCall was working on? It came down to his sister being gone again. Maybe McCall was just the sneakiest kidnapper who ever lived.

A movement up the hill drew his attention. He didn't make one single change in the way he rode or moved. He went on toward Penny's cabin until he came to a huge jumble of boulders. Swinging his horse behind them, he leapt down, lashed his stallion to a tree, and hit his belly, flat on the ground, all in nearly one smooth motion.

Dragging himself forward using his elbows, he got to the edge of the stack of rocks and, removing his hat, he eased out. Too low, the trees blocked his view. Inching up, his eyes riveted on the place where he'd seen that movement. He caught sight of a rifle with a scope on it. A rifle aimed at Cam's cabin. Where Gwen minded the children while she cleaned up after breakfast and got a start on the noon meal.

Cam felt the roar of rage press to get out. To draw the man's attention before he pulled the trigger. But he held off. As long as Gwen was inside, she was safe.

Cam saw no finger on the trigger. The man held the rifle by

the butt and barrel, yes, braced against his shoulder as if he was preparing to shoot. But he was looking down that scope.

Not aiming to kill. Aiming to watch.

Cam's mind worked fast—his army training kicking in. It came naturally to assess a situation and make swift changes in plans as things unfolded.

This man wasn't a killer, at least that wasn't what he'd come for today. And Cam knew Gwen had baking to do, and she had already had the children out to the privy earlier. No, she had no plans for a morning outside.

A chill raced down Cam's spine as he thought about how easy it would have been for this man to pull the trigger when Cam had come outside.

Instead of setting out to capture the man, Cam decided to learn all he could.

CHAPTER

14

"Boomtown." Penny said the word loud enough for McCall to hear, but only that. Nothing more. What more was there to say?

Penny glanced at him, amazed at the sprawling town carved out of the side of a mountain.

"You remember me saying I knew the wilderness and tracking and you knew cities, McCall? Do you really think you can find what you want in this place?"

The constant moving of horses, wagons, men on foot. The sound of hammers and saws, shouting. The smell of the place.

"Sure, I can."

"Virginia City is one of the biggest cities I've ever seen. I came from Philadelphia, of course, but out here? I can't believe this."

"Let's go down and see what we can find." McCall lifted his reins, then stopped and grabbed Penny's arm. "Wait."

"What's the matter?"

"I forgot I'm wanted for kidnapping and murder."

"Surely one look will convince them you didn't murder me."

"Yep, that is, if they bother to take one look. They might just come out guns blazing. We'd better call ourselves by a phony name in case you're still listed as a kidnap victim and someone is gunning for me. And I was here on my way to find Ronnie. I don't want to go anywhere I went before."

Penny frowned. "What if I forget your name?"

"Call me honey."

Penny looked sideways at him and grinned. "I'll be sure to forget that."

"I'll introduce us as Penelope and Jonathan Call. I think that's similar enough to remember and different enough we won't get arrested. You'd better start calling me Jonathan in front of people. We're a married couple, and I want everyone who sees us to know it and believe it."

"Jonathan, yes, and John is a common name. I can still call you that. If I slip and say McCall, hopefully no one will notice the first part of it. Anyway, a wife oughta call her husband by his first name, I reckon." She smiled at him, and he smiled back. It reminded her of that kiss, of all the kissing they'd done, in fact. Yep, she'd better start calling him John.

"And I need to get you out of those trousers."

That startled her into silence. She felt her cheeks heating up.

John said, "Uh . . . I mean into a dress. You should be wearing a dress."

The trail had turned into a well-traveled road, and they rode side by side. Penny had no desire to get separated from McCall . . . John, she corrected herself.

"Let's try and avoid the law. I don't want to talk my way out of another hanging. I've got too much to do and not enough time, and I don't want that kind of attention." John kept his horse moving, and Penny wondered how to find anything in this place. But from the first view of town it was clear there was a business district. Taller buildings, painted and more established. The edges of the town were being built, pushing the town's borders outward, but they rode past some neat homes on their way to those taller buildings. John rode straight up to a hotel, painted red with white porch railings on three stories.

"Let's go in here and ask some questions."

Tension climbed up Penny's spine as she thought of spending the night somewhere with John. She had no idea what it would cost, but if they had to search this whole town based on John's quick glimpse of a man's fancy boots, they could be here awhile. She might push to get out into the countryside and set up a camp, work from there.

Before John reached the glass-fronted door of the hotel, he stopped and stared down the boardwalk. A sign stuck out of a building a block or so down. Printed in clear block letters, it read *Virginia City Sheriff's Office*.

He hurried a pace ahead of her. "Let's get inside quick."

A realization hit Penny. "You might want to keep that fancy-boots information to yourself. The rich men in this town might be paying more than their fair share of the sheriff's salary."

John paused to let Penny come up beside him and shot her a smile. "Why, Penny McCall, what a complete lack of faith you have in human nature."

Penny rolled her eyes. "No, that's just exactly wrong, John.

I absolutely have faith in human nature. Have you noticed how natural it is for men to be dishonest, greedy, and selfish? I'd say being a decent, honorable man is, far too often, the exact opposite of human nature. And that's never more true than in a town built on a mining boom. That's why forgiveness is a cornerstone of Christian faith. Folks are always needing it."

"That's the truth. The truth and nothing but." John gave her a long look. Then his eyes narrowed, and he got a purely crafty look on his face. "And I've got another slice of truth for you."

"What's that?" Penny hadn't really spent much time thinking about what kind of man her husband was. As a detective, though, it figured he'd be plotting and planning.

"I just realized we need a little better plan than just bullying our way around town asking questions. It's not just the law that might take a coin or two in exchange for tattling about outsiders asking questions."

"What have you got in your head, John?"

"First"—his eyes rose to the fancy printing on the door to the hotel—"we're gonna need more modest accommodations than this hotel, so I can afford to arrange disguises."

"Disguises? What are you up to?"

"I'm up to buying you a new dress. I need to turn you into a proper city woman."

Penny snorted.

John grinned. "I find I like it when you snort."

"I'm married to a half-wit," Penny muttered.

He caught her arm as they went back to where they'd hitched the horses, and he led the way through an alley. They left the nice businesses behind and came to run-down buildings that were mostly saloons. He stopped in front of a shabby little two-story building with a hand-painted sign on its sagging front door that read *Room and Board Two Bits.*

John rented a room for one night using the name Mr. and Mrs. Call. Then he unpacked the strange number of cases and satchels he hauled around, and carried them upstairs. Penny had her usual trusty bag slung over her shoulder, and she'd brought along a satchel with a change of clothes. That was all she needed.

John unlocked a door that looked wobbly enough to be kicked open with little effort. "You stay here. I'll stable the horses and be back as soon as possible with a silk dress for you. Do you have a color preference?"

Penny glared at him. "Whatever's least expensive because I reckon I'll be tearing it up to make dishrags as soon as we're done with it."

Nodding, John said, "Fair enough."

"And why exactly can't I go with you?"

"I don't want anyone to see either of us until we're in city clothes."

Penny glanced down at her britches, brown shirt, and boots. "There's nothing wrong with these clothes."

"And besides, it's a rough-and-tumble town, especially in this area where the cheaper places to stay are. I want you to be safe."

"And I'll be safe in a silk dress?"

John's eyes slid down and up her body. Hair in braided pigtails, slouchy broad-brimmed hat, and buckskin coat. Those shocking trousers. "Oh yeah, you'll be safe."

A shouting match erupted from just outside the window.

Vile curses filled the air, then suddenly they were cut off by the thud of swinging fists.

"Well"—John shrugged his shoulders sheepishly—"safer anyway. Lock the door, and don't let anyone in but me."

Penny said, "Oh, I thought I'd just hold a big old party. I'm sure to make new friends around here."

A gun fired in the street below, and someone hollered something that broke about half the commandments in one go.

John gave her a narrow-eyed glare. "And while you're in here *all alone*, I suggest you keep your gun out and aimed at the door. I'll holler before I come in to keep my belly from being filled with lead."

She had a real mean urge to shoot right now. He seemed to realize that and left without further delay.

"Will you be staying more than one night?" A grubby little man stood behind a rickety little desk in Bolling's Boarding-house, one of the few places to stay in Ringo.

"Our plans aren't finalized," Florence answered with a smile, though her teeth were gritted.

She couldn't believe the West. It was nothing but an insult to be forced to deal with people such as Mr. Bolling and to stay in such a decrepit dwelling.

Years of experience lying helped get her through. Yes, she'd like very much to tell the man his filthy hotel and foul presence offended her and it was beneath her to have to speak to him. Appalling that she had to. But she kept those facts to herself, and the fool didn't seem to realize it, so she hadn't lost all her ability to lie.

Then the man sharpened his gaze. His eyes narrowed, and he straightened away from her.

She wondered what was the matter with him. With bitter amusement she considered whether she'd lost her desire to lie well. Maybe that was why Edmond was less obedient to her. Maybe he was seeing through her years and years of lies.

"We were summoned to the area by a letter from a woman named Deb Harkness. She said our grandson survived a wagon train massacre and is living with a man named Trace Riley, and we needed to come for the boy. I wonder if—"

"Trace Riley stayed in this very inn right before winter came barreling down on our heads. I don't presume to know him well, but I sure know 'im enough to say howdy. And his wife—"

The unwashed Mr. Bolling hesitated, then took the register book and flipped back one page. He jabbed his finger at a name. Reading upside down, Florence saw *Deb Harkness* with a line drawn through it.

"That's her. Miss Harkness checked in, but by evening time she'd married up with Riley, and we scratched her out. She spent her honeymoon night right here." Bolling smiled as if the memory was sweet.

Florence had to fight down the desire to reach across the desk and scratch that smile off his face with her fingernails.

"The woman who knows of my grandson is now married to Trace Riley. And do you know where Riley lives? I must find my little Cameron. I'm all he has."

Edmond chose that moment to walk in carrying a valise in each hand. Another man followed with four larger suitcases.

"That is, my husband and I are all he has in the world."

"I don't rightly know just where Trace's cabin is. Somewhere's around Tahoe, someone told me."

"Tahoe?" Florence shook her head, almost afraid the man had abandoned the language she was familiar with.

"Tahoe's a big beautiful lake just south of here. We get a lot of tourists. That's why I am able to make a living with this fine boardinghouse."

Florence concealed her reaction of contempt. But the man took a half step back from her, and she had to wonder if she'd concealed much of anything.

"How do you suggest we find him?"

The man gave her a strange look, almost smug, which simply could not be. It was obvious she was his superior in every way. Western people were fools. "I reckon Luth Payne knows best about newcomers 'round here. He's been here since the Rockies was foothills. He don't live none too far. Rich man, one'a them what built their big old mansions along the lake."

Fighting down her impatience, Florence didn't speak until she was sure something decent would come out of her mouth.

Mr. Bolling's expression changed again, until he almost looked dangerous. Florence was glad she carried her gun close to hand, in one of the satchels along with her gold. But she had no interest in digging out a gun just now. With a sniff she decided Mr. Bolling was probably a leading citizen of this miserable little town of Ringo.

Edmond said, "How do we get to Payne's house?"

The smooth smile from Bolling as he gave directions sent a chill down Florence's spine for no reason she could understand. All she knew was, she'd gladly go somewhere, anywhere, but here.

Nodding, Edmond said, "We'll plan to see him tomorrow, then we'll hope to go on from there to find our grandson. Thank you for your assistance."

Florence saw Bolling turn and reach for a key, then his hand hesitated, and he reached past the other five keys hanging on the wall to pluck the last one. "Follow me, folks. I'm giving you my finest room."

As well he should, Florence thought.

And then she saw the miserable little room half filled with wooden crates. Two rats zipped through a hole in the wall. She wondered in horror what the bad rooms looked like.

Penny threw John out of the room when he offered to help her change into her red silk dress.

He was still chuckling out in the hall when she had to face the fact that she couldn't button the stupid thing up herself.

He'd bought her new boots, a chemise, gloves, and a bonnet. All the trappings of a fine lady.

"Are you sure this shade of red is proper, McCall?"

The snickering from the hall broke off. "Call me John, sweetheart." And he was off laughing again.

She got as ready as she could, including twisting her hair into a knot high on the back of her head, then plunking the bonnet on the disheveled mess. There was no looking glass in the room, so she just did her best to jam the hair out of sight. Getting changed took all of five minutes . . . not counting the buttons up the back.

She swung open the door to see him still laughing. And then the laughter faded from his face, and his jaw dropped.

"What's the matter? Have I got the dress on backward?"

"P-Penny." John cleared his throat. "You're b-beautiful."

Penny couldn't manage much more than to blink. "Oh, go on with you. I know I'm a worn-out-looking woman. My hair's like a haystack."

"Muskrat nest," John said absently. "But no more. It looks nice now." He narrowed his eyes and looked closer. "Although—"

"My hands are callused as leather," Penny cut him off. "I've got muscles where a woman oughta probably have soft curves."

A smile crept back onto John's expression. But it wasn't that amused humor that'd set him to laughing in the hall.

"But this is the frontier," she went on. "I *need* calluses. I *need* muscles. I don't have time to fuss with my hair. I'm real happy with how I am."

Since Penny was a little unnerved by what she was seeing in his eyes, she turned her back. "Button me up. I can't figure why anyone'd own a piece of clothing they can't put on themselves."

Loud voices sounded from the lower floor of the boardinghouse. John shoved her firmly into the room and shut the door.

"What are you doing?"

Sounding shocked, John said, "You can't let people see your unmentionables right out in the hall."

"Oh no. You're right. I can't." Penny felt her face heat up. She slapped both hands over her cheeks. "I'm blushing. I can't remember that ever happening before I met you."

John's hands touched her back, and she felt a deeper embarrassment. And why? She had a chemise on under her dress. It wasn't as heavy of fabric as her usual shirtwaist, but it was perfectly modest.

And yet she knew why. It wasn't because of what she was wearing. It was because of whom she was with. His hands worked their way up her back, one button at a time, altogether too slow. Silence only made things worse. She cleared her throat. "Now then, what is the point of this silk dress?"

He fastened the last button at her neck. The raucous noise grew louder but it was still downstairs.

She started to turn, but his hands closed on her shoulders. "Hold still." He plucked her hat off her head and pulled a pin.

"What are you doing?" She reached back to stop him.

"No, let me fix your hair."

There was a long moment of frozen silence. Then she said, "You know how to fix a woman's hair?"

John chuckled to himself. "All part of being a master of disguise."

"So, you've disguised yourself as a woman, complete with . . . a long wig done up fancy?"

He laughed aloud this time. "I've never tried to get away with being a woman, but I've helped disguise a few. I'm going to see to it you look like a wealthy city woman before we leave this room. And they don't just jam a bonnet over messy hair."

Penny frowned and didn't fight with him anymore as he combed, smoothing her hair more than she ever bothered to. She occupied herself with wondering just exactly how much he'd helped women disguise themselves. And did he rent a single room with them, too? Just how well did he know these women?

It was a startling thing to realize the unpleasant curl of feeling was jealousy.

Jealousy. How ridiculous. Being jealous made it seem as if she had some true feelings for this man. As if she was possessive of him. As if she cared how he . . . involved himself with another woman.

She didn't like it. She didn't want it. Yes, he was her husband, but she didn't know him and couldn't possibly feel any such thing.

He put the hat on her head, adjusted it, then pinned it in place with pins she hadn't noticed, stuck right through the hat. She wondered how long she'd stood there stewing in the unpleasant thoughts about her husband and how he made her feel.

The hallway was still noisy. John said, "You're not the only one who needs a disguise. I was going to make you stand outside the door while I changed, but you can't go out there right now. We're married, so there's no reason not to change clothes together, but if you feel uncomfortable seeing me, you'd best turn your back."

She whirled to face the wall so fast she almost stumbled.

John laughed softly.

Penny ignored any rustling clothes and said, "Now would be a good time to explain your plan."

"Virginia City has been a boomtown longer than most any mining town in history. In fact, it's become more than that. It's the biggest city between Denver and San Francisco. And unlike other boomtowns that explode overnight then die almost as fast, Virginia City has been thriving for nearly ten years. There's an actual social scene here. There are churches and schools and fancy hotels, clubs, and restaurants. And there are levels to that social order. There are millionaires and a class of working men who have families and make decent livings. The highest wages of any miners in the world."

"Where'd you learn all that?"

"Lots of people willing to brag on their town wherever you go. I'm guessing our villain fits into the very top of the social order."

"You know that really is just what you're doing—guessing. For heaven's sake, he might've stolen the boots."

"Not the way they were shined. No, this is a wealthy man. I was stuck here the last week or so of winter, waiting for the trail to clear, so I learned a lot then. Today, I did some wandering while I was out. I looked at the businesses, and I've got a good enough feel for the town that I can tell you where wealthy people gather and where they shop. If someone in this town sells Hessian boots like the ones our kidnapper wore, I can find it. We need to go introduce ourselves to the right people, and we need to look the part if we're to fit in with rich folks."

He sighed. "You can turn around now, Penny."

Uncertain what she'd find, she turned slowly and saw John as she'd never seen him before. "Did you shop for that suit, too?"

He wore a well-fitted black suit and a string tie with a golden oval decoration. He had on his usual flat-topped, broad-brimmed black hat, but now he'd added a silk band with another golden oval to match his tie. With the tie, black suit, and sharp white shirt, the hat looked like one a rich man would wear. And he had on well-shined black boots. He'd been wearing those before, but he'd stopped and gotten them all shined up.

"Nope, I had it with me in the bag I left at your homestead when we rode to town."

"The hat and boots are the ones you always wear."

"It's what made me think of the Hessian boots as a clue. A man traveling by horseback, or even stagecoach, doesn't want to carry too much. And hats and boots take up a lot of space in a satchel or a bedroll. So, I don't switch those when I'm trying to fit in with Western men. Add in the tie with the bit of gold matching the hat, and all of a sudden I'm a fancy-dressed man."

"Do you dress like this back east?" He'd been in broadcloth and denim before this, dressed much like Cam and Trace.

"I have a few more choices back home, but I couldn't haul everything with me." He pulled one last thing out just as she hoisted her satchel to sling it over her head.

"You can't take that."

Penny looked down at her battered bag. "I never leave this behind. It's saved our lives at least once already."

He waggled some black velvet thing at her. "We can't get away with our disguise if you're carrying that bag. Use this reticule instead."

"*Reticule* always sounded a lot like the word *ridiculous* to me."

Nodding, John said, "I got the biggest one I could find, but your Army Colt isn't going to fit, so—" He tugged open the fancy bag and produced the littlest pistol Penny had ever seen.

"I can't stop much with that peashooter."

"I'm really hoping you don't have to gun anybody down, Penny. I'm going to do my best to keep this from turning into a turkey shoot. But I got this little pepperbox so you'd have some protection in this town. Lots of lawlessness left, even if the town is growing into a grand city." He handed over the gun.

"The aim is bad, so only use it at point-blank range." His eyes met hers. "Let's hope it doesn't come to that."

Penny nodded. "Tell me how to load it."

They spent a few minutes working over the gun. It fired five shots and rotated with each pull of the trigger.

"How much did all this cost?"

John tucked the gun in her reticule. Ignoring her question, he said, "Your gun is the hideout one I usually carry. It's from a matched set."

He made a sudden slashing motion with his arm and another gun, a twin to hers, appeared in his hand.

Blinking, Penny got close, while staying off to the side. "Oh, I saw that one before. How does it work?"

John showed her the little accordion holster. "And you remember the pistol strapped to my ankle and a knife in my boot and another one hidden in my hat? But your sleeves are too tight for the arm gun. You'll have to carry yours in the reticule."

"Any other surprises, husband?"

He smiled at her. "A couple. Let's go act like we're rich people. Try not to mention how well you can skin a buck in the middle of a conversation."

"But I'm really fast." She smiled back to make sure he knew she understood. "I lived in Philadelphia for years. Saw my share of rich, snooty folks coming into the store where I worked." With an exaggerated western slang, she added, "I reckon I kin purtend to be one rightly enough."

John rolled his eyes and took her arm. "Let us be off, then, madam."

He sounded like he'd stepped out of the pages of a fancy book.

Penny had her work cut out for her being close to as good with a disguise as her new husband. She refused to feel bad for not having a knack for being a sneak. Then she thought of all the time she'd spent sneakin' up on game in the woods. With a little practice, she might do better at this than she'd first expected.

16

The waiter bowed low. The man wore a black suit and white shirt, both made of silk, with a black vest and a little white bow tie. The restaurant was as fancy as any place John had seen on the East Coast, with white china and tablecloths—and silver everywhere John looked. The forks and knives looked like real silver, and there were crystal-footed glasses that were also rimmed with silver. The bright lights of the place drew his eyes up to silver chandeliers flaring with gaslight.

The waiter turned to guide them through the room, and an elegantly dressed woman rose from her chair and gave them a gracious nod.

"Carstairs, wait a moment." The woman halted the waiter in his tracks. "You're new in town, aren't you?"

John didn't let one bit of his tension show on his face. But there were a lot of ways this could go wrong.

Penny, with her hand through his arm, said with a remarkably civilized tone, "We just arrived. I am Penelope, and this is my husband, Jonathan Call. We've heard so much about Virginia City, we had to come and see it."

"Part of a short trip out of San Francisco," John added. They probably should have talked a little bit about what story they'd tell. "We're from Philadelphia, but business brought us west."

The lady gave the most demure gasp possible and rested one gloved hand on John's arm. She was a young woman, dressed in bright blue satin, with lace at her wrists and throat, and jewels gleaming with silver and diamonds, including a garish ring on the third finger on her left hand.

The woman looked at her companion. "This is my husband, Andrew, and I am Leota Wilkerson. We haven't been back east in ages. I think of myself as a welcoming committee to town, and we'd love to have you join us, wouldn't we, Andrew?"

Andrew was at least twenty years older than his wife. He had heavy sideburns on his jowls. He wore spectacles that didn't cover the shrewd intelligence in his eyes. He had neatly trimmed hair and a suit that was tidy but a bit out of date compared to John's.

John noticed he wore highly shined Hessian boots, but in black rather than brown. Holding his breath, John intended to get to know these people if he possibly could.

"Yes," Andrew said, "we've just been seated, haven't even ordered yet. You can tell us about yourselves and share any news you have from back east."

John felt Penny tense up. He rested his left hand on her right, where she held him. "We'd love to join you."

Andrew Wilkerson had shrewd eyes. John couldn't whisper to Penny any advice. He just had to hope she knew how to play along.

The waiter was at their table instantly, and he helped Penny sit. She handled it like she'd had a fancy waiter pushing in her chair all her life.

John began a lighthearted story about life in Philadelphia. Penny threw in enough details to make herself part of it. By the time the food came, John said, "Well, we can't do all the talking. We're here to see Virginia City. Tell us what you do here, Andrew?"

Andrew turned out to be a talker, and his wife went along with him. They were both as snooty as royalty.

John was an expert interrogator. And his best skill was getting information out of people without letting them know he was even asking.

Leota called people over to the table throughout the meal until John felt like he'd met nearly every important man in the city. He couldn't help but wonder if one of them was their kidnapper. He was sly about it, but he checked each pair of boots.

When he and Penny left the restaurant, they'd been invited to dinner at three people's homes. And they'd been invited to call for tea with four others. The only real problem he had was trying to figure out how he could make sure Penny had a new fancy dress at every home. And then he figured that out, too.

The Wilkersons left the restaurant with them and climbed into a black carriage trimmed in silver. "I can't believe," Penny whispered when they were a safe distance away, "that you offered to pay for that expensive meal. How much money do you have, anyway?"

John patted her arm and smiled into her alarmed eyes. "There was never any chance old Wilkerson would let me pay. The man was showing off for his fancy young wife and in front of all the other fine folks in that restaurant. I could have paid it if I had to, but I sure didn't want to."

"I thought you were broke. Didn't you try and steal my gun and money back in Dismal?"

"I was asking to borrow things, not robbing you. I wanted to get right back on the trail from Dismal. I had money in my pack that was left back at your cabin, but I didn't want to go back and get it, but it was good to get cleaned up and grab the rest of my supplies. And Cam gave me a few of those twenty-dollar double eagles, but I don't want to spend them. They're too unusual and might make someone remember me. But I have them if it's necessary. Even without them, I can fund our little operation. I'm not overly flush, but I have enough to keep up appearances. We have to be careful not to let on where we're staying, and normally a wealthy woman like yourself, Mrs. McCall, would need a different dress for each dinner. But we're going to invent a disaster with your trunk. I'm thinking it fell off the top of the stagecoach."

"My goodness, that's a terrible piece of bad luck," Penny said dryly.

"Wasn't it? That stage driver certainly got a piece of my mind." John could find a fine upper-crust accent if he wanted. "And we didn't even notice until we were unloading. You are so annoyed with me because you wanted us to buy a private carriage for the trip here, but I didn't want to take the time, so I insisted we take the stage. The driver has promised to search the trail on his return trip, but for now we're making do. That will even explain your dress, in case one of the ladies has seen it for sale."

"It makes me a little sick to my stomach to talk like such

147

a snob. That poor stagecoach driver. I hope he doesn't get in trouble."

"Hopefully they all consider stage riding beneath them and don't know a thing about drivers."

"You do all this lying a little too well for my peace of mind."

John smiled at her. "It's a disguise. And it worked."

The crinkled lines of her brow were a delight. John couldn't remember the last time he'd been around a woman so frank, so clearly honest. It gave him a twinge about all the falsehoods he told. He considered himself an honest man—a Christian man. But it was the plain truth that his job led him to do and say some dishonest things. All with a goal of solving crimes. But the twinge became more like a pang as he wondered how God saw him. Wondered it for the first time in a long time.

And now he was going to make it worse.

"Mrs. Wilkerson and her society ladies kept you busy talking."

"Mostly listening," Penny said.

"But while you chatted with them I found out something that is going to give me a direction for my investigation."

"What is that?"

"Well, I asked who sold good quality clothes here in Virginia City, and along with all the advice, I found the name of the only man who sold Hessian boots. They aren't a common item out here, though I did see a pair or two in there tonight."

Penny froze right there on the sidewalk, and her hand that had been loosely resting in his elbow tightened. "Are you saying you've found the name of the man who—" she glanced left and right before dropping her voice to a whisper—"the man who kidnapped us."

They were alone on the sidewalk, and John knew he needed to get them tucked away in their room before it got any later. They'd left the street with the fancy restaurant and were in a declining-but-still-respectable area between the wealthier and seedier parts of town.

He said, "Let's keep moving. We need to get tucked away for the night, before drunks start staggering out of the saloons."

With a guiding hand, he got her moving again. "I didn't learn his name, but I did find the man who almost certainly sold him the boots. His pair looked to be in good shape. Perhaps not brand new, but certainly not too old, either. And they were shined beneath a day's dust and dirt. I'm going to—" He hesitated, wondering if he should tell her more. But he needed to explain his coming absence.

"I'm going to, uh . . . visit . . . this store. The owner must keep records. I hope I can find the name of the man with those boots."

"You're going to question this man? At this time of night?"

Silence met her question. He kept her moving. He just needed to get her locked in that room, gun in hand, and be about his investigating. It also suited him to leave their room. It made him uncomfortable to think of spending the night in that small room with her, his duly sworn wife. A woman who kissed with an amazing amount of enthusiasm. It was all perfectly fine for him to be in there . . . with her . . . and their marriage license.

"No store is open at this hour." Penny leaned close and hissed, "You're going to break in."

John glanced at her and kept walking.

"Isn't that illegal?"

"I'm not going to steal or damage anything."

"Won't you have to break the door down to get in?"

"No." John didn't say more.

She rammed a fist into his shoulder.

"Ouch." He rubbed his shoulder. Cam did say she never learned to pull her punches. They approached the boarding-house. "Can you hold off punching me until we get inside?"

She walked faster, as if she could barely wait. She pounded up the stairs. He'd have criticized her ladylike act—she was failing at it—except they were staying in such an unladylike place that it hardly mattered.

She waited at the door, tapping her toe, arms crossed. He hoped she didn't confiscate the key from him. It was probably wrong of him to find all of this incredibly attractive, but he did. A strong woman had always interested him. Never to this extent, though.

He got inside and held up both hands, palms out, and he stayed well back. "We're not going to argue about this. I'm sure you can figure out that I have my ways of getting into a locked building. I am not going to damage or steal anything. I will slip in, thumb through the files until I find an order for Hessian boots, get the name or names if there are multiple orders, and slip out. Then we'll look into the background of the boot owners and see what kind of men they are. If that's not enough, we'll visit them and see how they act when they see us." He also hoped, with his visits, to uncover talk about the nature of his suspects that would narrow his search.

Penny crossed her arms. He braced himself for what she'd say. The woman was making him feel guilty for being a lying housebreaker. He resented it. Probably because he *was* guilty.

A conscience wasn't something he worried about much, since he figured he was fine in that regard. Until Penny started glaring at him.

Her mouth opened. He steeled himself to resist her appeal to his better nature, assuming he could even get any better than he already was.

"I'm going with you."

He was so ready for her to blast him for his behavior, he almost stumbled forward. "You can't go with me!"

"Why not?"

"B-Because women can't—"

"Can't what? Commit crimes? Break and enter? Lie? I assure you they can. And the only reason you don't want me to come is because you're trying to stop me from doing things you think are fine for you to do. How does that make sense?"

"No, the reason I don't want you to come is because I'm good at this. I'm sneaky. I'm quiet. I'm quick and a lot less likely to draw attention to what I'm doing and thereby avoid arrest."

"I can out-quiet you any day of the week, McCall."

He wished she'd prove it by being quiet right now. He was still wishing it when they were walking toward The Gentleman's Haberdashery.

"Gwen, we're going on a little ride."

Cam stopped his wife from tucking the children into bed for the night.

"You've been upset all day."

"On edge, ready for trouble. Not upset really." Upset seemed like something a weakling would be.

"What's going on?"

"*We* are going on. It's almost dark. We'll put the lights out in the cabin like always, then you and I and the children are going to slip away. We've had men watching the house. Three of them, though not all three at the same time."

"Three?" Gwen's eyes sharpened. "It was three men who kidnapped Penny and John."

His wife was a mighty smart woman.

"I can find no sign of a campfire or that they are watching through the night, and I've been scouting them all day. They break off the watch once we go to sleep, or so I'm thinking."

"We're going to run?" Gwen's voice had a snap to it.

Cam was pleased to see it didn't suit her to run from trouble. He'd been helping her learn to scout and shoot. It'd brought out a fierce side of his pretty little wife.

Cam liked it so much he'd've kissed her if he wasn't going to be real busy.

"We're going to Trace's as soon as I'm sure they're gone. I'm going to go out to the barn and then do some reconnoitering." That was an army word he'd always liked. "If Trace is willing, we'll trail these coyotes. Find out where they came from and maybe that'll lead us to the fourth man—most likely the one behind all this."

"I'd like to ride the trail with you, and face these men, but I reckon taking little children to a possible gunfight is a poor excuse for an idea."

He'd married a sensible woman.

"Pack some extra clothes. You might be at Trace's for a few days."

"Be careful and come get me if you find all three of them and decide this is going to end in trouble. I can get the young'uns to bed and come help."

"Will do, ma'am." And then he got his kiss. He gave Maddie Sue and Ronnie a kiss apiece, too.

Maddie Sue giggled. Ronnie rubbed on the whiskers of Cam's face. He hadn't shaved yet today.

Then just for his wife, he whispered, "I declare, I love you more every day we're married."

CHAPTER
17

❧❦❧

It was a fine hair she was splitting.

A baby hair.

A baby hair from a nearly bald baby.

But split it she did. Penny was a woman who believed in the Bible, and "Thou shalt not steal" couldn't be any clearer. And bear false witness? Well, what if someone caught them and asked what in the Sam Hill they were up to?

Of course, if someone caught them, what was the point of talking? Knowing all of that . . . she went right ahead and grasped that hair . . . or rather split it. She was bound and determined not to be left behind while John was out sneaking around.

After all the socializing at supper, it was already pretty late in the evening when they got back to their room. John wasted no time telling her to change into the split skirt she'd brought to help her be less noticeable. Penny figured she could run for it faster in the split skirt, too.

John stood outside for the outfit change, and when it

was her turn and he took off his fancy suit, she turned her back. He didn't want her out in the hall alone even though there was no fight going on at the moment. Then he'd made them wait for a couple of hours. When they finally left the boardinghouse, the saloons were still going strong in the seedy neighborhood.

Walking swiftly through the streets, Penny saw lights and heard tinny music from the saloons, accompanied by loud voices, outbreaks of laughter, and occasional shouting. They'd waited until it was so late that no one left in those establishments would have any interest in sobriety or work in the morning.

The neighborhood improved as they went along. The streets were silent, and the stores were all closed. John clasped her hand and pulled her along, intent on his goal. Suddenly, without her hearing anything, he stopped. She was being dragged just a bit, so she stumbled into him and noted his alert gaze well enough to keep quiet.

His gaze darted around, and she heard the scrape of a shoe on the paved streets. John's eyes landed on a spot behind them. Penny tried to look at what he was studying, but she had no time. He plucked her right off the ground and carried her with complete silence past two closed businesses and up three stairsteps and dragged her into a corner of a barely recessed entrance.

She needed to check his shoes. Whatever he was wearing— they looked like regular boots—made no sound.

He pushed her into a shadowy corner of the entry and pressed his body up against hers. What was he thinking? She shoved at him to get out of the too-close quarters.

He hissed, "Shhh. Be still."

155

The footsteps sounded closer now. Whoever it was had to see them there. The recess wasn't that deep. The shadows not that dark. John's eyes, mostly hidden by the night, were wide, and she could make out the whites.

And if they were noticed, there'd be no excuse for two people to be huddling here.

Or no, wait. There is one excuse.

She wrapped her arms around his neck. Yanked his head down and kissed him.

The ruse, the feigned kiss, lasted about two seconds. Oh, the kiss lasted longer—it was the ruse she forgot. His arms tightened around her waist, deepening the kiss, and Penny forgot about everything but how warm, how welcoming, and how fine this man was. This man . . . to whom she was most definitely married.

His arms pulled her closer, which shouldn't be possible considering just how close she was. But it was as if he pulled her closer to his heart, to his very life. And she went willingly, intrigued and charmed by this strong man.

Footsteps scraped louder, enough to penetrate her extreme distraction.

She heard a quiet chuckle from the man as he paused just briefly, then moved on. He'd seen them. He'd accepted that two people might seek out a dark quiet place for nothing more dishonest than a stolen kiss.

Except no one had done much stealing here. "Thou shalt not steal" definitely didn't apply because she'd certainly handed that kiss right over, and John had accepted it willingly.

The footsteps faded. Finally, John lifted his head, and she searched his eyes again. This time they burned.

He whispered, "I saw that man in the restaurant tonight. We

weren't introduced, but he was one of the few wearing Hessian boots. What was he doing out here this time of night?"

Penny realized that while she'd been pouring her heart into that kiss, he'd been checking around, looking, investigating. Checking boots for heaven's sake!

The kiss, well, he'd certainly thrown himself into it, but maybe that was strictly an act. It hurt to think a man could act in such a false way. Before she could tell him that, and maybe punch him, he grabbed her wrist and towed her out of their little hideaway and headed right back toward his goal. The Gentleman's Haberdashery. And his lawbreaking.

He reached the shop and headed down a walkway between two buildings. There were no windows on the walls that lined the passageway. John kept going to the back of the building, which opened into an alley. The back door was locked, as was the single window beside it.

It took a while, but John did find a window unlocked. It was on the second floor. They were entering, but no breaking had gone on. There was that baby hair again.

And they wouldn't take anything. So, there'd be no stealing.

That didn't stop Penny from praying for forgiveness and praying that they wouldn't get caught. She didn't hold out much hope for forgiveness from the Virginia City sheriff, but God was merciful. She'd find comfort in her spiritual redemption while the city did its worst.

She slipped in the window behind her sneak of a husband. Yep, sure as certain, he needed a new career. She was going to have to teach him the cattle business.

She threw in a prayer for patience for that, because she reckoned she was gonna need it.

"There's no one here." John spoke quietly, but it wasn't a whisper.

"Did you think there would be?" That was an alarming notion she hadn't considered.

"I wondered if the owner of the store might live above it. And it appears he does."

"You mean you thought you might be crawling in a window to a bedroom with someone sleeping in it?"

"We are in a bedroom, but no one's here. The owner could come back anytime. I doubt he's downstairs because there were no lights on, and I doubt he usually stays out this late. I told you to be quiet. Why did you think I said that?"

Penny saw the neatly made bed, and her stomach swooped to think of the man coming home. It was very late. If he wasn't here yet, maybe he wasn't coming. "Just hurry up."

They hurried past the bed, then descended the stairs. There were streetlights from outside that somewhat dispelled the murky darkness, and the front windows let in enough light that they managed to not fall tail over teakettle to the ground floor.

When they reached the bottom step, John paused for a moment to look back at her. "Why do you think that man was out at this hour of the night?"

"I have no idea." Penny hadn't thought much beyond being upset that John was so observant of their surroundings when she was wrapped up in their kiss.

"I suspect he was up to no good."

John led her through rows of good-smelling clothes, clean fabric, and new leather. He walked behind a counter and into a back hallway. A door to his right was open, and Penny peeked around him to see a desk and some filing drawers.

"His office, and there are no windows in there. I can close the door and turn on a lantern, and no one'll see it." His eyes glowed with an unexpected excitement.

He was having fun. She'd married a man who liked just a lick of danger. She knew the type from her years in forts. There were soldiers who always wanted action. She'd always thought those sorts were a nuisance.

"I just need a few minutes back here, to look through his account books. I should be able to find out quickly if he has orders for Hessian boots. Hopefully I can find someone's name on the billing records. You check the back door and inspect the lock to see if we can go out that way and leave the door locked behind us. I've seen locks that, if you set them right, will swing shut behind you and lock up. Climbing to the second floor left us too exposed. I'd like to go out a different way if possible."

Penny didn't comment. Honestly, she was glad he'd given her a job. It made her feel less useless. Like maybe he'd needed her to come with him after all.

He went in the office and closed the door. She stood in the hall and looked at the door on the opposite side from the one John was in.

She wondered what was in it and reached for the knob, but her hand froze. The doorknob, only a few inches in front of her, sent a chill down her spine. After all they'd done, why hesitate about entering a room? But there was something that held her hand back as surely as if the door was a solid rock wall.

Determined to look, but in no rush, she turned away and remembered what John had asked of her. She moved on down the hall to the back door.

First, she quietly turned the knob, but they'd done that when they were trying to get in. She already knew it wouldn't open. She couldn't figure what to look for in a lock. You stuck the right key in the right door, you turned it, and the door opened.

What kind of door locked behind you without a key?

She looked around a little and found a key hanging from a nail right beside the door. Well, that'd lock it, but how would they leave it behind? There was a small window beside the door. It was locked, but she twisted the catch on it and slid the window up an inch. It slid up silently. Closing it again, she mulled over how to use that information. Could they climb out the window and reach back to lock the door? But that would still leave the window unlocked. She decided she'd just tell John what she'd found, and that'd be that.

She reached up to turn the window lock. Just as she finished, a light gleamed in the alley. She jerked back her arm and dropped to the floor, curling low to get her head beneath the window. Gasping, she fought to keep her breath silent as the light approached. She twisted to look up and saw the shadow of someone leaning close, looking through the door's window.

Had the owner come back? Could he possibly walk past her in the dark without seeing her? Could he go straight up to bed—without checking the office?

Glancing down the hall toward the room where John worked, she saw the very faintest possible light coming from under the tightly closed door. The lantern he used was turned down low. She hadn't even noticed the light until now, this frozen moment. Would the man looking through the window notice it?

She didn't even breathe as she watched the knob slowly turn to the left, then the right. She braced herself, thinking frantically of what she would do when the door swung open. Then the light cast by the lantern shifted. She heard a tug on the window she'd just relocked.

Her heart pounded until she was afraid whoever it was might hear it even through the door.

Then she heard whistling. It was a tuneless noise. Footsteps crunched on the dirt and rubble in the alley. The lantern light faded along with the whistling.

It took her a moment for her panic to ease. It was just someone checking the windows. Probably a deputy doing rounds. There must be a patrol all night if he was checking alley doors and windows at this hour. And Penny and her lawless husband had to walk all the way back to their boardinghouse. They'd better be prepared to look and act innocent in case a deputy noticed them.

Penny looked down the short hall at that light again. The foot patrol hadn't noticed. But did he come by very often? It made sense that in this more exclusive part of town the night watch would be more vigilant. Would he check again? Would that faint light be niggling in his mind? Would that light bring him back for a closer look?

She nearly collapsed when the man was finally far enough away she couldn't hear him. Looking at the window, she realized she'd barely gotten it locked in time to prevent disaster. When she'd almost gathered herself enough to think logically again, the light beneath the door vanished, and John swung the door open.

"I've got the names, Penny. Where are you?"

"I'm crouched in a corner, near to having a heart attack."

In the silence of the hall, her hissed reply echoed like a shout. John rushed to her side as she stood.

Hearing about the night watch, he flinched. "Close call."

Then he studied the door and window. "We can get out this way, but we'd better make it quick."

"Wait, I meant to take a look behind that closed door opposite the room you were in."

"Why?" John asked, looking back over his shoulder.

"I'm not sure, something about it—" Penny realized she'd edged so close to John that his arm went around her. "Maybe I'm just nervous because of the night watchman. But . . . the door bothered me before that. I almost went in and decided instead to get on with checking this back door, but now I think we'd better at least glance inside—just because it's troubling me so much."

John looked down the hall, then nodded. "Let's go."

He moved toward the door, and Penny stayed in the circle of his arm. He got to the door, reached for the knob, and stopped.

He closed his hand and rubbed the fingers together. Then gave her a reluctant glance. "Wait for me by the back door."

His tone, the way he hesitated, everything about the flare of concern in his eyes—concern for her—sharpened her already razor-sharp attention.

"What's the matter?"

John gently rested his palm on her shoulder. "I'm afraid we're going to find a dead body behind this door. What you were reacting to is the smell of death."

And now that he said it, she realized that she did smell something. Blood and . . . something more.

"I'd spare you what you'd see behind this door, Penny."

The kindness in his voice was a new tone. It was the nicest thing he'd done so far in their short marriage. And she was tempted, so badly tempted, to let him take charge.

"It's going to be one of those things you'll live with. There's no forgetting it."

Nodding, Penny said, "I know you're right. But I know I need to stay with you right now. We are working on this investigation together, and I need to be a witness to as much as I can. It may help us get this solved more quickly." She didn't tell him that she had a little problem with the sight of blood. She'd just look quickly and leave before she fainted.

John held her gaze for a long moment. Then he said, "Let's go."

He reached again for the knob, and this time he twisted it and slowly pushed the door open.

They saw a single window. Moonlight streamed in to show a curtain hanging askew from one corner. On the floor, a dead man gripped the drape. He must've clung to it while he fell. He lay facedown on the floor in a white shirt. Penny stifled a gasp at the bloodstain high on his back. The blood was still wet and sticky. It looked ebony rather than crimson in the moonlight.

The smell grew stronger, and Penny took one long look, then turned her back and stayed at the door while John went to the man and crouched beside him.

Penny wasn't sure what all John was looking for. Penny didn't bother to chastise him or even ask what he was doing. She was too busy trying to keep down the rich meal she'd eaten earlier.

Then John was up and moving. "We need to get away from here. But first . . ."

He stepped into the office and came back out just as quickly, sliding a small book into his coat pocket. He caught Penny's hand and hurried them to the back door. She was still too befuddled from shock to move under her own power. He slid the window open, took the key, pushed her ahead of him out the door, and stepped outside.

"Aren't you going to get the sheriff?"

John gave her a bewildered look. "No, of course I'm not going to do such a thing. He'd probably arrest us for murder." He locked up, reached through the window to hang up the key, and pulled the window closed. He thrust a small metal object with a hook on the end through the tight space between the upper and lower window, and fiddled with it for a few seconds, then Penny heard the faint metallic slide of the window being latched.

"Let's go." He tucked his little tool into a leather pouch he'd produced from his pocket, and asked, "Which way did the deputy go?"

Penny pointed. He took her arm and got her moving in the opposite direction. They'd walked nearly two blocks before Penny said, "You need to find another line of work."

"You sound nervous. I never took you for a woman with faint spirits."

Penny slugged him on the shoulder.

"Ouch." John rubbed the injured spot. "You really need to learn to pull your punches."

He was ready to dodge, or she'd've landed a second punch. Instead, she marched on past him. "Don't you want to know whose house we're going to break into next?" he asked after her.

"What?" She whirled to face him. Her hands were definitely curled into fists.

"The files were empty. Nothing about purchases to specific men, and they were a mess, so I think the killer had already gone through them and taken out his name. But I found a record book tucked away." He patted his pocket.

"With comments from the bootmaker about his best clients and their preferences. I looked long enough to find four men who've ordered Hessian boots in the last year. I quit looking at that point so we could get going, but Hessians weren't a very common item, thank heavens. I wrote down the names. Once I've double-checked, we'll have our suspects, Penny. We're on the way to catching the kidnappers. And I suspect one of these four men is going to be who we saw on the street tonight. I suspect he's the one who killed that man at the haberdashery. I hope the things I found in the victim's pocket will give us the poor man's name, but I suspect he's the shopkeeper. I didn't get the murderer tonight, but I saw his face. And his name will be one of the men on our list." He waved the book in the air. "We have what we need to close in on him now."

"John, you can't go around breaking into people's homes and businesses. This is no fit job for a man of honor."

"*I am a man of honor.*" Fury broke over him in waves.

Even as he snapped at Penny, he knew he wasn't upset about his honor. His gut twisted with pure guilt. He whirled away from her. "That man's dead because of me."

His chest heaved as the knowledge swept over him. "I thought I did a good job of slipping questions in about Hessian boots. I thought I was so blasted sly and subtle. But I have to face the fact that something I said tipped someone off tonight. It's my fault that the shopkeeper was killed."

"Stop that." Penny turned and clapped her hands on his shoulders. "You know the fault lies with the man who slid a knife into a defenseless man's back."

John had to swallow hard twice to make his voice work. "I set the killer off. And think of this. If a murderer killed that man tonight just because he didn't like the way I was asking about boots, then he's a monster. And he won't hesitate for a second to kill again—including to kill us."

"He had to be in that dining room tonight, didn't he?" Penny asked. "Your few questions about boots weren't something one of those men would comment on. The killer had to've heard it." Then Penny's eyes got wide. "No, he didn't have to pick that detail out, not if he was our kidnapper. He recognized us. That's why he'd understand what our questions meant."

John's jaw tightened until he could barely speak. "And he knows exactly what we're here for. We have to stop him."

Penny hesitated, glanced at the book John had stolen. "I know we do."

"I'm gathering information on the sly, and not many lawmen would listen to my excuses about investigating a crime if they caught me in the act in that shop. But I believe whoever kidnapped us had every intention of murdering us right then and there. And after tonight he's got to be getting desperate. He'll have to kill us to silence us, and he'll very likely go after your brother and the rest of the folks who know about him. This is a wealthy, powerful man with a lot to lose, and he has no scruples about keeping his secrets. I won't apologize for hunting him down and bringing him to justice."

He nudged Penny to get her going, and she came along quietly. No fists in sight.

"I know we have to stop this man," Penny said. "If for no other reason than I'm sure you're right. He'll be hunting us now—as if he wasn't already. So, chasing him is going to give us a better chance of survival than if we wait for him to sneak up behind us. But there can't be a good reason to break the law. If that's what your job requires of you, maybe you need to rethink your job."

"I've been a Pinkerton agent since before the war, since before Allan Pinkerton renamed the agency after himself. Even when I enlisted, because it was known that I'd done some detective work, the navy used me for some spying and other sneaky tactics. I guess I feel like if the government can ask me to do these things, I'm not quite sure why they want to call it lawbreaking now."

He held up a hand. "But they do. I know they do." He was quiet for a stretch as they walked quickly toward their boardinghouse. The neighborhood deteriorated as they left the fancier part of town behind.

John hadn't caught sight of the night watch yet, and he was relieved. He didn't look forward to explaining why he and his wife had chosen the predawn hours for a stroll.

And if he wondered how he could come up with another reason to drag her into a shadowy doorway for a kiss, he shoved it from his mind.

The night was going to be long enough as it was as John strategized about how to best the man who recognized them at the restaurant tonight. Someone had to've. And he'd be intent on killing them. He might even try it tonight.

John had watched carefully on their way to the boarding-house from the restaurant, and they hadn't been followed. But they were on borrowed time. Borrowed from a man who didn't lend anyone anything.

"Wake up!" Cam Scott slammed his fist into the side of Trace's door. "Trace, it's Cam. Get out here."

There was a pause, and Cam heard the crack of a rifle being cocked.

"Cam?"

"Yep, hurry up. I've got trouble back at my place."

The door inched open. Trace stood behind the deadly muzzle of his rifle.

In the black of midnight, it was lighter inside than out. Trace was quiet for a few seconds, and Cam gave him the time. A nighttime visit like this could mean someone was forcing Cam to speak. But Maddie Sue was asleep in his arms, so Trace probably figured it wasn't big trouble.

Of course, he was wrong about that.

The door swung wide. "Get in here. What's going on?"

"We're being watched. I can't leave Gwen and the youngsters in our cabin while I tail them."

A lantern light behind Trace and Cam showed Deb, Cam's sister-in-law, in her nightgown. She asked, "Is Gwen with you?"

These two had spent more than a week helping Cam build his cabin, and they planned to come back and help Penny finish building hers. But add in that Trace had helped take Raddo to town, then he and Cam had spent days trying to find Penny and John. It'd been time for Trace to get back to his own ranch for a spell. And now here was Cam needing help again. But trouble for one of them was trouble for all. Or at least it had been so far. Trace had to get involved.

"Gwen and the kids are here with me." He turned to usher Gwen in with Ronnie asleep in her arms.

Everyone was on edge and worried about Penny, but there was no way to even know where she was to get her a warning. That edge was part of why he'd noticed the man in the woods by his cabin. Cam quickly told Trace what he'd already learned about the men who watched his cabin.

"The man ghosting around in my woods headed home for the night. He was alone."

"You're sure?"

Cam knew Trace was better in the woods than he was, but Cam was mighty good. "Yep, I'm sure."

Cam saw Utah and Adam coming toward the cabin. They'd read Cam's urgency just right. "I saw him leave for the night. Once he cleared out, we headed over. There might be someone watching here, too."

Trace's eyes narrowed at that.

"I want the women safe, and I need to be able to track. I'm leaving them here with you."

"I'll saddle up."

Trace's older cowpoke reached the door. "What's going on, boss?"

"Cam's got trouble. You and Adam stay here."

Utah frowned. Adam, just a step behind, clenched his jaw. Cam knew they both wanted to come. And he knew they understood why they couldn't.

Cam didn't bother telling Trace to stay home. Cam didn't mind admitting he needed someone to back him, and Trace was a knowing man. Having his help, with Utah and Adam on guard here, was the best they could arrange.

"You think it's got something to do with Penny?" Deb plucked Maddie Sue out of Cam's arms and led the way to a room for Gwen, the two women whispering. They'd grown to think of Penny as another sister.

"I wish we could just get settled," Cam said, regretting he had to worry the women. "Frontier life is just one thing after another."

Trace had a bedroll together and a satchel. He strapped on his gun belt and was heading for the barn. Wolf, his dog, or maybe his wolf . . . there was definitely some dog in him, but it was a mystery just how much . . . tagged along at his heels.

"Let us know if you need help, Cam," Utah said. "We've been keeping a close eye and have seen no one around here. Do your best to get back to your cabin without your watcher noticing you've been gone."

Nodding, Cam strode to where Gwen was heading into the back of the house. He caught up to her and gave her a hug, then he kissed sleeping Ronnie and the top of Maddie Sue's head, already resting against Deb's shoulder.

"You be careful, Cameron Scott." Gwen hugged him a second time. "And remember, if you run into trouble and need help, Deb and I are here for you."

"You've been gettin' a lot tougher, honey." Cam grinned, surprised he had a smile in him. "I've got a gunslinging wife. That's mighty handy."

He kissed her, then left the cabin and mounted up. Trace came out of the barn. He bent and spoke to Wolf, and though there was some whining, the critter romped over to the cabin and sat by the front door as if standing guard.

Trace talked quietly to Adam for a few seconds. Adam nodded and clapped Trace on the back and headed for the cabin. A lot like Wolf had.

Then Cam and Trace were on the trail, tearing toward his homestead.

CHAPTER

19

One room. One bed. Two people. Married.

Somewhat married.

Penny pushed those worries aside and almost ran to keep up with John as he rushed them toward the boardinghouse and off the streets. And while she ran, she prayed God could untangle her life somehow. She'd always done what she thought God would have her do.

Well, mostly.

She suspected God frowned on her inclination to punch her brothers.

But mostly.

Until these last few days. And just one thing after another had come at her and given her precious little choice in any matter.

And now she hustled toward her honeymoon-ish bed with a man who was a stranger. A man she didn't choose. A man she'd kissed with undue enthusiasm several times now.

Prayer was called for and plenty of it.

John hadn't talked about the sleeping arrangements as he

hurried her along, his grip on her arm just short of painful. She didn't try to slow him down.

Then they hurried up the steps to their room. As Penny rehearsed what she'd say, John closed and locked the door and, without turning up the lamp, stepped away from her. She could barely see his shadowy outline moving fast around the room. He was . . . "You're packing?"

"Yes. I don't trust the man who killed the haberdasher. I was careful not to be followed. But a ruthless man like that might well have informants all over town. Just because he didn't see where we're staying, doesn't mean he won't find out if he's of a mind to."

"Where will we go?"

John kept moving. Faster with every step. They didn't have much unpacked, and it didn't take him long. He'd brought her new silk dress in a gunnysack and he took a second to carefully roll the dress up, unlike the rest of his packing, which was wadding, stuffing, and rushing.

"I've got an idea. Something one of the men said tonight. But we need to move fast, quiet, and before sunrise." He grabbed Penny's bag that she'd taken with her since the beginning, and thrust it at her. Then he picked up the other things and guided her outside.

"No other way down than these steps." His hushed voice barely reached her ears. "We're going out the back way. Quiet, now."

The stairs creaked—in an old wooden building there was no avoiding it—but no one stuck their head out of a room to see who was moving around, just as they hadn't when Penny and John had come in.

John towed her along with that same unshakable grip.

She'd've been bruised tomorrow if she hadn't hustled to keep up with him. Lucky for her, she never for a second considered not hustling.

They went through the kitchen and straight to a door. In the darkened room, it occurred to Penny that John had planned for a quick exit before they'd even left the building tonight, probably before they'd even gone out for supper.

A Pinkerton agent probably had to make a run for it with some regularity.

She'd ask him later.

He grabbed a key off a nail beside the door, unlocked and opened the door, hung the key back up and eased open the door, and poked his head out just a bit. She could see outside over his shoulder, and she studied the shadows of the backs of other buildings and the alleys between them. John tugged, and Penny trusted him to be better at seeing into shadows than she was.

He moved along in the dark between the backs of two rows of buildings, laden down with his excessive baggage. She wondered about their horses and the plans they'd made to visit wealthy people in town. They needed to ask about that man they'd seen, to find a name and address.

They walked along, keeping to the shadows. Penny burned with unanswered questions. It was so close to dawn that the moon had set and the stars had faded as they often did just before the sun pushed another day over the land.

It was the darkest hour of the night.

Even in this wide-open town, in this unsafe neighborhood, everyone had gone to sleep.

Penny gave herself over completely to John. She just moved as he guided her and did her best to walk silently. The closely built buildings gave way to houses with yards around them. The houses grew smaller and tighter together, then even the houses were gone. And on and on they walked. Climbing, Penny realized. The path John led her along had a steep incline. She knew what the town had looked like, built down the slope of what she'd heard was called Mount Davidson. Apparently, they were climbing that slope.

She had no idea why. They came to a stretch without any buildings, and John now moved faster, almost at a run. Glancing back, Penny expected pursuit. She found it. They were being chased by the sunrise.

Precious time passed. Her breathing was labored. She did her best to be silent, but she hoped no one was too close. The pitch-black of night was giving way to the gray of dawn. The mountain they climbed was stripped of trees, no doubt all used for construction, so they were completely exposed. John changed directions and skirted a rocky stretch. His headlong rush had ended, and Penny realized by the slight lessening of his grip, the slower speed, that John didn't know exactly where he was going.

He zigzagged up and up. Then she heard him gasp with relief and looked ahead to see a building. In the faint light of encroaching dawn, all she could make out was a small mass, a jagged roof. The building looked ramshackle and abandoned.

They came up beside it, and John turned toward her. His eyes were intense. That's when she realized how well she could see him now. He touched his finger to his lips and urged her to the back of the small cabin. He pressed down gently, and she got the message. She crouched low behind the structure.

He dropped the baggage beside her and vanished.

She almost yelped. But from surprise, not from fear that he'd abandoned her. She trusted him completely to take care of her . . . realizing that was startling because Penny had some pride in how well she took care of herself.

But just being left alone, with the feeling of someone in that town hunting them—a man with wealth and power and so paranoid he murdered someone over a few overheard words—made her feel unnerved. It was a loneliness so profound it pressed against her belly, crushed her heart. She pulled her knees up and wrapped her arms around them.

She turned a bit and realized scrub brush had grown up against the little shack. Shifting to tuck herself between the bushes and the cabin, she felt like prey. Like an animal being hunted. Now in this little niche she could convince herself that she was hiding from the big, bad wolf.

Silence was complete. Not a bird chirped, not a bug buzzed nearby.

It all caught up with her.

Not just being up all night, but the long time lost in the woods after the kidnapping. The emotional upheaval of finding herself forced into marriage. Cam's anger and worry, coupled with the worry that her whole family was probably in danger. That man who kidnapped them *would* have killed them. He *would* have gone after her whole family.

The sickening sight of that poor, murdered man.

It had been nearly two weeks since it all began with Raddo attacking their camp, and it seemed like she'd been on a forced march ever since.

Now, wrapped in exhaustion, loneliness, and worry, and

surrounded by a silence so complete it pressed on her soul, she rested her head on her knees and slept.

———⊱❈⊰———

Penny was gone!

He'd left her, wanting to save time, knowing he had to do some serious scouting and do it fast to find what he was looking for.

But she wouldn't leave.

Had he gone to the wrong building? Heaven knew there were a lot of them up here. But no. Absolutely not. He'd left her right here behind this abandoned cabin, and she was gone.

"Penny."

Silence. He had to risk a little noise, he was running out of time.

"Penny, are you here?"

"Shhh . . ."

The hiss was more like he'd awakened a snake. But then, that was his wife for you. "Penny, where are you? We've got to go fast. We've lost the cover of darkness."

Penny moved, and he could finally spot her, tucked back in the bushes. Great hiding place. He'd compliment her on it as soon as his heart quit trying to pound out of his chest. Being afraid he'd lost the woman he was supposed to protect was bad enough, but this level of deep-seated panic could only be explained by his caring about her. And he didn't have time to care about anyone right now.

She stood and began picking up his bags. He got his share, then caught her hand and tugged. He'd been dragging the poor woman around for the entire night.

"I found us an abandoned cabin. It's not much. A lot like this one."

He saw her glance at the tumbled-down hovel, and she came along willingly. This wasn't a woman who'd fuss over rough accommodations. He admired that.

"Why not this one?" she whispered, and there was no complaint in it, just interest.

"I found one less visible from the town. The one I left you at is about the lowest one, and we're going to stay a lot higher and in a hut facing sideways, so we can come and go a bit without being exposed. There's even some furniture in it."

"More places for vermin to hide." Penny sounded groggy.

"Did you get much sleep?" He held her hand as they moved fast uphill.

"I went out pretty fast after you left, but I've got no idea how long you've been gone."

"Too long. I hated splitting up. I abandoned you for the sake of speed, but you're mostly more help than if I'm alone. I'm sorry about leaving you."

She squeezed his hand. "The sleep did me some good. Maybe you can get a chance to rest once we get under cover."

John rubbed one hand over his face as he moved along. The sun edged over the horizon. "I could use some sleep, but I have a lot of things I need to do today, and none of them allows for a nap. I need time to think and to examine that record book. And—"

Movement out of the corner of his eye shut him up. He moved sideways to put a pile of rocks between him and whoever was over there. He hunkered down, waiting to make sure the coast was clear.

"It's a cow," Penny whispered. "But hold up, maybe it's being herded."

John remembered how tough his wife was. This might almost qualify as the wilderness up here in these old shacks that were long abandoned as Virginia City climbed down the hill and prosperity brought bigger homes. The huts up here were mostly empty. He'd overheard that talk yesterday when he was shopping, so hopefully the killer didn't know John had heard of them.

The hovels that were inhabited mostly housed old drunks and ladies of the evening who were broken down by hard years and a fondness for gin.

"It's clear. Let's move." Penny must have a better angle on the cow than John did. He trusted her enough to not check himself. He headed onward, up and up. They reached their destination just as the first rays of the sun spilled over the land. The cabin had a door and most of a roof. Which was more than you could say for a lot of them. The thick dust and gaping squares where windows or shutters should have been attested to the building being abandoned. He got inside, feeling pursued.

The furniture was a sad thing, but there was a table and some kind of dry sink built into one wall. And in the back corner of the one-room shack was a bed frame with a moldering straw-filled mattress.

Vermin indeed.

"I promise if I showed you some of the others I found, you'd be thrilled with this."

Penny gave a soft chuckle. "I've lived rough on the frontier, John. I bunked with Trace, Deb, Gwen, and the children in a two-bedroom cabin half of last winter. I slept on the floor with a bedroll and a blanket and was grateful to be near a fire. Then on a bitter-cold winter day, that cabin burned down."

"You're lucky to have gotten out."

"Cam carried me out while I was unconscious, overcome by smoke. Then all six of us moved into a bunkhouse that already had three men in it, including my brother. This time I shared a room with Gwen and the two youngsters. I got the floor again. A beat-up mattress and a cabin with a faulty roof doesn't scare me much. I can face discomfort and harsh weather. It's men that seem to be where most of the trouble comes from."

"That's the plain truth." John slid one arm around her shoulders. "I need some time with this notebook."

She felt the weight of his arm, drawing her attention because it was so heavy. She saw lines of exhaustion on his face. She wasn't sure how long she'd slept, but he hadn't gotten a moment.

"You're so tired your eyes are gonna cross trying to read. It's still mighty early. Let me beat on that mattress and drive out any critters, then you can get some shut-eye. Even an hour or two will help. You're not going to get through the day without sleep."

John nodded without comment. He dropped his satchels, including that gunnysack with her dress. She wondered what he'd draw out of those magical packs next.

She made sure the mattress didn't have any visitors. And it didn't. This hovel was so bad even mice and rats were too good for it.

But the dust had settled in happily.

She cleared it out without being a fanatic about it, and John lay down and said, "Come here. I wasn't gone that long, about half an hour. You need sleep, too."

She'd worried about sleeping arrangements before, hesitating over two people and one bed. But right now, she was so tired that she didn't think twice. She lay down, with her back to him. He wrapped his arm around her waist and pulled her close, and she marveled at how nice it felt to be snuggled up against him on the cool mountain morning.

"This can't be the trail to Payne's mansion." Florence snorted. Perfect name for this place. "No man living in a mansion would put up with it. Not only that, he'd have workmen hauling in materials and furniture. He'd need a wide enough trail to get a wagon through."

The trail was so steep and narrow that branches slapped her in the face and scrub brush underfoot threatened to trip her horse.

"You're the one who got directions." Edmond—in the lead—fought the reins of the nag he'd been given. Florence had trusted him to get the horses. He'd gone to a big barn in town and come back with these two ancient mares. Clearly he got cheated. The horses were balky, given to biting, eager to stop. Florence wished for a riding crop and the English saddle she'd ridden in back east—on the rare occasion when she'd ridden at all.

"You saw him point to this trail the same as I did. And he said it'd take us right to the house. He said there weren't any forks in the trail so just keep going up, then down the other side." Then Florence reached a high peak and gasped at her first sight of Lake Tahoe.

Edmond had gotten there first, but she hadn't paid attention to his silence. Now she understood it. In a reverent voice

Florence barely recognized, for there wasn't much reverent about him, Edmond said, "This is the most beautiful thing I've ever seen."

Even she, who'd seen the most beautiful things money could buy, had to pause and absorb the shining lake up here at the top of a mountain. The crystal blue water reflected everything perfectly. The stones surrounding the lake, the ring of pine trees. Beyond the trees, the snowcapped peaks of the Sierra Nevada Mountains. Clouds scudded overhead, and as they moved through the sky, they sailed across the surface of Lake Tahoe.

When she finally managed to look somewhere besides that pure picture reflected in the lake, her eyes dropped to the shore right beneath their feet, and she saw a huge wall. No house was visible, not even from where they stood on high ground. But a wall this massive had to guard a mansion.

"We've found it, Edmond." Finally, someone worthy of the Chiltons' social position. Someone with taste. Someone wise enough to show the world how wealthy he was.

Her husband, still stunned by the view of Lake Tahoe, tore his eyes away from the beauty, saw her pointing, and followed the direction.

"That's nothing but a giant fence. . . . Can we get through it?"

Florence scowled at her husband. "Bolling wouldn't have sent us here if we couldn't. There must be a gate."

"I don't see a gate anywhere." Edmond shook his head, frowning.

"We just have to get closer." She was so excited that she quit paying attention to the trail. Florence kicked her horse to get moving toward the mansion, and the horse balked, kicked out its heels, and tossed Florence right over its head.

She landed hard right on her back and got the wind knocked out of her. Skidding down the slope she'd so recently stood atop, she hit a tree, grabbed at it—missed— rolled like a log down the stony hill, and then went airborne. Bushes and branches clawed at her skin. She struck rocks and flew over drop-offs. She was battered all the way down. Fighting to draw breath, she barely saw the water as she plunged in.

Freezing cold, brutally cold. What little breath she had whooshed out. She hit the bottom and shoved herself up. She couldn't stop the gasp for breath.

Drowning was a terrible way to die. Except . . . she wasn't drowning.

In fact, her head was above the water. Scrambling, she got up on her hands and knees in about two feet of water. Really cold water. She'd inhaled enough of it that she coughed and heaved. She staggered to her feet, her dress limp and weighing three times what it should.

She stumbled toward the shore, only a few steps away, hacking up water. She was knee deep, then ankle deep, and then she tripped over a boulder and landed on sand.

Warm sand, thank heavens. Her coughing fit slowed, and she got breath into her aching lungs.

"Florence, are you all right?" Edmond picked his way down on foot very carefully, and that was probably necessary. But he'd done a fine job of taking plenty of time. She'd had to take care of herself just like she'd done her whole life. Shivering from the drenching ice bath, she used another boulder— heaven knew there were plenty of them—and got to her feet.

Edmond arrived at her side just as she looked up and up . . . and up . . . at a massive wall made of the same kind of boulders she'd been bouncing off of a few seconds ago. The wall looked absolutely impenetrable. The woods had been cut back well away from the fortress. On her left, climbing the steep incline, the wall went on for maybe two hundred feet, though Florence was no judge of such things. To her right, the wall stretched into the lake, far enough out that it was most likely in deep water. Cold deep water, and she saw no way around it.

"Get off Payne land." The shout was followed by the crack of a rifle. A rustle from above drew her attention to see the horses they'd rented bolt for town.

Florence had little experience with guns, but she turned to see a large man striding toward them, his gun aimed and cocked. Without being asked, Florence raised both hands high in surrender. She watched the man like she'd watch an approaching rattlesnake.

Florence also noted that Edmond had kept his head enough to grab the satchels containing their gold and jewels. It was the first sensible thing the man had ever done. And that most definitely included marrying her. That hadn't shown much sense at all.

And now an armed man was going to rob them or kill them or both. And while she watched him and tried to decide which he'd do, she began to shiver with a cold so bone-deep she wondered what she'd die of first.

———❧———

"You're searching for a woman named Deb Harkness and a man named Trace Riley?" Luther Payne did his genial best not to let the gloating show on his face. "To retrieve your grandson from them?"

"Yes, do you know these folks? Can you tell us where to find them?"

Luther started to speak just as a quiet knock came on his office door. "Come in."

The man who'd brought these two useful fools in at gunpoint was now serving them coffee and sandwiches. Luth had sent his cook and daily maid home with instructions not to come back until they were summoned. The Chiltons seemed to be over the gun and eager to be treated as honored guests.

Luther wondered if anyone back east would notice when they went missing. He made a note to himself to sink their bodies deep.

"I know Trace Riley. Not personally, of course, but it's a small world out west. We country folks know our neighbors for miles around."

Truth was, Raddo had mentioned Riley and Harkness. Two witnesses he wanted to kill. Luther knew Riley had helped bring in Raddo's body.

The two folks he kidnapped had escaped and were now asking awkward questions in Virginia City that would almost certainly lead them to him. And he knew of Cameron Scott and his new wife, Gwen, and their two children . . . including one, Ronnie Scott, whom these people wanted. Now he had the perfect people to blame when his fist came crashing down on all of them.

Luther liked to think he was subtle. Ruthless, but subtle. Most of the wealthy mine owners in Virginia City knew him well enough to never cross him and to keep their mouths shut and look at anyone but Luther when a competitor had a convenient accident or vanished.

"Between them they live in two separate locations, though not that far apart. Riley's place isn't where the children are staying. They are in the care of Cameron Scott."

Florence Chilton shuddered. "Dreadful man. He can't be allowed to raise our grandson. He's been gone from Ronnie all his life. A complete stranger."

Luth wondered how well the kid knew these two.

"Let's eat and relax while you tell me what you know about your grandson. We'll have no trouble collecting him. I'm personal friends with a few lawmen, so we'll have the authority to get your grandson back. It shouldn't take long, and in the meantime you can make yourselves comfortable. I live a rustic life here, of course, but I value privacy, and the beauty of this place is spectacular."

In truth, the beauty wasn't something he thought about. But the privacy was unequaled. It suited him to live in an easily guarded backcountry within half a day's ride to Virginia City and a couple of hours to Carson City. Pushing hard on a fast horse he could make it even faster. And he often did. He wasn't that far from the Cameron Scott homestead, either.

"I have only a cook and maid, but they don't come in today." The Chiltons didn't know what orders had been given.

Florence nodded her head with the dignity of a queen getting her due. "I'd appreciate it if you'd send one of your men for our bags at the boardinghouse in Ringo."

"The men are out working right now." Spying on Cameron Scott. "But I'll send one as soon as he's available."

Gruffly, Edmond said, "Thank you."

While he entertained them with stories of the Wild West,

he noted the way Florence had clung to her two satchels. They seemed unusually heavy, and since she admitted she didn't have any clothes, he had to wonder what was in them that she valued so highly. Considering the type of greedy fool she appeared to be, he could only guess she'd laid up significant treasures here on earth.

Luth would enjoy confiscating whatever wealth she'd clung to. He'd wait and take it after she and her husband were beyond complaining about its loss.

20

"Five names in all." John snapped the little book closed. "And these records look thorough. I'm guessing these are the only men who bought Hessian boots from that store in recent years. And I was told last night that this is the only man in town who sells them."

"I'd have said we can't be sure our villain hadn't gone to San Francisco to get his boots, if not for the murder last night." Penny dug food out of her bag. She'd restocked at home and was glad for it now. "Killing that shopkeeper showed the kind of ruthless, cold-blooded villain we're up against. But it was also foolish. That murder is an admission that we're on the right track, don't you think?"

John opened two of the cases he'd been dragging around after him for years. "I have no absolute proof . . . nothing that would hold up in court, but yes, we're on the right track. That man dying last night proves it to me beyond any doubt. And I'm going to find the man who killed him and see him hanged."

He pulled out a coat, worn but high quality. A specially

made vest, a white shirt, and the small hard case that held one of the great tricks of his trade.

"What are you doing?" She glanced up from where she dug in her bag.

He had married a marvel. That woman could keep them alive forever with the contents of that old leather bag.

John smiled at his wife. He'd just slept next to her for the first time, not that anything had happened, but it was a turning point. It was trust.

He'd savored the comfort of having this pretty, tough, smart, likable woman in his arms. He intended to keep her there, but right now he didn't have time to do more than solve this case.

"I'm turning myself into a sixty-year-old fat man who's down on his luck. A completely unremarkable, unmemorable man who can walk around Virginia City and listen and learn without anyone knowing."

Penny continued her diligent search for whatever it was she had in there. He had no doubt she could find anything. But she delicately cleared her throat. "Um . . . I'm sure you know your business, John."

With every heavily doubtful word she spoke, she said she was sure he did *not* know his business.

"And maybe in the dark, among strangers, for a short time, someone will believe you're an old fat man. But you are a young, fit, handsome man. Intelligence shines out of your eyes. No one could be near you for long and not notice."

He smiled, loving every word. She might not exactly know it, but she'd just said words that made a man feel proud. Of course, she was wrong.

"Would you like to place a bet on that?"

She sat up straight and her brow lowered. "I don't gamble. It's sinful."

One corner of John's mouth curled up when he thought of all the chances they'd taken lately and how willingly she'd gone along. She gambled, all right. A person didn't need a deck of cards, a saloon, or a roulette wheel to be a gambler.

John had shaved just last night for the restaurant. He regretted not having a couple of weeks to prepare for this new disguise because a neglected, unshaven face was the most natural makeup in the world. But he simply didn't have time.

He opened the first case and pulled out the theatrical whiskers and the stage makeup.

"Prepare to be amazed, Mrs. McCall."

* * *

Penny had entered this cabin with a young, handsome, intelligent man. Now she shared it with an old, really tall, and fat and . . . yes, she had to say it . . . stupid . . . man.

And she didn't mean stupid as an insult. In fact, it was amazing. Somehow, he'd wiped that gleam of sharp wit from his eyes. He walked differently. He talked differently.

He'd added dirt and some of the contents of the mattress to strange padding he pulled out of his suitcase. Then he donned that padding like a suit of clothes. He showed her something he called lifts, which he put in his shoes to make him taller . . . and he was already a tall man.

He stuck wads of what looked like cotton bandages rolled in small, tight balls into his mouth. It fattened his face and slurred his speech, adding to the impression of low intelligence. He put grizzled hair on his face that looked like neglected, shaggy sideburns. He'd smeared dirt and some strange pot of something on his face, so he looked like he hadn't washed in weeks. A droopy, bedraggled hat helped shield his face and cast shadows on his handiwork.

All the little bits added up to him becoming someone she might well have walked right by on the street without recognizing. She had no doubt he could walk right by the folks they'd met last night in that restaurant.

And then he left to gather whatever information he needed. Now it was her turn to help. She opened the record book John had taken from the murder victim and several other papers John had given her and went to work. She'd definitely gotten the boring end of this investigation.

But boring didn't mean unimportant. She settled in to study, grimly determined to prove she could help.

John meandered around the shabby neighborhood near his boardinghouse. He found diners and saloons filled with gossip. He also found quiet men, idlers with piercing eyes. Informants . . . whether to one man or many he couldn't say, but he was mindful of his own acting skills showing disinterest, an idler himself.

Of the five names he'd found in that record book, he'd heard mention of four. He also picked up information about the night watch and where they were most vigilant.

And he'd learned that at least one of the five men was feared.

Feared to the point that his name had been spoken in whispers. Torn, John tried to decide if he should just get busy finding out where this man lived and go straight there, before the merciless killer stabbed anyone else to death, or if he should be more thorough. Just because they were unusually afraid of the one man didn't mean they weren't all hard men. In fact, he got the impression they were, and he suspected no one made it big in a boomtown without being hard.

He waddled along, staring down, all part of the demeanor he'd taken on, until he reached an area of town that bisected the richer and poorer parts. Here he found a diner just filling up with men hunting a noon meal.

Sitting down at a long table, next to a man dressed in a similar fashion to him, John ate and listened and found the last man.

Lake Tahoe? One of the men had a mansion out there? Mr. Payne, co-owner of one of the biggest mines. Luther Payne. That jiggled something in John's mind, but he wasn't sure what. He set it aside to keep listening and gathering info.

No one mentioned Payne much, and his name was one of dozens he heard, mostly not connected to John's work, though he paid attention to every word.

When John returned to wandering the boardwalk, his thoughts were haunted by that poor murdered man. John didn't think he'd ever done anything, outside of wartime maybe, to get an innocent man killed.

And then he walked by a mining office. With a few names painted discreetly on the window of the front door. One of them Payne. Luther Payne.

And he thought of something else he'd found in the haberdasher's desk and it clicked. He turned and headed for home. Penny had some information John needed badly.

⁓⊙⊱⊙⁓

Penny could find no notes about any other buyer for the boots John had noticed, though she went through everything carefully.

She also couldn't resist being curious about all John's luggage and went through it, just plain snooping. It must all be disguises. Some of the wisps of hair and other strange objects were a mystery. She was careful to return everything just as it had been. Not that she didn't want John to know she was going through his things. She planned to ask him about it and admit what she'd done. She was bored, after all. But she didn't want to mess up what were very carefully packed cases.

Once done with that, she debated whether it was important to keep watch. Would it be better to post a watch in the night? Now she was alone and maybe more vulnerable. Later John, who might be out kicking up suspicions, would be here. If someone followed him back they'd need a sentry through the night. Finally, after several painfully dull hours, she was falling asleep anyway, so she decided not to fight it. She'd rest now so John could sleep later.

Besides, that solved the very uncomfortable question of sharing that bed again. In the breaking dawn, they'd both been so tired it hadn't mattered. Tonight might be different. And, she admitted, John's strong arms around her felt better than Penny had realized anything could.

She found her husband's strength and warmth appealing. But that wasn't love. And until she could say she did at least plan to stay with him and commit to a true marriage, there could be nothing more intimate between them. It would be a travesty of what God wanted after wedding vows.

As she lay down to sleep, she regretted that those strong arms were the last things she thought of before she slept because they followed her into some very restless dreams.

CHAPTER

21

"I'll head back before first light, Mr. Payne. I found them,
counted how many were there. One man, one woman, two
little ones."

"The rest of them went back to Riley's house? Riley with
his wife and the hired men, too?"

"Yep. And the man—that'd be Cameron Scott, I checked
in the land office, and that's his homestead right beside his
sister's. She's the woman we had in our hands, who brought
Raddo in with Riley and another man we haven't identified
yet."

"Jonathan Call. I saw him in Virginia City last night. Along
with a woman he introduced as his wife, Penelope Call. It's
the same pair." And they were hunting him. Luth had moved
fast to close down their line of investigation. And he'd tossed
his favorite boots aside until this was settled.

"Scott is out and about working. I saw his wife when Scott
opened the door, but otherwise she stayed to the house. He's
built a cabin, and I can see the start of a second one. His sister,

Penny Scott, got a homestead and so did his wife—Gwen Harkness was her name before they got married. Saw that at the land office, too."

"The woman who Raddo hunted was Deb Harkness. Sisters probably." Luth could use that if he needed to. He paused in his thinking for just a few seconds as he remembered Raddo coming, wounded, to this very house and blackmailing him. Luther had given him enough to live on for life, but Luth had told his old partner in crime, who was his little brother besides, to get out of the country. Raddo had agreed, then ignored that agreement to go after Deb and Trace Riley.

Deb had witnessed Raddo massacring a wagon train. Something Luth and Raddo had done together, with a gang, years before. Then Luth had gone straight. Gotten in at the beginning of the Comstock Lode silver boom.

Luth suppressed a smile. He hadn't exactly gone straight. He'd just gotten smart and real sneaky. A few men had died in accidents when they were in his way, or when they owned a share of a mine he wanted.

There'd been talk because Luth had gotten too rich too fast and the deaths had been too convenient. But there'd been no evidence, and he'd made sure folks feared him, which kept the talk down.

Now he could see why asking Raddo to let witnesses live was foolish, because Luth didn't consider doing it for a second. Luth and Raddo were cut from the same cloth.

His hired gun went on. "Scott put his cabin up right on the property line so they got away with only building one, but the sister's cabin—"

"Can the three of you handle them?" Luth knew enough about Trace Riley, and he'd heard things about his hired man

195

Utah. He knew if he killed the Scott family, which included Trace's sister-in-law, Luth would have to face Riley.

It didn't matter. He had to do it anyway. Scott was a tough man. He'd as soon not have them all to deal with at the same time.

"Won't be a problem."

"I'll need you to bring the children back here."

His guard's eyes snapped wide. "Bring them? Won't they be crying and carryin' on?"

"Having them here is part of dealing with the Chiltons. I need those children to—"

A sharp rap on the door startled Luth. He didn't like anyone in his office, and one of only two people might be so bold as to interrupt him. Both of them uninvited guests.

"Come in." He fought down the urge to pull the gun out of his desk drawer and finish with Florence Chilton right now.

But he also really liked the rug in here and would regret bloodstains.

He and his hired man exchanged a quick look.

Luth said, "The three of you handle it. I can come along if—"

Florence smiled that brittle, arrogant smile at him. The one that said she thought she was better than him. "Have you had time to get our things from Bolling's Boardinghouse?"

"My men are occupied with important business this morning, but perhaps this afternoon." Luth sure hoped it was that simple.

Florence sighed dramatically, like she was being put upon. Luth looked at his beautiful rug and controlled himself. Besides, he'd need her to wrangle the children until their usefulness was at an end.

"This afternoon will have to do. I appreciate the help, though Edmond could go."

Florence didn't realize it, but she'd been seen for the last time by anyone outside this house. Edmond, too.

"My men will handle it," he snapped, wanting her to get out.

Florence lifted her chin and looked down her nose at him.

Luth hadn't meant to sound quite so sharp. He'd done a poor job of covering his irritation at her interruption.

"Well, thank you. That's fine. I'll go now." Florence smiled with rather phony politeness and backed out of the room.

When the door shut, his hired gun said, "We can—"

Luth swiped one hand at the man. Silence dropped like a shroud over the room. Luth didn't trust that woman one bit. He doubted she was above eavesdropping.

"Handle it. And get it done today."

With a short nod, his man left the room. Luth had an internal wrestling match with his temper. He needed to be sure Florence hadn't been alarmed. He didn't want her running off.

Time to be a genial host. He rose from the chair, and it slammed back against the shelf behind him.

Then he waited. He needed another minute so he could come up with a smile that didn't look like he was baring his teeth.

CHAPTER 22

"I found him."

Penny stood from the dirt floor and barely stopped a scream when a strange man burst into the cabin. A fat, slovenly old man who moved and sounded . . . exactly like her husband.

Slapping a hand on her chest, she said, "Good night! John! I didn't recognize you."

He grinned. "Glad you didn't shoot me. You'd have some explaining to do when some judge accused you of finding a fast way to divorce me."

She'd been sitting in a corner for the last few hours . . . ever since she woke up. The whole day dedicated to rest and silence. It didn't suit her.

Then she realized what he'd said. "You found who?"

"Whisper Man. The man who kidnapped us. His name's Luther Payne."

"Are you sure?" Penny rose to her feet, excited and impressed.

"I believe so, and that means it's almost for sure Payne

killed that shopkeeper last night. And if that's right, then I've seen his face and know his name. I found out he's co-owner of a mine. And I found out he's a feared man. I decided it was him from the way the men didn't talk about him."

Narrowing her eyes at the strange statement, Penny said, "That doesn't make sense."

John smiled. He was almost buzzing with excitement and energy—completely at odds with the disguise. Then he set aside a gunnysack he carried and started shedding his old man costume, one garment at a time. The way he moved fast and sure, as if he couldn't contain his thoughts and remain still, reminded her of the way he liked to pace when he did his thinking. She'd never had much use for a slothful character, and John showed plenty of signs that he was an energetic man.

"Did you find any other names in that record book?"

"No, just the five you found before you left this morning."

"I heard all five men talked about. These five are all rich, powerful men. Not all with the mines. One's a banker. One's a lawyer. One handles timber and shipping. Another is a railroad man. And one, Luther Payne, owns a mine. Rich men get their names mentioned, and it wasn't long before a few names from my list popped up. There was good-natured complaining, and a few complaints not so good-natured. Payne only came up a few times and then with a kind of fearful neutrality as if no one wanted to get caught mentioning him. I think Payne's the kind of man who has eyes and ears everywhere."

"Eyes and ears?" Penny asked.

"Informants. I'll bet word is out that he'll pay for information, and particularly when it is information about himself.

He's probably got a reputation for retaliating against men who blacken his name. And that retaliation must be so harsh no one risks speaking ill. I got a strong impression of that."

While he talked, John finished turning back into himself, carefully repacking every piece of his disguise. Then he picked up the gunnysack he'd carried in, loosened a string tie at the top of the bag, and pulled out a plate wrapped in a red-checkered cloth. He unwrapped it and handed it to Penny. A meatloaf dinner complete with potatoes and a big hunk of bread. He even had a knife and fork. Then he reached back in and pulled out a similar meal for himself.

"I promised to return the plates. She made me leave a dollar for each set, and if I bring her all the plates, napkins and utensils, she'll give me my two dollars back."

Penny hadn't realized how hungry she was. She snatched the plate from John, plunked herself back on the floor, and picked up the fork.

"Keep talking."

John sat on the floor beside her, eating his own meal like a starving man.

He finally must've taken the edge off his hunger because he swallowed a bite and said, "Do you have that paper with you that Cam copied off Raddo's arm?"

"The tattoo?"

"Yep, I think I remember what it said, but it didn't make much sense, and I'm not sure if I have the right words in the right order. It might matter."

Penny took her last few bites. She'd eaten that meal like a hungry wolf and felt a pang of embarrassment about it. She set her plate aside and went to her trusty bag.

Rummaging deep, she finally produced the small strip of

paper. Staring at it, she said, "Luth. The word *Luth* is on here."

With satisfaction, John said, "I thought so. I was sure I remembered the word *Luth*. Luther Payne."

He set his plate aside, done eating, and stood. "Read it to me."

"Cam copied it off as best he could. Remember how faded it was? And the words made no sense, so it was hard to know if he got it down right. One of the reasons we copied it was because it was so odd we weren't certain of remembering it right."

"Let's hear it."

Penny cleared her throat as she looked at the mysterious line of words. "'Luth if I die Revenge Watchbook Tahoe Jewel Overlook.' Most of them are right, but some were so faded, I'm not sure." Her brow furrowed. "What can it mean?"

Chewing, looking thoughtful, John said, "Luth is there. 'If I die Revenge.' That part makes me even more certain I'm on the right path. I've got our suspect, but I need proof I can take to the sheriff. From the questions Payne asked when he kidnapped us, we know he is worried. He wanted to know if Raddo had told us anything. That was the whole point of snatching us."

"The tattoo would be a good way to leave behind blackmail material." Penny stuffed her plate back in the gunnysack. It didn't sit right to not wash them up, but they had only a bit of water in their canteens, and she wasn't wasting it. "All he had to do was keep his arms covered, and he had a threat to hold over Payne that couldn't be stolen, forgotten, or bribed out of a greedy lawyer."

John nodded. "A man as mistrustful as Raddo might well have tattooed his proof right onto his skin."

Penny looked at the line of words again. "'Watchbook Tahoe Jewel Overlook.' Good grief, what could that be?"

John shook his head, but he had a smile on his face. "I don't know."

"Then why are you smiling?"

"Because it's a clue. It's another thread to pull as we unravel this mystery. If they knew each other from long ago—and that tattoo looked old—then Raddo's got reason to hold a grudge because somehow Luther got rich and Raddo got left with nothing."

"So, we don't know what 'watchbook' means, but 'Luth' and 'if I die Revenge' are easy enough. 'Tahoe Jewel Overlook . . .'"

She looked up and their eyes met. She could see his mind working and found she liked the expression. He was really good at this.

Penny, who had mostly been around soldiers and frontiersmen, found admiration for a city man with a crafty mind.

Admiration and attraction.

To distract herself from that, she asked, "Could that be a place? Maybe Raddo hid some evidence about Payne?" Penny looked up from the note. "I know it'll be a challenge to your conscience, but it looks like you're going to have to do some more snooping."

"Do you think *overlook* is right? Did Cam copy it down right? I mean, *overlook* could be two words: *over* and *look*. It changes the meaning of the phrase."

"The phrase had no meaning, so it changes it from nothing to nothing."

"Good point." John paced and talked and rubbed his chin.

"To the best of our ability, this is what we decided the words said."

The small hut was silent for a few minutes as they mulled . . . silent except for the sound of feet treading back and forth.

Penny asked, "Could it be some spot by Tahoe that's known, an especially pretty view?"

"Possibly. I can ask about it. I'll need to be careful though." John stopped and focused on her intently. "Anything you think of make sure and say out loud, even if it seems silly or outlandish. I'll say what pops into my head. Either a new idea or some idea spurred by what you say. We bounce ideas back and forth like a rubber ball until we have a few different possible things to check. I do that some with the detectives I work with, and it's surprising the ideas we come up with that way."

"Two heads are better than one?"

John smiled. "It's better than too many cooks spoil the broth."

"I've always thought that was a stupid saying. Broth is broth. How can extra cooks spoil it?"

With a shrug, John said, "Maybe one wants to put too many onions in, another too much salt. Have you ever tasted those fiery hot peppers from down Mexico way?"

"Yep, Cam spent time in the southwest desert, so I lived down there."

"Those can have a strong effect on a broth."

"Okay, but oversalting broth is just wrong, no matter how many cooks you've got in the room. So, the saying should be 'too many cooks spoil the broth if one or more of them are bad cooks.'"

John's smile widened and since he was pacing again, he paced right up to Penny and kissed her. She was taken by surprise.

And then she was kissing him back.

Penny's arms came around his neck. Then John lifted his head so there was a whisper of space between them. She saw something in his eyes she couldn't quite define. Intensity, interest, perhaps affection.

"Penny, I've decided we need to figure out a way to make this marriage work. I'm going to have to stay, or you're going to have to come away with me. I find myself very interested in being . . . um . . . that is, being . . . married to you properly."

"Properly?" She was a little dazed. The kiss had muddled her thoughts. Either that, or he was making no sense.

"I mean, well, this is what I mean." He lowered his head and quit talking.

John only confused things when he talked. When he kissed her, things seemed very simple.

He deepened the kiss, and Penny figured out what he meant when he said "properly married." Part of her was all for it. And they were already married, after all.

But there was a small place in her heart that balked.

A small but very stubborn place.

It took a huge act of willpower to pull her arms away from where they clung to him and press her hands flat against his chest. She tilted her head enough to break the kiss, to put a stop to the sweetest, most wonderful moment of her life.

"John, wait."

He didn't try to pressure her. Instead he held her close and rested his forehead against hers. He breathed deeply, but he didn't speak.

A surge of something flashed through Penny like a bolt of lightning. Something strong and bright and heated.

Not love, it couldn't be that. They were too different, and their marriage was not one they chose.

But maybe . . . fondness. That wasn't love, was it? But it was a good way to feel about a husband. It struck Penny that love was a confusing, rather mysterious thing.

Of course, she loved her brothers and her niece and nephew. She'd loved her parents. But that was almost born in her. She'd never really thought about it beyond knowing family loved each other.

But a husband. Loving a husband . . . that seemed like something to discover through a tidy courtship. Long conversations and a deep knowledge of each other, followed by *choosing* to get married.

No noose or gun involved.

And now she felt a great fondness for him. She'd even go so far as to call it a burning fondness.

She stepped away from John. "I slept a few hours today so I could sit up and keep watch tonight. In case anyone spotted you today and followed you . . . home." She said the last word with a complete lack of conviction. Was this now her home?

John smiled. He was generous with his good humor, and Penny appreciated that about his character. Cam was a man with a very serious nature, so a man who saw the humor in life was a nice change.

"I was careful not to be followed." He reached up a hand and brushed a hair off her forehead, then with gentle fingers, tucked a strand behind her ear. "Do you really want to keep watch, or were you just planning ahead to have a good reason to be on the other side of the room from me?"

Penny felt a blush warm her cheeks. John's eyes didn't miss

much. His caressing hand brushed over one cheek, then he leaned in and kissed the spot he'd just touched.

"It might be best if you do keep watch awhile. And do your very best to sit silently and not attract attention."

That was alarming, and she forgot her blushes. "You're afraid they might be watching up here and see me moving around inside the cabin, maybe even hear me? Are they that close?"

Another mischievous smile. Another sweet kiss on the cheek. "No, I'm thinking of myself. Every move you make, every sound, is going to keep me wide awake wanting to lure you into my arms. It's going to be hard to get to sleep with you this close."

Penny smiled and stepped farther away. "Get on to bed, McCall. I'm going to hide in a corner still and silent as a church mouse. Don't blame your sleeplessness on me."

"Why not? It's all your fault." He stole a quick kiss and turned away from her. He trudged to the bed. And that wasn't easy to do since the room was about ten feet square.

He lay down on the wrecked, lumpy bed with his back to her. It got cool up here at night, but they had the blankets from their bedrolls. She hunkered down in a corner with her own blanket pulled up to her chin and wondered if she'd made a mistake in turning her husband away.

It might be time for her to be properly married. If not tonight, then soon.

CHAPTER

23

He woke up in the still, gray light that came just before sunrise. He found a warm, sweet woman wrapped in his arms and wasn't sure when she'd come to bed, nor when he'd pulled her close.

But he was very sure he liked it. He was very sure she fit in his arms with absolute perfection.

It wasn't a full, complete marriage yet, but he saw now that it could be. They didn't really know each other well enough that more intimacies should happen. But all in all, he thought he just might bring the treat of a good dinner for his wife every night. In fact, he was tempted to wait on her hand and foot for the rest of their lives, to advance the cause of their marriage. He even had a notion about the rest of his life that might make them both reasonably happy.

He slipped out of bed and dressed as silently as possible. He was hard pressed to be completely silent though.

"A new disguise?" Penny's voice, husky with sleep, sounded from behind him.

"I didn't mean to wake you, but I was a bit slow getting into town yesterday morning. It's a crowded, bustling town, especially when the men are heading to the mines and back. I feel like I can slip into that flowing crowd and not be noticed this early."

"What are you going to be today, the old man again?"

"I'm going to be old. Graying my hair and adding whiskers are a handy way to disguise myself, but today I'm going to be thin and a bit taller and quite a bit older. And I probably should be a drunk."

Penny sat straight up in bed. "If you're planning to come home reeking of gin, you're going to need to get your own hut, husband."

John laughed. He was amazed anew at all the things she did that charmed him.

"I never drink, Penny. And most certainly not when I'm working. But I've been known to sit with a glass in my hand to make people think I'm a sot. It helps them to ignore me. They certainly never take me seriously. And that helps me to ferret out clues."

Penny shoved back the blanket and stood, fully dressed except for her boots. Maybe she'd worried about kicking him in his sleep.

"How are you going to be taller?"

John lifted up a pair of floppy leather shoes she hadn't seen before. Almost moccasins, but a darker leather. "I put lifts in these shoes—higher than the ones I wore yesterday." He held up a leather pad about two inches thick. "I can fit this into the bottom of my shoes and lace them up looser than with the lower lifts."

He adjusted the shoes and put them on, then stood.

With a gasp of delight, Penny said, "You really do look much older. What's that in your hair?"

"It's talcum powder. I streaked it in to make my hair look gray. And this coat is tighter and cut in a way that makes me look thinner."

"This business of disguises is really interesting. I wouldn't think two inches taller would be that noticeable. But you also look almost gaunt. And much older. And you move as if you're older." Penny's eyes sparkled. "Do you think you could teach me this? I don't even know as I'd ever have a reason to actually be disguised, but it's so interesting."

John shrugged one shoulder and smiled. "It can be a quirk of our marriage. One night a week we can come to the supper table dressed in disguise."

Penny laughed. "That would definitely qualify as a quirk."

He kissed her pretty, laughing mouth, and she fell silent and kissed him back. When the kiss ended, she said, "The disguise doesn't reach to your kissing, John. That was all you."

"That was all us." He snuck in one more kiss. "I brought a loaf of bread and a bit of cheese and a couple of apples. They are in the gunnysack." He nodded his head in their direction, and Penny brightened.

"Thank you. I have jerky and hard biscuits, but this will be much better."

"Remember that," he said with a wink. "I am a fine provider."

She laughed again and punched him in the shoulder.

He tossed something at her, and she caught it by reflex, "What's this?"

"Oh, didn't I tell you?" His grin said he knew he hadn't.

"Tell me what?"

"That's your disguise. Today you're going with me. Hurry up."

———⚜———

Cam had slipped into his house before sunrise, leaving Trace to ghost around in the woods. Unfortunately, they hadn't found much new information. But today they planned to confront the spy.

At the crack of dawn, Cam left the cabin, carrying his rifle, hoping the man on lookout would assume his family was still here, just staying inside. Clouds gathered overhead, barely visible in the first light of the morning, but a storm was coming, and it suited Cam. That would be ample excuse for Gwen and the youngsters to keep to the house.

They'd been watching, one at a time, and not taking any action against Cam or his family. He stepped out boldly, planning to saddle his horse, ride away, and circle back.

The clouds sifted and cruised along, and a gap opened up that let a few rays of sun through. The sun hit something in the woods that grew thick on the rising mountain outside Cam's cabin. A flash of light caught his eye, and his old soldier instincts took over. He twisted sideways and threw himself back.

A crack of gunfire sounded a split second later.

The heat of a bullet burned Cam's side under his right arm, inches from piercing his heart.

He landed, grimly ignored the pain, and scrambled for cover. A rifle—sounded like a Winchester—blasted away. He dove around the corner of his house. Another bullet fired, then another. A second gunman opened fire, splattering chips of wood just above Cam's head. Two men, and the second one was on this side of the cabin.

It turned his shelter into a shooting gallery. He moved, clawing his way fast, keeping low to make a poor target.

A boulder just ahead promised refuge . . . maybe. A bullet kicked dirt into his eyes. Blinded, he rolled and leapt for the stone. Another bullet pinged the stone, ricocheting inches over Cam's head. Now he was in a narrow alley between the cabin and the boulder. Safe, unless the shooters changed positions. Or unless there were more than two men.

There should be three of them. Where was the third?

A new rifle opened up. One shot, then silence. With grim relief, Cam hoped he was hearing Trace's Winchester getting into the fight. It was the second Winchester he'd heard, but the single shot sounded like Trace's gun. Cam knew guns, and he hoped he was right.

The man who'd been aiming at Cam shot in a new direction, aiming high, up toward where the second Winchester had sounded.

Taking advantage of the distraction, Cam jumped up and ran for the edge of the woods, sprinting for all he was worth. He charged past the first big trunk of an ancient oak before bullets peppered the ground he'd just covered. Plunging into the forest, Cam was now surrounded by places to hide, which left him free to maneuver.

Gunfire above, two guns, at least one a Winchester for sure. Trace drawing fire. Cam ran toward the closest assailant, the dry-gulching skunk who'd covered the back of the house.

Silent as a ghost and fast as a striking snake, he closed in on the first man. Easy to stay out of sight in the woods and still go in the direction of the gunfire. He finally saw a barrel poking out from behind a massive ponderosa pine. He circled the tree to come up behind the coyote, and without one second's hesitation, he slammed the butt of his rifle into the man's head.

The man went down without a whimper.

Cam had come prepared to take prisoners. He uncoiled a short length of rope from his waist, whipped the man's hands and feet together as neatly as a hog-tied steer, tucked the man out of sight in a copse of aspens, and moved on.

More gunfire. It sounded like only two men. Cam hoped that meant Trace had taken an outlaw down. There should have been three men after them. Cam had gotten one. Trace hopefully had taken down the second. That left a single out-law still firing.

He listened to the gunfire. Cam only had a second to make a decision. Knowing he was running straight into a blazing shootout, Cam charged forward and hoped he wasn't running toward Trace. Not being sure would force him to hesitate.

And that hesitation could be the difference between life and death.

CHAPTER

24

The skinny old man with the aching joints and the fat old lady with an extra chin went into the diner and glared at each other through breakfast.

John had told her to be grumpy, like they were in the middle of a fight. It kept people away, and it gave them an excuse not to speak. Which gave them more opportunity to listen.

Penny had never heard the poem about Jack Sprat and his chubby wife. John quoted it to her word for word as they walked down the blasted hill to the town.

"If I'd've tripped and fallen, I'd've rolled like a barrel all the way to town."

"I'd have paid good money to see that." John had a flare for acting because he was a man prone to smiling, and he was teasing her, but he did it without giving up being grouchy as an old bear.

Penny didn't have much acting skill. She was a straight-forward, plainspoken woman. Luckily for John, she was irritated at being made fat, so it wasn't hard to maintain the correct attitude.

He gave her a few pointers about how he wanted her to act. Shrewish, critical, whiny. "In fact, just be yourself."

She looked closely, but he never cracked a smile.

Then he ordered her a double breakfast. She saw the glint in his eyes, but he was careful that no one else did.

Penny didn't hear anything interesting, but John set out after the meal. He clearly had a target. They walked along the sidewalk. Him bent over, moving slowly like his joints ached. Her waddling along like a duck.

She really didn't think anyone gave them a second look. As ridiculous as she felt in this outfit, mostly they just looked boring and regular, like many other people in this town.

They reached a building, and John said, "Remember how I told you to act. I'm a broken-down old man with outrageous demands, you're the wife who's goading me into making them. But don't talk much. Mostly jab at me and mutter dire insults. I knew Payne was the name of the man who was so feared. But I couldn't get anyone to tell me how to find him. Then I found this building. I'm hoping someone in here will tell me where he lives."

Penny looked up at the words *Payne, Logan, and Pratt Mining Office* painted in what looked like pure gold on the window of the front door.

The killer owned a mine.

And he had the people in this town too scared to do more than breathe his name.

John went straight in. Penny forgot all about being annoyed with her husband and tried to be ready to react to whatever John said or did.

In other words, she got ready to tell a passel of lies. Another sin.

Penny had corralled herself a very different kind of husband than she'd planned on.

John walked a bit more unsteadily than he'd been doing a few steps ago. It aged him. What a strange talent her husband had.

A man sat behind a desk, the only person in what had to be the front office, because the building was imposing, yet this first room was small. The desk was to their right when they stepped in. An elegantly paneled wall, with a beautifully carved oak door, cut the room off just a pace beyond the desk.

Penny wondered what business went on in the back room.

The man had the look of a secretary. Account books lay open on his desk. He had a pen in hand and held it poised over the book as he looked up.

"This is a mine office. We have no services here for customers."

Not much about that to encourage talk.

"Name's Mack Johnson." John's voice cracked with age. "This here's my wife, Mayme Belle."

Oh, for heaven's sake. He'd named her after that crazy woman who'd forced them to get married. He had a pure knack for irritating her. And since she was supposed to be cranky, she didn't bother to hide a scowl.

"I left off mining a few months back but find myself short of money and unhappy in idleness. I want my job back."

The man's lips curled in a sneer as he ran his eyes down John's bent-looking body. Calling him too old and disabled for any use without saying a word.

"If you're hunting work, you need to report to the mine."

"Speak up, sonny." John leaned forward and said in a voice that vibrated from his elderly, feeble throat, "I'm nigh onto deaf from all those years working with loud equipment in your mines."

The man raised his voice. "Go to the mine. There are people there who deal with hiring. As I said, this office is strictly for the business of mining, buying and selling, ordering equipment and supplies. We handle the payroll, but it's all given out up at the mine, as I'm sure you know."

"Well, now, that's the thing. I been to the mine. They don't want me. I came here to talk to the big man. I said as how I was gonna get Mr. Payne to hire me on, then he'd be out there and tell 'em what's what."

"Uh, sir, I'm afraid—"

"Now, I put in good years." John talked over him, like he was an old man who couldn't hear. "Gave you the best years of my life, Mr. Payne. I think your company owes me. I've slowed down some in recent years, I know, but there's always work a man can do."

"I'm not Mr. Payne, I'm Howard Lund. I work—"

"My Mayme Belle here'll tell you I can still do a man's work."

Penny nodded her head, still scowling. She daydreamed about getting the old codger out of the house, because he was a nuisance to have around after all these years of her having the house to herself while he was in the mine. She decided if she could read Lund's mind, he could just as well read hers.

Lund barely spared her a glance. Then he nearly shouted, one slow word at a time, "I am not Mr. Payne."

John jerked as if the words were stones pelting him. "Oh, sorry about that. I know he's the big man around here. I reckoned you was him. If I could just talk to Mr. Payne, I can't believe he wouldn't know my name. I worked for him for years."

"You can't talk to him." Lund sounded very satisfied to deny the request at the top of his lungs. "He's not in."

It wasn't really yelling, no anger behind it, rather a nasty pleasure in brushing off an old, crippled man who'd fallen on hard times after giving his life to a company.

Penny would've liked to slam a fist into Lund's smug face.

"Could you tell us when Mr. Payne will be back?" Penny asked, keeping her voice as thin and soft as possible, a bit high pitched. She had no idea how to sound old . . . so she settled for quiet.

John turned in a painfully slow way to look at her. "Good idea, Ma." He turned back to Lund. "We'll wait."

John turned to look at a chair near the wall. "I don't mind sittin' a spell. Knees are actin' up."

He turned toward the chair. Penny looked around the room and saw no other chair besides the one Lund was polishing with his backside. "I can get a chair, too. There's bound to be one in the back room."

She headed for the door, curious about what filled up this building. "I'll be glad to get it on my own."

Lund was out of his chair like a shot. He jumped in front of Penny to block her way. "That room is private."

Penny narrowed her eyes and dropped her head like a maddened bull. "You're lying to us, Mr. Lund. You won't let me back there because Mr. Payne is here, and you're just denying us a chance to speak to him."

"I am not lying." The man looked flustered, and suddenly Penny was more than curious about what was in that room. She was sure there were secrets back there.

Because she figured John could just break in later, she didn't push to get past him. "What about Mr. Logan then, or Mr. Pratt?"

"Logan is dead and Pratt spends the winters in San Francisco. He isn't back yet."

John had come up beside her. "We'll be glad to wait. We don't want to have to come back."

She gave Lund an expectant look.

He erupted. "No. You can't wait here."

John shrugged. "Well, I'll go to his house, then. Is it a far walk? Because my joints are aching something fierce."

"Mr. Payne hasn't lived in town since he built his mansion on Lake Tahoe." Lund said it with pride, as if he owned it.

"A mansion?" John said. "He lives in a mansion while Ma and I can barely afford food?"

It crossed Penny's mind that if John wanted to make them poor to the point of hunger, he shouldn't have made her fat.

"Surely a rich man like that would offer a man a chance at honest work. If you could tell me where on Tahoe, maybe someone would give us a ride."

John sounded afraid and sad and doubtful that anyone would help. How did he do all that with only a few words? Penny clearly needed acting lessons.

"Mr. Johnson, I'm sorry." Lund sounded sincere. He had a spark of humanity in him after all. "There is a society here in town that works with injured miners and people in need—"

"Charity." John spat the word. "I'll go without before I go begging to them."

"No, they don't just give charity. They can help you find a job, perhaps one that doesn't require hard work like lifting and swinging a sledgehammer, for example. They are kind, good people."

Lund gave out those directions generously, and John and Penny went on their way. When they were a few steps away from the mining office, John looked sideways at her and grinned. Anyone with working eyeballs would've known that grin was from a young man. But they were alone on the street, so it was probably all right. Still, she thought she should have a serious talk with him about maintaining his pretense at all times. The character he played needed to be kept in place.

"Let's get our horses out of the livery where I stabled them. We need to get to that hut, pack up, and head out."

"Head out?" Penny had been thinking about being a detective, not about the actual case.

"Yep, we're going to Ringo, Nevada."

"Ringo?" Penny felt her brow furrow as she thought back. "I think we went through there after we were driven off of the land we were homesteading in California. We picked new plots of land, then headed for Trace's ranch to get Ronnie and Maddie Sue. But why go back there? What's in Ringo?"

"You were on your way to homestead, so you weren't asking questions, but Ringo is a town close to the north shore of Lake Tahoe."

"Yes, Lund mentioned that. But Tahoe's got hundreds of miles of rugged forest around it. It could take us years to find a house tucked up along that lake."

She realized they'd reached a building with a corral off to the side. John had stabled the horses when they first arrived while she stayed in their boardinghouse room. She didn't even know where the horses had gone and realized now she hadn't given them much thought. Proof, she realized with a start, that she trusted her husband.

It was a wonderful thing to discover. But that didn't change her doubts about going to Ringo with the minimal information they now had.

"We don't have years, John."

He hooked his arm through hers and guided her around to the side of the livery stable, made some quick adjustments to his clothes, and turned back into a young, thin, fit man.

"Can I take off my disguise now, too?"

"Nope. The liveryman never saw you. He'll probably think you're my mother."

She punched him in the arm.

He beamed at her. "Hey, that must mean you're really starting to care about me."

"What are you talking about?"

"You've finally learned to pull your punches."

Cam rounded a boulder, low as he could bend, and came nose to muzzle with a Winchester rifle. And not Trace's, either.

The man had it turned aside from where he'd been aiming, and when he saw Cam, he brought the rifle up and pulled the trigger.

On an empty chamber.

Cam's rifle was loaded, but instead of shooting an unarmed man point-blank, he brought the butt of his gun down hard and fast. When the outlaw collapsed to the ground, Cam yelled, "Trace, I got him."

Then Cam wondered if he'd been right about three men.

He ducked behind some scrub pines and waited as fast, quiet footsteps closed in on him.

Trace appeared out of the forest.

"I'm back here," Cam hissed. "I've got one tied up here and another back in an aspen copse."

"I got one right at the beginning. He's tied up over yonder."

"I reckon we'd best haul them into Dismal."

Cam lifted his Stetson off his head and brushed his brown hair back, then anchored his overlong hair with his hat. "Let's haul them in. The sheriff can lock them up. We can try asking them a few questions, maybe they'll name their boss, but they're hired guns, which makes them guilty enough to lock up and throw away the key. Reckon they won't tell us much."

They were a while scouting out the men's horses, then throwing them over the saddles. Cam and Trace searched them and found gold coins in their pockets. Probably taken as payment to find and kill Cam. The coins were strangely carved twenty-dollar gold coins of the same type they'd found in Raddo's saddlebags.

"Will you look at this?" Trace had a small paper sack he'd found in a saddlebag and was staring down into it.

"What?" Cam tightened his last knot and went to Trace's side.

Trace slapped the sack against Cam's chest in an outburst of temper. "It's candy."

Cam looked in and his temper exploded. "This is the kind of candy a child would want, not an adult."

"Yep, they were gunning for you as cold-blooded as can be. To kill you."

"If you're coming to kill, why bring candy unless—" Fury closed Cam's throat. He wanted to roar his rage into the sky.

He wanted to tear their prisoners apart with his bare hands. Instead he went silent and cold as ice.

"They were coming for the children," Trace said.

"Has to be. But why? Hostages? To use them as bait in a trap for you, your men, and Deb?"

"No, I don't think so." Trace looked from the bag to Cam. "The only one who wants those children is John."

"John's working for the Chiltons," Cam reminded him.

"Have we been suspicious of the wrong people? Could there possibly be *two* sets of three men causing trouble at the same time? Penny said their kidnapper wanted to know about Raddo. But these men, we've assumed they were the three that took Penny and John, but maybe not." Trace shook his head, skeptical. "But what are the chances of that?"

"You think these men were sent by the Chiltons?"

"They'd already sent John, though." Trace rubbed the back of his neck in an agitated way as he looked at the bound outlaws. "Why send more men?"

"John couldn't be behind it, could he?"

Trace shook his head. "John might push hard if he wanted to solve a case or do a job he was hired to do. But hiring out murder? I think I'm a good judge of men, and I don't believe it."

"So, then, are the Chiltons behind this?" Cam tried to believe it. "They made Abe's life a misery. I want to believe any awful thing anyone says about them."

"But not this?" Trace must've heard Cam's doubts.

"They badgered Delia to the point she refused to see or speak to them. But hiring murder?" There was silence for a few long moments, then Cam said, "Honestly, I'm surprised they even hired John. And he told me they paid him ahead

of time, gave him money for expenses, too. The Pinkerton
Agency insists on that. They wanted Ronnie mighty bad,
and I never got the impression they cared one speck about
the tyke."

"They planned to haul Ronnie across the country. In the
care of a man he doesn't know. I'd say they aren't overly
concerned about the boy."

"They want him bad for some reason. The Chiltons are
nasty people, and they're certainly fools. But murderers?"

Cam thought a moment longer, then shook his head. "I
just can't see it. All those years they hated my brother mighty
bad, but they never tried to have him killed. At least there
were no attempts Abe ever spoke of, and he'd've told me.
So why now?"

Cam stopped talking, stopped moving, almost stopped
breathing. His head came up, and his eyes met Trace's.

"What is it?" Trace asked.

"Why now?"

Trace caught Cam's tension. "What happened that made
it so important to get Ronnie?"

"They've never wanted to even know the child."

"But you said they always wanted Delia back. Maybe that
wanting just extends to their grandson."

"Wrong way to look at it."

"Then what's the right way?" Trace's eyes snapped with
impatience.

But Cam needed a few minutes to sort it out. Finally, he
said, "What happened is, Delia died. Deb wrote me a letter
right after Abe and Delia were killed. I got to your place
right as winter was slamming down on our heads and got
trapped. McCall didn't make it. He had to wait for spring.

Your wife's letter to the Chiltons got to them, and they sent McCall right away. The Chiltons wouldn't spend that money out of sentiment."

Trace nodded thoughtfully. "What if you're just trying too hard to explain something simple? With the boy's parents dead, they saw themselves as the natural custodians. They got Deb's letter and took it as their duty to fetch the boy home."

"Maybe it's that simple, but Ronnie came from that marriage. If they thought Abe was beneath them, then wouldn't his son be also?"

"He's their only grandson. The only one they'll ever have. Why wouldn't they want to raise him?" Trace seemed to be enjoying arguing his side of things.

"No, I think we need to look deeper. We need to see if the Chiltons had a solid reason for wanting their daughter, and now their grandson, back. Something more substantial than love or hurt pride. From what I've heard of those two, it probably comes down to money."

"What money? You said Abe was poor and the Chiltons are rich."

Cam dragged his hat off his head and slapped his thigh with it as he thought it all through. "Maybe there's . . ." Cam stopped and thought for a few more seconds. "Could there have been money left for the boy? Maybe by a grandmother or another family member?"

"You're just guessing now."

"I am, but knowing the Chiltons, there has to be gain for them. It's got nothing to do with loving a little boy." Cam slapped his leg with the hat again. "I know some honest folks back in Philadelphia. I'm going to send some wires. Find out if Delia had a claim on anything. And after she died, Ronnie inherits that claim. That would be a good enough reason to send McCall, and maybe others."

"You've conjured up a decent story, but it might not contain a bit of truth. If you've got it wrong, maybe your friends back east will know something that'll explain what's going on. Let's get these men to town." Trace started moving. "Once you've got your wires sent, we'll do some tracking. We'll see who we find at the end of the trail these varmints left."

"I'm interested to see who we find at the end of the trail."
John came out with their horses.

Penny was still fuming about the fat clothes. They were
warmer and harder to maneuver in than her regular split
skirt, but she could shed them in just a few minutes, and in
the meantime, John fought down a smile, not wanting to set
off any yelling or punching.

He couldn't figure out how to boost her up on the horse
dressed like she was, and he didn't want her to remove her
disguise just yet. She was too pretty and too noticeable. Without the big, baggy dress, she might be identified as Penelope
Call from the restaurant on their first evening in town, only
two days ago.

Penny tried to hurry, but the waddle slowed her some. Still,
she pressed on, and John could see that the time she'd spent
moving around with soldiers had trained her well.

"Shouldn't we take what we know to the law instead of
just riding out after Payne?"

"As a rule, I'd talk to the sheriff." John stayed with her, leading both horses. "But I got such a strong impression of fear when Payne was mentioned yesterday. It gave me a notion that those folks wouldn't expect the law to be on their side in any trouble they had with Luther Payne. And that makes me hesitate to go to the sheriff."

John looked over at her. She met his gaze, and they walked a few paces in silence. When they reached the edge of the main part of town, they left their mounts behind. There weren't any riders up on these slopes, so their horses would draw notice. They staked out the horses to graze and headed up to the hut to fetch their stuff.

"I'd prefer to turn this over to the law. I don't want to set myself up as a vigilante. Let's just find where Payne lives, and once we know that, I can see how a lawman in Ringo acts. Maybe Payne's influence isn't quite so strong away from the mines." John frowned as he considered with some doubt whether Payne would leave much to chance.

Inside the hut, Penny shed her oversized dress and the padding, then they made short work of packing and were back to the horses in no time flat.

Then they hit the trail for Ringo. John had a few ideas about how to ferret out the information about where a mansion might be located on that big old lake. He had a feeling it wasn't going to be hard to find. How many mansions could there be?

"Florence and Edmond Chilton?" Penny staggered back, and if the wall hadn't been there, she might've sunk to the floor. "They're registered here?"

Mr. Bolling's eyes gleamed with bright pleasure. "Sure enough. And they headed out of town for Luther Payne's house early yesterday and haven't come back."

Bolling pointed to a stack of luggage. "They left their belongings behind, too. Maybe Payne took 'em in, but why wouldn't he have sent his men back to get these satchels? Those fussy city folks'd be wanting a change of clothes."

Penny glanced at John, who glanced at her and then looked right back at Bolling. "I can tell there's more, Mr. Bolling. By your tone and the way you're fighting a smile, you know a lot more about this."

Bolling chuckled, and for a peaceable-looking man, there was a mean ring to it. "Those Chiltons came in here with their noses in the air, insulting me and my place and this town and the whole western part of the United States. I took 'em to the worst room I had. The one where I store some of my supplies, a room where I fight the rats to keep them away from the food."

"You figured if they wanted to believe this was a bad place to stay, you'd make it as bad as you could." Penny grinned. "The Chiltons treated me and mine like we were the dirt under their feet. I'd've made them sleep with the rats, too."

"I know them, too. And they treat me the same." John shook his head. Penny realized in their search for Payne, they hadn't spent much time thinking about the Chiltons and John's mission out here.

"What made them want to go out to Payne's house?" John asked. "Had they heard of him? Were they on their way to his home?"

"Nope, they were just so snooty, and Payne's mansion, well, I mentioned it just to goad them, to let them know there were plenty of fine rich folks about. When they heard the word *mansion*, the woman's eyes lit up. It was like she hoped that finally she'd find someone decent enough for her to talk to."

Bolling looked down at the open register book with the Chiltons' name clearly signed. "Payne is a man who likes his privacy. He guards that castle of his like he's the king of that whole lake, and I'm surprised he didn't build a moat around it. What he did do was put up the biggest, toughest fence I've ever seen. Solid rock, more than ten feet high. It took men years of hard work, all during the short good weather seasons, to get that fence up to suit Payne. They built the house first, using a road that comes in from Carson City. Then when the fence was up, they tore the road up and put boulders close up to narrow the road and downed trees, everything Payne could think of to make it real hard for folks to get in. It's barely passable by a man on horseback."

"He can't even get in with a wagon? How does he get supplies?"

"A pack string mostly, but he built his house on a deep water shore, so he can get a fair-sized boat in if he needs something bigger than a horse can handle. That fence of his even reaches out into the lake. And he hires men to patrol his grounds and watch the trails with spyglasses, or at least that's the rumor. I've never gone out there, except once to see the fence, just so I could see if the gossip was true."

"And it is?" Penny asked.

"Yep, and he's got these men, hard men, always on hand. They come into Ringo now and again to sit in the saloon and such, but they aren't drinkers and they never come together. Folks are mighty careful in what they say about Payne when those three are in town. For that matter, folks're cautious about Payne all the time. Men who get on his bad side tend to disappear."

Penny thought of Payne's dead partner, Logan. And Pratt, who lived away from his mine.

"Three of them?" John's voice was calm, but Penny knew he'd heard that just as clearly as she had.

"Yep, a bad bunch. Word is, Payne wouldn't trust them if he didn't have to. He has a couple of local women come out to clean and cook for him. Daily help, they don't live out there. When they came home the day the Chiltons headed up, it was with instructions to not come back until they was sent for. It's just the Chiltons, Payne, and his three guards out there now."

"Is there any gossip about Payne?" John asked.

"No one gossips about him. In fact, no one around has a word to say against Luth Payne. That whole outfit has a fearful hold on the town."

"What about the sheriff? Is he afraid, too?" John watched Bolling's face carefully.

"We don't have no law in Ringo. There was talk of hiring a sheriff, but Payne put a stop to it." Then Bolling quit talking beyond giving them directions, though he admitted he hadn't told the Chiltons about the fence.

"I expected them back within an hour, once they saw the way that fortress is set up, but they never came. Payne either took them in or killed them. I can't work up to going out to hunt for them. Figure I won't find nuthin' but trouble. I reckon that makes me a yellowbelly. Ain't proud of it."

John had more questions, but Bolling was done. He fidgeted like he was scared he'd said too much already.

Eyes and ears. Payne must have spies in Ringo, just like in Virginia City.

"We won't tell anyone anything we've learned from you," John said.

Bolling calmed a bit, but he told them no more, and considering how secretive Payne was, maybe Mr. Bolling didn't know any more.

John nodded. "I think we'll go see if we can find out what became of the Chiltons, and then have a talk with Luther Payne."

Bolling nodded. "If you manage that talk, you'll be the first. He's a man of business and goes into Virginia City, but he ain't a man to sit down to coffee and tell you about himself."

Penny remembered the paint on the building that read *Bolling's Boardinghouse*. It was long faded, to the point of being hard to read. That meant Bolling had been here awhile.

"Have you owned this boardinghouse long?"

Bolling nodded. "Came out heading for the California gold fields in '50. I got stuck on this side of the mountains when winter caught us. I found a little color and settled on a claim near Virginia City. I never had a real taste for the madness, so I didn't go on to California. I worked a claim here for a few years. Made enough to feed myself, then saw the men charging me for supplies getting rich while I scrimped. When the big rush came here, I opened a boardinghouse right by the Comstock Lode, and was gettin' fat in the pocketbook for a while. Then one day, some big strike came in and the town threw a party the likes of which I've never seen. Came close to gettin' myself killed trying to fight a pack of drunks busting up my place. Decided I liked life more than being rich. By then Lake Tahoe was drawing in tourists from San Francisco, so I came here. A much calmer crowd, tourists."

Bolling looked around his modest boardinghouse with pride. "Ringo barely existed at the time, but it's about as close as you can get to the lake on a good trail. I tucked away the money I had from Virginia City and used the least possible amount to open this place. No sense flashing money, it only draws thieves. I've been here for years. Married a fine woman and had a few youngsters. Makin' a living, but not gettin' rich. Not gettin' killed neither, so I'm a contented man."

"And has Payne been around all this time?" Penny thought of Raddo and their theory that Raddo and Payne were old partners. Raddo must've had some hold on Payne.

"Yep, a miner like the rest of us at first. But he kept making all the right deals." Bolling glanced around him. They were completely alone. He whispered, "You swear you won't repeat anything I tell you? Not to anyone?"

John said, "You have my word."

"Mine too." Penny nodded.

"Well, Payne's got some partner in his mines, but he runs it. No one dares challenge him about anything. He started building his fortress ten years back. Now he's only rarely seen out and about, but he'll pay to hear of those who speak against him. Pay well. I'm only talking because I reckon I'm a coward, and that's a shameful thing. I've got a young wife and four sons born too late in life for an old codger like me. If I've misplaced my trust in you, well, I've lived a long time, but what will become of them? I suppose someone else'd have the sense to marry her and take care of her, and she's a fierce woman, she'd fight for her family."

As he shook his head, his shoulders slumped, almost as if

232

he expected the worst, and he said, "I'd rather have the conscience of an honest man than live to a doddering old age."

"You really think you'll die if word gets out you've spoken to us?"

"Yep, and I'm afraid you young folks are headed for a bad end. So, it's a warning. You might want to let this go and leave that old surly wolf be. Word to the wise." Then Bolling turned and walked away, leaving them in the small entrance of his boardinghouse.

"That's a brave man." Penny looked toward the door he'd taken into the back of the building. "He knows when it's just common sense to be afraid."

"I'd probably take his advice and leave Payne alone. Grab you and drag you back east with me. But it's too late. He's coming after us, and there's a good chance he'll take on your brother next, then Trace and his outfit. We can stop Luther Payne, or we can be stopped, but I don't think we can just leave it be. And considering the way he kidnapped us, it was already too late before we started."

"Let's go take a look at this mighty fortress Payne has built for himself. I wonder if we should tackle him ourselves or go get my brother?"

"Let's go by ourselves first. That gives us a back-up plan . . . if we live to use it."

26

"I can't believe you got a wire back already." Trace scratched his head while Cam read the longest telegraph he'd ever gotten.

"It wasn't that fast. I thought Sheriff Walters would keep asking questions all day."

"He might've if Mayme Belle hadn't come and dragged him off for dinner." Trace had a look of wonder on his face.

Cam was pretty sure it didn't have to do with the formidable Mayme Belle.

"I got stranded out here after my pa was killed in a wagon train massacre, years ago. You know that."

"Sure I do. What'd you say it was, two or three years before you saw another human being?"

"Longer than that. I barely survived my first winter. I've been to town since then, mainly here in Dismal, but last summer I drove cattle over the Sierra Nevadas and then did some wandering. Saw the ocean, saw a big city. Still, I've lived a pretty quiet life. I can hardly imagine that you sent a

telegram all the way across the country to Philadelphia and
got an answer back the same day. It seems next thing to a
miracle. It's for certain a modern-day wonder."

"Lots of telegraphs went up during the war, but it is a
marvel, I reckon," Cam said. "But we got lucky, too. No
lines were down. And the man must live or work close to the
telegraph office. And he had things to say about the Chiltons
without having to do much asking around."

"They've vanished, then?" Trace read the telegram again.
"And they've left creditors behind howling about unpaid
bills."

"The interesting part is the money left to Delia, though."
Cam tugged the telegram away from Trace to read it again.
"And tied up tight enough that the Chiltons couldn't get
their hands on it. Delia even owned the house they lived in
And the Chiltons managed to find a gullible banker who
loaned them money against the house. But that's even done
now. The house is mortgaged up to the hilt so they're out
of ways to get money."

"Not including getting a job," Trace said dryly.

Cam shrugged. "They haven't tried that yet, I reckon.
Anyway, that's why they wanted Delia back so badly, and
why they've been after Ronnie. To get their hands on a fortune left by Florence's mother. A wise woman who knew her
daughter well and went to great lengths to protect the money
from Florence. I'll bet there's a whole lot more to this, but
it comes down to Ronnie being a rich little boy. No wonder
the Chiltons moved so fast and spent so much to send John
out here. They were probably hoping he'd get here and back
with the boy before all their bills came due."

Cam fell silent and met Trace's eyes.

Finally, Trace asked, "Are we going to find the Chiltons when we backtrail the men who attacked us this morning?"

"I hope so." Cam crushed the telegram in one gloved hand. "I've got a few things I'd like to say to them. Let's ride."

"Have you ever seen anything like that?" John looked at Penny as they stood at the base of a massive wall right where it went into Lake Tahoe.

"It makes the walls built around the army forts look like a child's toy." Shaking her head, Penny glanced behind them.

John followed the direction she was looking and saw their horses, up at the top of this steep slope, standing contentedly. The horses were going to have a tough time getting down here. Maybe a really bold, mountain-bred mustang like Trace's black stallion could do it without breaking a sweat, but neither of them had such a horse.

"It had to take years." John heard the wonder in his own voice. He'd heard of the Great Wall of China and had to wonder how this compared. "Bolling said it was huge, but I never pictured this."

They'd gone down to the water's edge. Now they turned and climbed up, not all the way back to their horses, but following along the wall.

"He cut the trees back thirty feet, too." John couldn't imagine it. None of this had been visible from the trail above. The wall and the stretch that'd been cut back were tucked deep behind a thick stretch of forest.

"How did he pay for all of this work?" Penny asked.

"He's a wealthy man according to Bolling, and according to the folks back in Virginia City who dared to speak his name."

"You can just see the treetops." Penny pointed at where they started up, beyond the strip of cleared forest. "Cutting the trees back gives Payne a perfect field of fire. And no one can get high enough to see the house, which means no one can shoot from a distance."

"The house might be visible from a boat on the lake." John looked behind him.

"Something we don't have."

Which set John to thinking.

Penny interrupted the plotting going on in his head. "I'd say Luther Payne is a suspicious man."

"Or a man with a lot to hide," John suggested.

"Or one with dangerous enemies."

"If we stay up right against the base of this wall, no one can see us." John took a few steps along the wall that ran parallel to the shores of Lake Tahoe.

"What about our horses?"

John stopped and looked back. He frowned at Penny. "We won't be gone long, will we?"

Penny looked down the long stretch of wall, then looked up, overhead. "If he's got only three men, they have to take shifts so they can eat and sleep. And they can't watch in three directions at once. If there was a watchtower, it'd have to be high enough we should be able to see it, and I didn't."

John's eyes met Penny's. He said, "I'll go. Just calm as can be, I'll walk over to the horses and lead them back here. If someone sees me, I hope they shout out a warning before they open fire."

"Only if they don't recognize you."

"Yes, only then."

"I'd better go with you."

"Nope, no sense both of us being ducks in a shooting gallery."

"But if I'm with you, I can shoot back, or you can. It makes it so they can't just open fire on us with no risk."

"Good point," John said. "I'm starting to think you're about the smartest, toughest wife a man can have." He kissed her soundly and said, "Let's go get those horses."

They raced across the open stretch, and no one started raining down fire. Penny pulled her rifle out of the boot on her saddle. It took some work to lead the horses through the tight forest that sided the trail, but they made it to the open space and ran again.

John slammed his back against the wall, and the horses almost ran him over.

Penny said grimly, "Does it strike you that we had it a little too easy?"

"Cheer up, Mrs. McCall, I'm sure there's a chance to dodge bullets in our immediate future. Now watch this wall for a gate. There has to be a way in."

"There has to be a way in, but good grief, look at this thing." Cam pulled back on his reins until his horse backed out of sight of any watchtowers atop this thing.

Once he was no longer visible to someone on top of the massive stone barricade, he said, "There's gotta be something huge behind this wall."

"Yep," Trace said. "But they're short three lookouts."

"And with a short supply of guards, the wall blocks their

view of us as surely as it blocks our view of them. Unless I
miss my guess, we just turned three of the sentries over to
the sheriff in Dismal." Cam dismounted and walked back up
to study the wall. "This reminds me of a fort. They usually
had stockade walls with trees lashed tight together. This is
stone, but the idea is the same. A wall so strong and high no
one can get over it."

"There's a way," Trace said. "I'll stash the horses, and
we'll move closer on foot."

Cam slipped his rifle out of the scabbard on his saddle.
Trace vanished into the heavy woods with the horses. While
Cam waited for Trace, he checked his rifle and pistol to make
sure they were fully loaded. They were, he knew that already,
but a smart man got into the habit of checking his weapons.

Trace emerged from the dense forest. "Let's scout around.
Look for sentries, gates, handholds on the wall. These stones
aren't that smooth. We'll get in."

Cam and Trace set to work. Scouting, climbing, digging
even—though they had no shovel. But poking with sticks
convinced them the wall was sunk deep, so no shovel would
help.

Trace got about eight feet off the ground climbing before
he could go no farther.

Cam walked to the water's edge and tried to wade out,
hoping to get around the wall that extended out so far. But
the icy water got deep so quickly he knew the location of
the house . . . assuming there was a house behind this monstrosity of a wall . . . had been chosen to be impossible to
reach by the water. Maybe with a boat or swimming—but
Cam couldn't swim.

They walked for a stretch and finally found themselves

in front of a solid iron gate with no way to look through or climb up. Trace morosely sat down and leaned his back against it. "I wonder if he brings in supplies by boat? The water is deep enough."

"Nothing of any size could get through that gate." Cam studied the massive lock—for the tenth time. "A person or a rider could get through, but not a wagon."

"The men we trailed got in and out. How did they signal someone to open the gate?"

"We went through their pockets. There was no key." Cam's time in the military had trained him to be thorough, so he'd had both of them check the pockets to be sure nothing was missed.

Rising to his feet, Trace said, "You reckon they'd hide a key out here somewhere? We might be able to find it and unlock that door and walk right in."

"Or, you could let me pick the lock."

Trace and Cam whirled around, guns drawn, as John stepped out of the woods with his hands up.

Penny stepped out of the woods behind him. "We trailed the man who kidnapped us right to this house. And we found out something mighty interesting in Ringo."

Cam holstered his gun, bulled past John, and hugged Penny. "Are you all right?"

She froze.

Cam wondered if he'd ever hugged her like this before, so freely. He was just plain relieved to see her alive and well, so that was probably it. Though it was possible that marriage was making him soft.

Then she thawed and hugged him back hard. "It's good to see you, brother."

240

"You too, Penny. I had plenty of time to imagine you coming to harm. Glad to see you made it through, too, McCall." Cam took a moment to offer John his hand. "What's this interesting thing you found out?"

She patted him hard on the shoulder, then stepped away. "Florence and Edmond Chilton came through Ringo just a day ago, and they headed out to this mansion."

"It looks like the Chiltons got tired of waiting on you, McCall."

Trace snorted. "Or they had to run from the bill collectors and decided to run this direction."

"It's all connected—it's got to be." John started pacing.

"So there's a mansion behind this wall?" Trace asked. "It stands to reason there is, but we can't see anything behind it."

"That's what we were told in town by Mr. Bolling at the boardinghouse. And he said they built the house first, then the wall, so he saw it. They had decent trails in, too, but once the house was up, they filled in the trails and blocked them to make it hard for anything but a rider to pass through."

"Mighty strange behavior," Cam said. "Did you see the Chiltons in town?"

"Nope. Bolling had their baggage in the hallway. He said they haven't come back for it. They rode out to see the place. Bolling admits he was hassling them by sending them out, figured they wouldn't see a thing but this big wall. But they never came back. They've either gotten themselves taken prisoner or been invited in for a visit."

"Unless they're dead," John added.

"We've learned a lot more about the Chiltons since you two left," Cam said. "They ran off, a step ahead of creditors in Philadelphia. And we found out that Delia and now Ronnie have a sizable inheritance they'd never gotten word of. It's a sure thing that the Chiltons want Ronnie so they can get their hands on his money. Oh, and we took three men in to Sheriff Walters, then backtrailed them to this place. We're just here from Dismal. Are the three men we caught hired by the Chiltons?"

"Three men?" Penny's eyes went sharp.

"Yep, we reckoned these were the same three men who kidnapped you and the fourth man was behind this wall, but couldn't quite figure what the Chiltons have to do with it."

"The fourth man"—John walked while he talked—"is named Payne. Luther Payne."

"Luth?" Cam exchanged a quick look with Trace. "The same name that was tattooed on Raddo's arm?"

"Be mighty unlikely if there were two Luths in this business," John said. "Let's fall back from this wall and compare notes. The one that I found most interesting is that Payne is known to only have three men working for him. If you took them out of the picture, he might be in there with only the Chiltons."

"What else do you know about this mess?"

The four of them spent a few minutes learning the details each had found out. Trace led John and Penny's horses off to hide them with the others. Then John pulled a small leather packet out of his satchel and extracted a small metal tool. "Let's just see how tough Mr. Payne's locks really are. Sometimes the big ones are the easiest."

John spent an hour muttering and fiddling with the lock before he gave up.

CHAPTER

27

Penny was surprised how much she was hoping John could get that lock open. Not just because they needed to get in, but because she was proud of her husband's dubious skills and wanted Cam and Trace to be impressed.

She'd have to hope he impressed them later. Now wasn't going to work.

"You're welcome to try climbing," Trace said. "This is at least fifteen feet high. I gave up at about eight feet, and eight feet was my hands, reaching high overhead. I'd say whoever built it spent time checking for details like making sure it can't be scaled. Even if I stood on my horse's back I couldn't reach it, 'cuz I considered trying that."

"There has to be a key hidden out here somewhere." Cam began moving through the rock and scrub brush nearest the gate. "The men didn't have one with them, and they have to come and go."

John folded his arms across his chest and began pacing. "I'd say it's more likely there's a way to signal someone to come and unlock this thing. I doubt Luth would trust anyone with a key. So somewhere there's a cord to pull or a way to send a flare up, something like that, to alert those inside to come and let them in."

"Help me hunt." Cam kept searching.

"No, it's a waste of time," John said. "We've got to figure a way over it."

"I've already told you," Trace snapped. "We've tried."

Penny got food out of her pack and passed it around. She could tell by their shortening tempers that the men were hungry. She was hungry, too. But she had more sense than to snarl at someone because her belly was aching for a meal.

John chewed and paced as he studied the wall.

Cam ate while he turned over small rocks.

"We've been so busy trying to breach this fortress of Payne's, we forgot about the tattoo." Cam quoted the ink they'd read on Raddo. "'Luth if I die Revenge Watchbook Tahoe Jewel Overlook.'"

"The mansion could be Tahoe Jewel." John walked a little slower. "A big old mansion could be considered a jewel. That could be what he meant by Tahoe Jewel . . . but overlook. The house overlooks Lake Tahoe."

Penny said, "Take the words separately. 'Luth if I die Revenge' makes sense. He's saying he's got a way to get revenge against Luther Payne. 'Tahoe Jewel Overlook' could be this house."

"That leaves *watchbook*." Trace quit studying the wall and looked in the other directions. "What in the world can he mean by *watchbook*?"

"Is it some reference to a book Raddo kept and hid around here?" Penny mused. Talking more to herself than the others.

"Some evidence against Payne? It has to be that, but what evidence and where is it?"

All of them thought in silence for a full minute.

"Could be—" Penny hesitated, and they all looked at her. John even stood still. "Could be what?"

"It could be"—Penny looked sheepish—"a rock shaped like a book hidden in a spot that overlooks the mansion? Tahoe Jewel Overlook. Watchbook . . . maybe he found a flat, book-shaped rock and used it to cover a hole he dug for his evidence?"

They all stared at her until it was a little embarrassing. She began to regret speaking. Then they pivoted in three directions, ignoring the wall since there was nothing to see there.

"Why would he call a book a watchbook?" Trace shrugged. "No one else has any suggestions."

Penny pointed to the west, up behind the wall. "Whatever it is, if it overlooks Payne's Tahoe Jewel, figuring that means his house, it should be up the hill."

"And the ground has been cleared of trees all the way to the top of the hills. No real rocks or boulders in the open area." Cam crossed his arms. "Payne was mighty careful to give no one cover close enough to fire a gun."

"So maybe there's something in the tree line? Where it wouldn't be noticeable?" Penny started up the hill. "If Raddo wanted to hide blackmail material on Luther he might like the idea of his secret looking down on Payne's fortress."

"He might indeed," John said and started up.

Cam and Trace came after them. Penny had to hustle to stay ahead. She almost said words like "I could be wrong" or "I'm only guessing." But what did it matter? They'd either

245

find a stone that made them think of a book, or they wouldn't. And right now, no one else had any better ideas.

And while they searched, maybe they'd find a catapult or some such device to get them over this blasted wall.

----❦----

"Mr. Payne, has our baggage arrived yet?" Florence's irritated voice worked like a cheese grater on Luth's ears.

It occurred to him briefly that the selfish woman had morals similar to his own.

With one big difference. Florence was lazy. Luth might've cheated and murdered his way to the top, but at least he was ambitious.

The thought sent a chill of icy pleasure through his soul—where he should've been warm. Well, he figured himself bound for the devil, so he'd better enjoy the cold now. When he met the devil, he'd strike a bargain, and Old Scratch would make room for him to rule in hell.

"My men had things to see to this morning, Mrs. Chilton." The woman considered herself his better. Maybe she thought he was more servant than host.

Let her enjoy that for as long as she could.

"I'll send them for your things as soon as they come back."

"Edmond and I would be glad to ride into town to get them. You'd have to lend us horses, of course, and let us out of that massive gate. Goodness, the West must be dangerous. Did you build that wall fearing Indian attacks?"

"I prefer privacy, Mrs. Chilton. And I was sure once I built this house people would have a hard time not stopping in to visit. They might figure I'd welcome company. I don't."

Florence sniffed. "People can be so presumptuous."

Luther almost ground his teeth to dust to stop himself from snarling that she hadn't been invited. But he wanted that kid because he wanted all those who protected and championed the little boy, so he'd keep Florence around. For now.

He never let anyone inside his fortress walls if he didn't want them.

The woman had missed that sly insult.

He added stupid to the list of faults this woman possessed. Irritating, stupid, and rude. Not to mention greedy and ruthless—a willingness to kidnap a child couldn't be anything but ruthless. That meant he and Florence had a lot in common.

It was enough to make a man change his ways.

CHAPTER

28

"Does this look like a book to you?" Trace stood looking down doubtfully at a rock.

John thought it looked like a one-hundred-pound potato. A bigger problem than that was, it looked like pretty much every other rock they'd seen during their search.

Which meant Trace was just plain grasping at straws . . . or John was getting hungry and things were starting to look like food.

John rolled his eyes, but he did it before he drew Trace's attention. "Not really."

Trace looked back at his discovery.

Penny came up beside John.

Trace shrugged one shoulder.

John looked at the huge potato. "I've got no idea where a man like Raddo would get his idea about what a watchbook looks like. I mean, what is that really, anyway? Why would he pick that word to ink into his skin as a clue?"

Cam came up to the rock and arched one eyebrow. Without commenting on its bookish shape, or the lack of such, he said, "A *watchbook* isn't really a military term, but we posted a watch and we kept a book we called a duty roster. Could Raddo have something like that in mind?"

"I'll look around this wrinkled, rounded-off rock, see if anything's buried under it."

John exchanged a look with Penny. "We haven't found anything better, so why not?"

Trace turned to his rock, looking glum. "Or maybe I'll just mark it and keep looking. If we don't find something better I'll come back."

Penny found herself muttering, "Watchbook, watchbook. It has to mean something. But maybe it doesn't. My idea about something being buried up here was nothing but a guess."

Then she shoved irritably at a scrub pine that scratched at her leg and saw a pointy rock. It gave her a whole new idea.

"We could barely read that faded tattoo. What if it didn't say *watchbook*? What if it said *witchrock*?"

John, Cam, and Trace all turned to look at her, saw what she was pointing at, and moved closer.

"A rock shaped like a witch's hat," John said. "That's something that makes sense. Especially when you look at this pointy-topped stone right here."

The witchrock was a real different shape than the rest of the rocks. It was rounded on the bottom and turned narrow as it went up about two feet tall to the point of its hat. They were back in the woods about ten feet past the tree line, and looking at the rock, Penny said, "You can tell this is new growth close around it. Raddo found this and used it as a marker. I'll bet we find something we can use to have Payne arrested under this rock."

John slung an arm around Penny's shoulders and gave her a loud, smacking kiss on the cheek. "You're gonna make a good detective. I need to get you to a town where there's a Pinkerton office. We can work as a team."

She kept her face straight. She didn't want him to even suspect how interesting she found that idea.

"I wish I'd brought a shovel," Cam muttered.

John said, "I've got one."

Penny chuckled. "Of course you do."

"I'll get it." Trace headed for where he'd stashed the horses.

"I'd better go with him. He'll have to dig through everything to find it." John headed out after Trace.

For a second there was silence, then Penny turned to Cam and hugged him again. It was Cam's turn to be startled, but she noticed he got over it quickly and hugged her back.

Then he stepped back a pace, looking serious. "What are you going to do about being married, Penny? You know you've always got a home with me."

"John and I decided we'd give ourselves time to get to know each other. We wouldn't run off from each other, but neither are we carrying on as if we're married. It's been interesting watching a Pinkerton work. But I'm not sure if it's a sinful life. I feel like it is, but John with his sneaking and lying is trying to solve crimes. I've decided he's a good man, but should he be doing such underhanded things for a good cause?"

Penny looked at Cam, hoping he had the answers.

Cam stood silently, but Penny was used to her brother thinking things through carefully before he spoke.

Then he shook his head. "Is he breaking commandments?"

"He sneaked into a business after hours, but he didn't steal anything. Well, he took a record book, but the owner of the store was dead. We found his body. And he lies. We went by false names and told a pack of lies to find out where Luther lives. But the commandment is to not bear false witness against thy neighbor. That probably has to do with a court, lying to get a neighbor in trouble. We—we—" Penny paused, then threw her arms wide. "Do you hear me? Trying to justify what he does?"

"You're doing a fair job of justifying it. Do the police tell lies to solve cases? Do they tell lies to trick suspects into confessing?"

"I don't know. The only sheriffs I've ever dealt with drew a gun and marched people off to jail. I don't know much about solving a tricky crime. Maybe that's why there even is a Pinkerton Detective Agency." Penny grinned. "Honest, Cam, it's kind of exciting. We sneaked around. Hid from a deputy. We pretended to be young and wealthy, then—because John carries disguises in his bags—he dressed us up so he was an old man with crippled knees and I was his fat shrew of a wife."

"I'd kind of like to see you being a fat, old woman. I can picture you acting like a shrew, though."

She punched him in the arm.

"Hey." Cam looked down at where the blow had landed. "You pulled your punch. Marriage must agree with you."

She made another fist, but Cam jumped back, and they both laughed.

Then Cam took her into his arms again.

"You've never been a hugger, Cam. Marriage must agree with you, too."

"Not sure it's got anything to do with being married, but I suppose it might. Mostly, I've just been real worried about you. Kicking myself for letting you go haring off with a near stranger."

With a little jerk of one shoulder, she said, "A stranger I'm married to."

"That didn't make me worry one bit less. I figured you could look out for yourself. Leastways, I sure hoped and prayed you could."

"So, what was the hug for?" Penny asked.

"I'm just mighty happy to see you alive and well. You're looking pretty happy, too. I reckon you and McCall can figure out a way to get along. I'd sure like to see you stay around here. I've been away from family too much in my life, and I've enjoyed having you close by."

"I'd like to stay close, too. And John is going to have to be worth it for me to give up on you and the little ones. I'm uncommon fond of them. And I was there with Maddie Sue a lot when she was real little. I can tell you stories about those years that you've never heard."

"I'd love to hear every word you've got to say."

The snap of a twig told them someone was coming. Cam's hand went to his gun. Penny reached into the bag she always carried.

"He really had a shovel." Trace emerged from deeper in the woods. A man wise to the ways of the frontier, he warned them of his approach with the twig and by calling out.

John followed him out from behind a tight clump of trees, carrying a small shovel. He went straight to the rock and started digging. Then he stopped and looked up at all three of them.

"I just figured out how to get inside that wall, too." He went back to digging with such energy that they didn't have time to fire questions at him.

Penny was just thinking he was a handy guy to have as a husband, when his small shovel hit something with a sharp clank. Metal striking metal. He'd found buried treasure.

———✦———

John dropped to his knees and pushed dirt aside, uncovering more of a chest with every sweep of his hands.

The gray steel box was a foot wide, eight inches deep, with a lid that arched on top like a small trunk. It was heavy for its size, and John had a fight on his hands to get it out of the ground.

"This isn't some tin box, either. It's an iron chest." John dragged it free of the ground and plunked it right in front of the stone that stood guard over it. "A sturdy container that'd make a pirate proud."

He fiddled with the latch. The lid was rusty, but it flipped open, hinges screeching. "Not locked."

Cam dropped to his knees on John's right. "Let's see what you've got."

"I'm betting it's not gold and jewels." Trace went to the other side of the witchrock. "Not much use for them out here anyway. Deb sure would look silly wearing diamonds to cook biscuits."

John looked straight at the pointy stone. "Good grief, it looks more like a witch every second."

Penny crouched beside John and reached into the open chest without pausing to savor the moment, which John thought wasn't very fun of her. She pulled out something wrapped in oilcloth and tied with string like a parcel headed for the mail.

Cam got involved. He produced a razor-sharp knife so fast John almost flinched. He was dealing with some tough men—and woman—out here in the West.

Not wanting to be left out of his own discovery . . . not counting that Penny had figured out where to dig . . . but honestly it was his shovel . . . John unwrapped another packet wrapped in oilcloth to find a leather pouch.

"Gotta give him credit for trying to protect it," Penny said dryly.

John flipped open a leather flap and reached inside to pull out papers. And another smaller leather pouch.

Trace must've figured he should get to help. He moved to kneel shoulder to shoulder with Penny and lifted a piece of paper off the top and unfolded it and read, "'Wanted: Dead or Alive.'"

It was a wanted poster for murder. And a picture.

Penny gasped. "I remember him from the night at the restaurant."

"That's the man I figured to be Luther Payne. He was at the restaurant wearing Hessian boots, and he's the one we saw later on the street, when we hid in that doorway."

"On his way back from killing the shopkeeper, calm as you please." Penny sounded sick. "Remember he laughed? He saw us there kissing and laughed."

Cam swatted John on the back of the head.

John scowled. "What? She's my wife. And kissing her probably saved both our lives."

"This is from back east. Ohio. And the poster calls him Lewis Posner."

Trace lifted the wanted poster away and another one was revealed. This one with a picture of Raddo. Also wanted for murder. His name was really Randy Posner.

They all exchanged looks. Cam asked, "They're brothers?"

John looked at Penny. "It's possible. I only saw Raddo that one time for a second, then he was dead. And I saw Payne those two times, and not close, but I'd say they're both the same size. Both have dark hair. Hard to judge a family resemblance when one man is draped over a saddle."

Trace moved to the next in the sheaf of papers. This one was a picture. A stiffly posed family portrait. A father and mother and four children. The two oldest were boys, nearly full grown. In front of them were a little girl and another boy.

Pointing at the younger of the two mostly grown boys, Cam said, "That's Raddo."

"The oldest kid is Luther," John said. "And this is a nicely staged picture. It's mighty worn from being carried around, but it has to be a family picture, and those folks are Mr. and Mrs. Posner. I wonder if the other youngsters turned to a life of crime, too?"

"Keep hunting. What's in that leather pouch?" Trace sounded impatient.

John pulled out several sheets of paper covered with writing. He began reading out loud. It was a list of the crimes the brothers had committed: where they'd stolen money and when they'd killed men. Raddo listed men who'd ridden with them back east and told of them heading west, running from the law. They'd found new hunting grounds for their robbery and murder.

"Look at this," Penny said, reading over John's shoulder. "Raddo says the wagon train massacres were all Luther's ideas. And he said they did a few back east, too, but it was harder, the wagon trains were too big. Luther thought it'd be easier pickings once they got farther west. The men were tired, and their guard was down. Then the gang quit the wagon train massacres and turned to robbing miners caught out alone. Finally, they both turned their hands to mining."

"What's this talk of a guardian?" John asked. "Raddo sounds like he's getting a little bit touched in the head. He talks of ghosts haunting the trail. Superstitious nonsense."

Trace looked across Penny and John to meet Cam's eyes.

"Oh, tell him." Penny nudged Trace.

Trace tipped his head sheepishly. "I'm who he's talking about. I'm the ghost who haunted that trail. They called me The Guardian. The first couple years out here, after these coyotes killed my pa, I was madder'n a bear with its tail on fire. I stood sentry over that trail. I thinned out the outlaws some, but mostly I just scared them away."

John stared at Trace, then read the letter again, then stared at Trace some more. "Raddo acts like he's scared of you. Like he thinks you're the ghost of someone he killed and you were out to get him."

"I never showed myself. I moved quiet . . . except when my gun started blasting. I reckon I drove Raddo and Luther into another line of work. But I sure didn't change the kind of men they were. I made the trail safer, but I didn't solve anything. He's telling here about robbing miners. Then stealing whole mines."

"Yep, Raddo has a list here of Luther's victims. The last killing is dated ten years ago. I'm guessing that's how long ago he buried the box."

"Mr. Bolling said Payne started building this fortress ten years ago." Penny sifted through the papers.

"And he's been holding this over Luther's head ever since." Cam looked up from the wanted poster he was holding. "Remember when we caught up to Raddo in that cave? He ran and left everything behind—and everything wasn't much. He was dressed in rags. He was wearing those skis, no sign of a horse. He had a bullet in him, too."

Trace handed the wanted poster with Raddo's picture on it to Penny. "Then a few weeks go by, and here he comes at us again. Only he's got gold in his saddlebags. He's all healed up and wearing fine clothes, riding a fine horse. He went here, to Luther."

"And Raddo blackmailed Luther into helping him."

John tapped on a few lines at the bottom of the page he was reading. "He says Luther was fierce about not leaving any witnesses." John handed off all the papers and stood.

"Well," Trace said, "we know that Raddo wanted to silence witnesses."

Penny expected John to start pacing, and he didn't disappoint.

Cam said, "What we need to do is get the army in here with a cannon and blast our way through that wall."

"Arresting a killer isn't a problem you take to the army, Cam." Trace studied the papers some more.

"Then we need the sheriff and a posse." Cam glared at that huge fortress wall. "And an army with a cannon."

"I've met two sheriffs around here. The one in Dismal I wouldn't trust to water my horse." Trace shook his head. "The one in Carson City is a good man, but he doesn't look for trouble outside of town."

"We avoided the law in Virginia City," Penny said. "We didn't trust the lawmen. They might be fine, but Luther's gotten away with his crimes right under their noses for years. They're either poor at their job, afraid, or they've been bought and paid for by Payne."

"Add to that," Cam said, "John was wanted for kidnapping and murder."

John kept walking back and forth. "For all those reasons we weren't inspired to take our troubles to the law."

John happened to walk past Cam at that moment, and he slugged him in the shoulder.

"Sorry about that." Cam didn't hit back, which meant he knew he deserved one good punch for reporting John as a kidnapper. "So, it's left to us to do what I think needs an army." He rubbed his shoulder and added, "You said you had a plan?"

John stopped and turned to face the wall, just visible through the trees. "My plan is to go for a swim."

Penny threw herself in front of John and spread her arms wide like she was heading off a stubborn bull.

"You're not swimming around that wall. You have no idea what you'll face when you get inside. Luther could be standing there waiting for you with a rifle. You can't take a gun with you because it won't survive getting wet. No, absolutely not."

John looked over his shoulder at Trace and Cam. "I need rope. At least thirty feet of it. I have some but not that much. Did you carry some on your saddles?"

"Yep, we have more than enough." Trace didn't go for the rope yet. He was busy shifting his eyes between Penny and John.

"That wall is fifteen feet tall, I'd estimate. I'll swim around the wall with the rope, toss it over to you, and you'll come over. I'll be fast. I won't take any chances I don't need to, and I'm a good swimmer so I can—"

"This isn't about being able to swim," Penny shouted. Then she dropped her voice, but the anger was loud and clear. "This is about a multiple murderer waiting for you when you surface. We'll find another way in. We can . . . can . . . We can build a ladder." Penny gave him a firm nod of satisfaction. "Have you got an ax in your pack?"

"Remember me telling you about the Anaconda Plan?"

"Stop talking and get the ax. Cam can ride home and get one if we finally found something you don't carry with you."

"I've heard of the Anaconda Plan," Cam said.

"What's an anaconda?" Trace asked.

"It's a big snake. Some say an anaconda can get twenty feet long and weigh one or two hundred pounds, and they can drop out of trees and crush you in their coils. I've even heard they can swallow a man whole."

Trace looked overhead. "I've been out here a long time. I don't think we have any of those. In fact—"

"The Anaconda Plan," John interrupted firmly, "was a tactic they used in the navy during the war to cut off ports to end trade and shipping. They created a long blockade and wrapped it around the East Coast, Florida, and up the Mississippi River. I was in the navy, and I was involved in it. We meant to bring the South to its knees without a bloody, vicious war with Americans on both sides killing each other."

His expression grim, Cam said, "They failed at that."

John nodded.

"Stop trying to change the subject," Penny interjected. "You're not swimming around that fence alone, unarmed, with nothing but a rope you hope to have a chance to toss over the wall."

"I was a spy for the navy. I didn't just sit on a boat. It was common for us to launch small boats, dock offshore, and swim to land. As part of the Anaconda Plan, I'd spy on the officers while they concocted battle plans. I'd locate troops, count their numbers, and see how well-armed and supplied they were."

"Decent work for a man who's a trained detective."

"I was perfect for it. I also on occasion blew up munitions, stole papers, spiked cannons, destroyed supplies. Oh, I caused all sorts of mischief."

"I'll bet you were good at that," Penny said dryly.

John grinned. "So, I'm an excellent swimmer, and I'm used to making it to land quietly, cautiously. I won't just stand up on the beach and shake the water off me like a dog. I'll slip in, keep low, see where the house is, find a place I can toss this rope over the wall without being too noticeable, and get all of you and your guns in there. It sounds like there's a good chance the only people in there are Luther and the Chiltons. I'll be careful. I'll be all right. I'm good at this."

"Take someone with you at least. Cam, you were a soldier. Trace, you know the frontier like few men alive. One of you go with him." Penny snapped her fingers, and her eyes blazed. "I know. I'll wrap the gun in that oilcloth that Raddo had in the treasure chest. There's not a whole lot of it. But enough to keep at least one gun dry."

She looked from John to Cam to Trace. They stood, three in a row, right in front of her. The last two looking a little uncomfortable.

"What are you waiting for? One of you volunteer to go."

Cam opened his mouth, closed it, and shrugged. Trace exchanged a glance with Cam, studied the sky, then clasped his hands behind his back and looked at the toes of his boots.

"What is it?"

"I oughta go, but the thing is . . . is . . . well, I . . . I . . ."
Trace shrugged and said sheepishly, "I can't swim."

Cam heaved out a sigh of relief.

Penny glared at her brother. "Why are you happy to hear that?"

"Because I can't swim, either. I don't feel like I'm the only failure in the group now."

Penny looked at John, who arched one brow and fought a smile.

She said, "Fine, I'll go. I can swim like a fish."

The two nonswimmers looked stunned.

All amusement faded from John's expression. "You're not going."

"You can't do this alone, and neither of these two half-wits are capable."

"Hey," Cam growled.

"I'll take that little pepper gun with me, there's plenty of oilcloth to wrap that up. Okay, we're burning daylight. Cam and Trace, get down there close to the wall so you don't have far to go when the rope comes over. John—"

"Will you just hold on a minute? If I let you go, and I'm thinking maybe I will, then I'm sure enough not going to let you be in charge."

"I'll fetch the rope." Trace walked into the woods.

"There are a couple of things I wasn't going to bother to tell you about the swim, since I planned to go alone."

"What's that?"

"I don't want to be stuck with cold, wet clothes while I'm hunting Luther and the Chiltons."

"We don't always get what we want in life." Penny sounded like a philosopher now.

"I do, in this case."

"I don't see how."

"I do it by . . . ahem . . ." He glanced at Cam, then Penny. "I do it by swimming . . . in my drawers."

With a gasp of outrage, Penny said, "If you think I'm going to be in my undergarments in front of three men, I may have to use that little pistol on all of you."

"Trace and I could turn our backs away from the lake. John could face the water, then wade straight in without a single backward look."

"You picked a great time to start coming up with ideas," Penny snarled at her brother.

Trace came back with the rope.

Penny said, "I'm not swimming in my undergarments and neither are you. We'll just have to get wet."

"Cam can throw the rope back over the wall and have our clothes tied in a bundle. We can get our clothes back on first thing."

"First thing is way too late."

"It doesn't matter because you're not going."

Trace handed John the rope. John studied it a second—it looked like three lassos tied together to make enough length—then slung it over his head and under one arm. He said, "Turn your back, Penny. Even though you're my wife, we don't know each other all that well yet."

"I'm mighty pleased to hear that," Cam said with a smug smile.

"I'm going," she said. "And I'm keeping all my clothes on, and so are you, McCall. Being wet isn't as important as being modest. I'm sure we'll dry quick enough."

John glowered.

Penny said, "Wait a minute, why'd you say Cam can throw the rope over the wall. What about Trace?"

"He's not going to be here."

"I'm here right now." Trace crossed his arms and glared at John.

"Someone"—John's voice got deadly earnest—"needs to take that evidence and ride to town. We can't take a risk like we're getting ready to take and end up not proving Luther's crimes."

"You'll have a lot better chance of winning this fight with me."

"I know it, and I've tried to figure out a way to ride to Carson City, hand that proof to the sheriff, and get back here in time to capture Luther. For that matter, I'd like to wait until dark to try this stunt."

"It's the middle of the afternoon." Penny looked at the sun, still high in the sky. "Dark is hours away."

"I'm hoping we can just slip around that wall, underwater, find some cover, and get Cam inside without being noticed. But our chances of success drop with every moment that passes, because Luther is going to be on high alert when his men don't come back."

"He may start shooting at anything that moves," Penny said. She was afraid he was going to do that anyway.

"Trace, you know Sheriff Moore best. You're the man he's most likely to trust. Get this evidence to Carson City and tell the sheriff what's going on. Then bring back a posse. Ask the sheriff to bring the most uncompromising, honorable men in town. Men Luther can't buy or frighten. It won't be that easy to find men like that, but if we trust the sheriff, then you'll have to trust him to select good men. Things should be over here, and I'll have that gate open. You can come in and collect our prisoners."

Trace looked at the little chest. "It sits wrong to leave you here."

"I'd send Penny if I didn't hate the idea of her riding alone . . . and the sheriff doesn't know her . . . and neither of you can swim."

"I'm probably tougher and a better shot than you anyway, Trace," Penny teased.

Trace snorted. "Not likely."

"You know we need to get that evidence somewhere secure. If we all die, then Luther gets away with murder . . . including the murder of your pa, Trace. And he may go on to murder Deb, Gwen, and the children. In fact, I can promise you he will."

Struck by John's words—the obvious truth—Trace's muleheaded look faded.

"I think that's his plan, just like it was Raddo's plan. They're all witnesses."

Grimly unhappy about it, Trace said, "I'll go. Take as long as you dare to get around that wall, but I agree, we can't wait until full dark." Turning on his heel, Trace said over his shoulder, "I'll be back as soon as possible."

Then he was running for his horse—and Trace could run faster than anyone Penny had ever known.

CHAPTER 30

It'd be uncomfortable to have wet clothes, but Penny had her trousers at least. She wouldn't have a skirt floating in her face while they swam.

He got what he needed from his packs, shed his boots at the lakeshore, and waded in. John was tempted to ask Cam to bring dry clothes, but he didn't want to take the time to go dig a change out of his baggage.

"John, wait!" Penny said.

"What?" Everything about this investigation irritated him. Now here she was slowing him down.

"You said you needed to tell me a couple of things, but we got caught up arguing. What was the other thing?"

He'd forgotten to tell her because he hated the very thought of her being in danger.

He'd spent enough time with her to know he was better with her at his side. She was strong, fast, quick thinking. Yes, he had a better chance of success with her along.

But the thought of her being shot, maybe dying, was unbearable.

Instead of saying that, begging her to stay behind, stay safe. Instead of admitting he cared about her, he'd gone around making outrageous suggestions. Now if something happened to him, her last memory of him would be of what a thoughtless polecat he was. He should drag her into his arms and tell her he loved her. Tell her she was more important to him than any woman he'd ever known.

And he might've done it if her big brother hadn't been standing right there. He found it impossible to declare his love right in front of his brother-in-law.

Instead, his mouth clamped shut on words of love, and he answered her simple question, hating every syllable.

"The other thing I needed to warn you about was that Luther's bound to have set traps. No self-respecting Confederate city left their shores unprotected. They could get pretty creative about their defenses. Luther will have done something real mean and sneaky."

"That sounds like him."

"So be careful and stay behind me, and keep your eyes open for wires and jagged rocks and nets or ropes that might tangle you up. Who knows what he's come up with?"

"I'll stay behind you and keep a sharp eye out."

John looked past her and saw Cam watching with eyes like an eagle. It was no time for words of love, but he did slip in one kiss. It wasn't nearly as long as he wanted it to be. Then he headed into the water. He was up to his waist and already shivering when he heard Penny wade in.

He was over his head in the water and had started to swim, ready to dunk his head and move faster, when shocking sudden pain jagged through his left shoulder.

"Back! Stop, Penny!" he hissed, not shouting like he wanted to.

Sound carried far over the water—he'd learned that lesson well.

Watching, looking for what had stabbed him as he stroked backward, he could see nothing. To his very sharp eyes, there was nothing there.

He bumped into Penny.

"What is it, John, what happened?"

"Shhh, hold on. Give me a second." The water was clear, and he hadn't seen anything below the surface.

His left arm worked, but pain radiated from his shoulder down to his hand . . . and sideways into his chest.

Penny's alert, dark brown eyes went to his shoulder. John followed her glance. Blood oozed out of a puncture wound high on his left arm. Crimson coursed down his arm, mixing with water, staining the lake red. Penny's eyes rolled back in her head, and she sank.

John caught her. The cold water must've revived her, but her eyes went right back to the blood, and she whirled around.

"I'm sorry. I can't stand the sight of blood."

"What? A tough frontierswoman like you?"

"Shut up. It's a strange thing that's been a problem all my life. You'll have to bandage your own wound."

"I've got a better idea." John sounded aggravated.

He put his hand on top of her head and said, "Hold your breath."

He dunked her again.

She came up gasping and whirled to face him. "Why'd you do that?"

"I need some help here." He pressed his right hand hard

against his wound. "Now if I have to, I'll dunk you every few seconds to bring you back around, but between faints, put a bandage on this."

Without saying a word, Penny swallowed hard and nodded. "Talk to me. Tell me what happened."

"I don't know. I'm going to look."

Penny grabbed the coil of rope looped over his neck and under his arm to stop him. "Be careful. Whatever you hit, there's bound to be more of them."

"Good advice." John submerged his face and stared. It took him a while to see it. Then he saw another and another. He came up.

"There are spikes down there, stuck in the sand, I suppose, and they're painted a light gray color. Real close to the color of water. It makes them almost impossible to see."

"Do we go back?" Penny could have said that differently. She could have made it a demand. Instead she seemed to be wondering if this could be handled.

"No, we go on, but slow."

"I'll make a bandage." Penny produced a knife from somewhere and cut at the fabric from his sleeve while he talked.

"I'll have to feel my way along. These are really thin wooden stakes." He reached for the closest one and yanked. It came right up out of the water. "I'll use this to swipe back and forth and find each spear, yank them up, and clear a path for us. But I don't trust myself to see them in time, and I don't want to put my head under because I don't want to get poked in the eye."

"Okay. I'll stay right in your path." She got a long enough strip of cloth she could wrap around his arm, then up over his shoulder so it wouldn't slip off.

"You've always had trouble with blood?"

269

"Yep, when Cam got his leg caught in a bear trap last winter I completely abandoned him to Deb and Gwen's care."

"Cam got caught in a bear trap?" John winced.

"Yes, set by Raddo. I'm not proud of how I acted, but I can't seem to get over it. When it came to shooting trouble at the fort, they liked everyone to pitch in to help the wounded, but I never did."

"You saw that shopkeeper stabbed to death."

"I saw him for about a second, and you were busy enough examining the crime that you didn't notice I turned away to keep from upchucking or fainting."

"I was bleeding after we got kidnapped."

"I turned and ran and didn't really look at you again until after dark." She worked fast, and he was glad the cloth had covered the wound.

"I can shoot, skin, and butcher an elk without a speck of trouble." She shook her head as if disgusted with herself.

"Thanks, Penny." He fastened his cold hands over hers, noticing how delicate they were. Strong, callused, competent, but fine boned and feminine, and right now, shaking hard. He kissed her fingertips and turned around to advance. He heard muttering behind him.

"What's that?" He didn't look back. He was afraid he'd miss a spear.

"I said, try not to stab anything vital."

Inching along, he waved his spear back and forth, yanking out any new ones he found, and he found a lot, about every few feet.

"Look at that," he whispered. Penny came up beside him.

"What is that thing?" Penny leaned her face close to the water.

"I think it's a long-dead otter. The poor animal was probably playing and got impaled." Next, he saw a good-sized fish. Then a bald eagle. All dead. All trapped underwater and left to drown or die of their stab wounds, whichever killed them first.

"What if some tourist wanted to go swimming?" Penny said quietly. "What if someone boated up, thinking this clearing of Luther's would be a good place to come ashore? What if they jumped off their boat to take a swim?"

"Luther didn't worry one whit about people he might harm. They mean no more to him than these animals."

"And he had plans to bring the children here, at least Ronnie." Penny's voice was tight with rage. "He might've waded out into the water and found himself in deadly danger."

Looking at the bald eagle, John's stomach twisted as he imagined a human killed in such a way—a child—an innocent little boy. If Luther'd had his way, John and Penny would have been his victims. John pulled the next spear out of the ground and handed it to Penny.

"It wouldn't bother me overly," she said, gripping the spear so tightly her knuckles turned white, "to use this on Luther Payne."

With a nod of agreement, John moved on in the chilled water. He already knew the kind of man he was up against, but the cruelty of this trap was sickening. John wanted to take the time to cut out every one of these spikes. Get rid of them so they'd stop killing animals and endangering people. And he would, but for now he had to keep moving.

John hoped Luther entrusted his safety to his hired guns. Maybe he'd gotten soft, and learned to leave those defensive things to others. Maybe John could just walk straight into the mansion and pull his gun—or rather, Penny could pull her little derringer—and this would end.

He didn't believe it, but he could hope.

John got near the end of the wall, ready to round it and be on Luther's side of it. He cleared out the last of the spears, figuring they'd start up again once he rounded the wall, and signaled for Penny to swim up beside him.

"We're probably going to be visible from the house in the next few feet." He produced two reeds. He handed Penny one and said, "Watch this."

He put the reed in his mouth and sank under the water, breathing through the little hollow tube. When he came back up, Penny was under, the reed showing a few inches above the surface. Then she came back up.

Water streamed off her hair, which was in her customary twin braids. Her long dark lashes glinted with water. Her eyes flashed with trust . . . all aimed at him.

"The spikes seem to be gone, but I suspect we'll find more once we round the wall. This is taking forever, and the cold water is taking a toll, but we have to move cautiously."

As one, they turned to look at the sun. It had slipped behind the peaks of the Sierra Nevadas. The surface of Lake Tahoe became a pure mirror of the blue sky. It would be impossible to see anyone standing on shore from beneath the surface.

Thinking the word *shore* had John turn to where they'd just come from. He saw nothing on the outside of the wall. Then Cam stepped out from behind a tree. He'd obviously been watching them while keeping himself concealed. He waved, then vanished back into the forest.

"Let's go. No sense waiting any longer." John kissed her

again. "You're beautiful when you're soaked more than a wet hen."

She grinned. "Get going." Then she leaned close. "You are, too."

John shook his head once, then turned and swam forward—inched forward. The water was deep here. When he rounded the end of the wall, he sank beneath the lake. If he was above the surface, he'd be clearly visible now from the house. Using the reed to breathe, he swam on, swiping back and forth with the spear he'd kept to search for the next trap.

—⁂—

Penny stayed directly behind John. It took no thought, which unfortunately left her plenty of time to rage against Luther Payne.

She touched the little gun tucked inside her shirt to make sure it was still well wrapped and hopefully dry.

They rounded the wall that had tapered down to nothing about twenty yards out into the water. With her head submerged, the water was almost as clear as air. She marveled at breathing through the reed. How had he known to do this?

But of course, she knew. He'd learned it being a navy spy. Handy.

And if it wasn't so blasted life and death, it'd be interesting. It was beautiful down here. With the reed, she could stay underwater all day. Fish swam by. There were pretty shells gleaming with color on the sandy bottom many feet down. She'd come back and spend some time underwater in Lake Tahoe. The water was cold, but she didn't think it was dangerously cold. She hoped.

She stayed alert. A deep chill could addle the mind, make

someone sleepy when sleep was a terrible idea. So far, she felt nothing like that. She still had the spear John had given her, and she waved it out to the side, feeling around for the camouflaged spikes Luther had put in. She hadn't found any in her path, though she saw some off to the side. She couldn't reach them and stay behind John at the same time, so she followed him.

Ahead, she saw John jerk one of the spears out of the sand. He'd found more, which meant the water was getting shallow. Then her feet touched the ground, and after a few inches she realized her head was coming out of the water so she ducked down. She had to crouch to stay under the water. Moving faster now, John reached back and tugged her to her knees, then she watched him and saw him lay flat on his belly with his head tilted up to breathe.

John caught her wrist and this time tugged her up and forward. They were out of the water only inches from the wall. They rushed for a clump of cattails and ducked out of sight. Penny searched the grounds of the mansion for any sign of a witness to their invasion.

John said, "I'm going to get Cam in here right now. I don't see anyone coming, yelling, or shooting. So, let's get this done. Stay low. Get your gun unwrapped. Cover me."

Penny had the derringer out in no time flat. She looked at the house, and merciful heavens, what a house. She'd seen pictures of castles in England, and this reminded her of that. Payne must be stunningly rich. Stupid, too. How did he heat this thing?

John rushed the wall, whipping the coil of rope off his body. He tied it around a handy rock and tossed it up and over.

Cam would be watching for it.

Penny kept a sharp eye on the house. She couldn't believe the arrogance it would take to believe you deserved a home this size. A man alone, if their information was correct. If he planned to marry late in life and have ten children, this would still be a fool's house.

She thought of the very tidy little cabin being built on her homestead. It would have two bedrooms and be spacious and lovely.

She'd lived in an attic with one bedroom with Abe and Delia and the two children. It had been terribly crowded, but they'd loved each other and been polite and careful, and they'd made do.

This was two full stories with windows coming out of the steeply pitched roof. It had a central house, then two wings that angled back from the shoreline. It was made of the gray native stone that surrounded them. Set back about fifty feet from the lake and up a slope. Lake water could rise and lower, so building up high made sense. There weren't a whole lot of windows. That would be wise for protection against harshly cold winters. But why build here and then block off the view?

Penny suspected the lack of windows wasn't a decision between saving on firewood or getting a lovely view. It was about defense. Fewer windows made it harder for anyone outside to shoot someone inside.

Considering the massive wall, defense was probably at the root of every decision Luther made while building.

He was a man suspicious of everyone.

As well he should be.

He hurt so many people that she'd bet he had more enemies than there were trees in the Sierra Nevada Mountains.

A scratching sound from behind her drew her attention. Sparing a quick glance back, she saw Cam top the wall. He swung over and dropped, hand over hand, to the bottom of the rope, fast as a running squirrel.

He had Penny's pack over his shoulder. It bulged, and she knew it had guns for all of them. Including her trusty Army Colt. She liked her little pepperbox, but for stopping power, she much preferred her Colt.

Cam was at her side, the three of them crouched behind the succulent reeds and marsh grasses on the sandy soil, right against the wall. He'd brought their boots, and Penny pulled them on her chilled feet.

Wrenching open the pack, Penny grabbed her weapon, checked the load, double-checked that her derringer was dry, and said, "Ready?"

"I'll take the back of the house, see what entrances there are." Cam's cold eyes surveyed the monstrosity of a house.

"I'm going in that window low on the south side." John jabbed a finger at the closest window. "I'm betting that's an empty room. Oh, for heaven's sake, they're all empty. There aren't enough people in all of Nevada to put a person in every room in that house."

"After he's dead," Penny said with an anger colder than the lake water soaking her clothes, "maybe Mr. Bolling can knock some holes in these walls and use this for his next boardinghouse."

"Bolling strikes me as a reasonable man. He might see it as a good investment for the tourism business."

Penny brought them back to the goal at hand. "I guess that leaves me to go marching right in the front door."

"No," John snapped.

"You're coming with me." Cam spoke at the same instant.

"We'll do better split up. We can sneak up on them. And if they get one of us, the others have a chance to stage a rescue. And if I happen upon Florence Chilton, I'm going to take pleasure in having her arrested, and I might knock her in the head before I try and take her captive."

"Get in line," Cam said, sounding like the whole idea suited him perfectly.

"You know, Raddo killed Abe and Delia," John said softly. "He's the one who left Maddie Sue without guardians and little Ronnie without parents. Luther hasn't really done anything to the two of you. When you got Raddo, you got justice for the crimes against you. Trace is the one who should be here."

Penny gave John a disgusted look. "Then why'd you send him to the sheriff?"

"I already told you why. I just said that because I want you to go in calm, thinking sharp. Don't let anger get the best of you."

Penny nodded. "Good advice."

"We'll come in from two directions. Penny, you stick with me."

She obeyed him because he made sense, not because she liked taking orders. But refusing to obey for no good reason made her stupid, and she wasn't. She slid along behind John. Crouched low.

Cam led the way, and when they were close to the window, Cam said, "Give me a few minutes to get around back."

He went on ahead to find another way in.

John looked at Penny. "Are you ready?" His hands were fisted until his knuckles were white.

"Yes, and don't you dare give Luther even one chance to get the upper hand. If ever a man was completely ruthless it's Luther Payne."

"We agree, then." John looked all around, alert to any danger, then put his hands on her shoulders and pulled her close.

"This isn't the time or place for anything but focusing on taking Luther prisoner, or stopping him however we have to."

Penny knew John was saying they might come to a shootout, and they didn't dare hesitate. They didn't dare give Luther a chance.

"But, Penny, go in there knowing—that is—I want you to—" John didn't go on. And she knew what she wanted to hear . . . words of love . . . words of how he wanted them to be together forever. She didn't push him. She was afraid she'd hear that he wanted her to stay outside and take cover or run for help or some other half-wit thing like that.

"Let's go, John. We can talk later when we've got Luther and both of those awful Chiltons tied up and draped over a saddle. I'll enjoy that."

He shook his head just a little as if she was the one around here who was ridiculous. "Your brother's had enough time. Let's go."

John turned to the window, small and about shoulder height. It was locked. He pulled out his little metal tool and had it open in a few seconds. "Maybe we should have gone with Cam and made sure he could get in."

"He'll get in. He can't pick a lock, but he can put his boot through a door."

"I was kinda hoping to go in quiet." John hopped up, going headfirst into the window. Penny was anxious while he was out of her sight.

She scrambled after him. The window was higher on her, but before she could begin to struggle, John reached out and dragged her through.

She looked around as she righted herself. "What kind of stupid room is this?"

"Billiards. A piano. I think those tables are set up to play poker."

"He lives alone. Who does he play poker with?" she whispered. Luther was an idiot.

"I reckon he saw a fancy room like this somewhere."

"He's short a few dancing girls, or it'd make a nice saloon. All the red and velvet puts me in mind of that."

"Probably just what would appeal to him. He had a greedy urge to put one in his own home. Get moving. We can take a tour later."

The room was bigger than Penny's whole cabin would be. Carpeted floors, high ceilings, chairs and lamps. Red flowers on the wallpaper. Red velvet drapes. Gaudy.

John crossed the room, Penny on his heels. She said, "It's just starting to occur to me that we might have trouble finding Luther in this huge place. Can you imagine going into Cam's cabin and having trouble finding someone in there?"

"Shhh." John opened the door a crack and looked out. Then he swung it wider and looked in both directions. He caught her hand and pulled her out of the room. They were in a huge entry hall. A stairway was at Penny's right hand. It swept up with shining oak banisters, to an upstairs hallway lined with doors.

John didn't go up.

He crossed the huge entrance and looked into a room with double doors, wide open. A fancy room full of overstuffed couches and chairs. Penny saw another set of doors that must lead into the far wing of the house. John looked but didn't go in. Moving along the entry, he came to a second room, this one with its door closed. He leaned close, listening.

He looked at Penny and barely moved his lips. "Someone's in there."

A gunshot exploded in the back of the house.

Right where Cam should be. And it wasn't Cam's gun. Penny recognized a different weapon. She took a step toward Cam, and John grabbed her wrist, pulled her back, and pressed her against the wall, his body shielding hers. Footsteps pounded from behind the door.

Penny shoved at John. He met her eyes, then moved away. They both had their guns out and aimed.

Luther burst out of the room, and John grabbed his right wrist, the one holding a pistol, and twisted it with brutal strength. The gun in Luther's hand went clattering to the floor.

Then Luther came up slashing a knife. Without one second's hesitation, the man stabbed at John.

John went from still to a madman in the wink of an eye. His arm lashed out and blocked the descending knife. He kicked at Luther's knee. Punched him, left and right, then brought a fist up so hard into Luther's chin that the man went down backward into the room he'd come charging out of. Luther hit the floor. The knife skidded right to Penny's feet. Penny snatched it up. She wasn't sure how to use it in a fight, but she tucked it in her pack for safekeeping.

John charged in swinging his fists. Luther had the vicious fighting skills of a dockside ruffian. He rolled over on his back and jumped to land his foot square in John's gut. John dodged and grabbed Luther as he came in and the two went flying. John landed a fist that stunned Luther, who collapsed on the floor, taking John with him.

Penny had her gun aimed at the scuffle, but a hard arm wrapped around her neck from behind before she could swing her gun around. Her attacker roughly grabbed her arm and knocked her gun to the floor.

"Get off of him or she dies."

John was on his feet and had taken a step toward Penny when the pistol cocked and jammed into her temple.

"I mean it. I'll kill her and then you."

The utter panic and rage in her attacker's voice must've been convincing because John stopped.

"Edmond Chilton." John stood, staring, shaking his head, arms at his sides, those whip-fast fists relaxed. But Penny saw the cool light in John's eyes. "I didn't think you'd even carry a gun, let alone know how to use it. I figured you for the closest to innocent in this whole mess. Let her go, and we'll forget this. You can run, and I won't chase you."

Penny thought John sounded completely truthful, which just proved what an excellent liar he was, because she knew him well enough by now to know he'd never let any of these criminals roam free. If he had to let Edmond leave Luther's house to defuse this mess, he'd go after him again.

"No. I won't let her go, but if you are really careful, really obedient, when we lock you up, I won't shoot. It'll take a long time for you to get out. We'll collect our grandson and leave the area."

Edmond tightened his grip around her neck until she couldn't breathe. At odds with his violent treatment, he said,

"We'll be good to Ronnie. You have our word. You knew Delia." Edmond jerked at Penny's neck to make her realize he was talking to her. "She was a good woman, and we deserve credit for that. Ronnie will be treated well, and none of you gets hurt."

John looked at Penny, and she braced herself, preparing to shove at that gun.

It was time.

"Another Scott. Good." Florence came down the hall with a gun held steady in her hand.

John froze an instant before he'd've leapt at Edmond. He'd've gotten Penny shot, and himself, too. Now their chance was gone, and the odds were much worse.

Then Luther groaned and rolled to his side.

"I shot her brother coming in the kitchen window." Florence came down the hall from the side of the house where Cam had entered. "I heard what Edmond said. It's true. We just want the boy. Your brother is unconscious. He staggered into the hall, which made it easy to shove him into that locked closet right off the kitchen. My bullet won't kill him . . . if he's lucky." Florence moved closer until the hallway was clear. Her gun was aimed right at John's belly.

"Head down this hall." She gestured with her head. The gun didn't move. "You and Penny will go in there with Cam, and we'll ride away. Everyone lives."

John wasn't sure where Luther Payne came in, as far as killing witnesses. But Edmond and Florence might consider their promise of safety to be only for themselves. Whatever

Luther did wasn't their problem. Right now he was still out of the fight, but John didn't figure that would last long.

John started forward. Edmond tightened his grip on Penny's neck. She grabbed at the choking hold to loosen it—she needed air.

"I'm cooperating. If you strangle her, she can't walk." John's voice snapped, and he fought to remain calm so he could think clearly.

Edmond relaxed his hold by the tiniest bit, but it was enough. John saw her drag some air in.

John went ahead of Edmond and Florence.

"Hold up." Florence's cold voice froze him in place. She took his gun from the holster but didn't search him beyond that.

He had gotten most of his hideout weapons back from Cam, but he didn't dare use them. Not now. John's mind rabbited around, trying to be his usual smart, fast, and sneaky self. All his plans ended with Penny getting shot, probably himself, too. Cam left to bleed to death.

He walked ahead of them until he reached a door that stood open to see Cam, sprawled on the floor, bleeding from a bullet in his back, in a closet barely big enough for the three of them. He went in and knelt by his brother-in-law.

Cam lay facedown, unconscious. John reached for the wound just as Edmond shoved Penny forward hard enough that she fell over John's back.

He twisted and caught her before she hit the floor. The door slammed shut, plunging them into darkness.

Penny hissed, "I have my pack. Florence took our guns, but she didn't search the pack."

"I have come to love that bag you carry around." John

couldn't see, but he heard her rustling around. A few seconds later she struck a match.

In the dancing light, Cam's eyes flickered open.

Penny took one quick look at the blood, then jumped to her feet and turned to face the back of the closet. She found a stack of cloths on a shelf, grabbed a couple, and tossed them at John. "You bind up his wound, and I'll do everything else. This is a storage closet. I see a candle up there."

John went to work while Penny lit a candle.

Cam started to come to his senses. "Fl-Florence Chilton shot me."

"Yep," John said. "And Edmond got the drop on us."

"John knocked Luther out," Penny added. "We were so sure the danger came from him."

"I wouldn't count him out yet," John muttered.

"Save your strength, Cam. We're getting out of here soon."
Cam's eyes fell shut.

"I can't believe I let Edmond get the drop on me," Penny said. "I took him for a soft, spoiled layabout. I didn't think he had a dangerous side."

"Maybe the West has changed him. One thing for sure, this solves any dilemma I had about who gets Ronnie. I'll be his champion, protecting him from those two."

Penny glanced over her shoulder and said, "I've known you'd side with us almost from the beginning, but it's nice to hear you say it."

She added, "How fast do you think they'll leave? Then you can pick the lock and get us out of here."

"We're not waiting." John tore the towel into long strips and used them to stop the bleeding. "They might be right outside the door with a gun trained on it. But they probably think they have things under control and won't stand guard. If we wait too long, Luther will come around and get back in the fight. I bested him, but he didn't expect me. This time he'll be on guard. I hit him hard, though. He'll be addled for a while."

John finished tying off the wound. Then he looked at the bandage on his own arm. "Your brother and I match."

"I thought after I bandaged you up, I might be cured of fainting at the sight of blood, but nope."

"Let's go. Cam, can you get on your feet, or do you want to stay here and we'll come back for you?"

Cam gathered himself, got as far as his hands and knees, then collapsed again.

Penny gave him a long look, as if she was being torn in two. But she had to leave him. "Hang on, Cam. We'll get these fools under control and be back to get you to a doctor."

"Be careful, Penny. Both of you be careful." Cam's voice was no more than a whisper.

John was already working on the door. It wasn't a fancy lock. "Do you want me to lock it behind us?"

"No point. They've got the key." Cam tried again to stand and slumped flat on the floor.

⁌⁘⁙⁘⁌

A few seconds with that lockpick tool and Penny heard a low snick.

John opened the door a fraction of an inch, then looked back at her and nodded. "I can hear them talking back in the room where we left Luther. Have you got your pepperbox?"

The hallway was full of shadows. Night had finally fallen, and none of the lanterns along the wall had been lit.

Penny nodded, then produced another gun. "You take this. It's the match to your peashooter. It was in my bag. I've got the derringer. Let's go."

John smiled. "You're a handy woman to have along."

He pulled a gun from his boot and gave it to Cam. "Quiet now, and when we get in there, be mindful of Luther."

They inched down the hallway slow enough to hear the Chiltons.

"He's got a fortune in gold in his desk." Edmond's words were accompanied by the soft thud of bags, no doubt heavy with gold. "We tie him up and leave him here, then hit the trail for San Francisco."

"He'll come after us," Florence whined.

"He might." The thuds kept on.

How much gold was Edmond finding? "Maybe we should kill him. That'd stop him from hunting us."

"If we leave him tied up, the law will handle things."

"Maybe. But he was going to kill us, Florence. Are you so stupid you don't know that?"

Edmond had always been the weaker of the two. Somehow since the last time Penny had seen them, Edmond had grown a backbone. A crooked, evil one, but he had one.

"Leave him alive, Edmond. So far, we haven't done anything worth hanging over."

"You just shot Cameron Scott."

"He might live. If we run, neither Luther nor the law will come after us."

"All right." Edmond sounded disappointed. "Let's go. Did you get the key to the gate?"

A low groan told Penny that Luther was still only partly awake.

"Yes. It was in his pocket."

"We'll steal a couple of horses and be over the Sierra Nevadas by morning. We'll ride straight through to the coast and take a ship around South America. I think we should head for England, maybe Paris. Luther may dodge the hangman's noose, but he's still a man of the West. He won't want any part of Europe."

More thuds clinked. They sounded like the pouches of gold Raddo had in his saddlebags. "That's the last of it. We should swing by and nab Ronnie, so we can get his inheritance, but I don't want to stop in Philadelphia to claim it. Besides, that boy's bloodline is tainted. I'd've taken him in for the money, but I see no reason to worry over him now that we're rich."

Penny wanted to shove a fist into Edmond's nose. How could someone so vile talk about someone else having tainted bloodlines? She gripped her little gun tightly. She needed to get close to use this, and though she sure as certain didn't want to kill anyone, if she had to fire, she didn't want to miss.

Footsteps approached.

When they came near, John stepped into the doorway and said, "Drop your guns."

He stepped in and to the side. Penny came in right behind him, her eyes on Florence, the old witch who'd shot Cam, hounded Abe and Delia, and paid the Pinkertons to kidnap the grandson she'd always ignored. All for money.

She remembered Edmond and his new fierceness, but she could only look at Florence.

"Drop it right now!" John's voice cracked like a bullwhip.

Florence's gun hit the floor.

Penny hurried to get her hands on Florence's gun. And to get close enough that hers had some use.

Edmond's gun hand came up, and Penny leapt at Florence and drove her backward into her husband. The gun fired as the three of them went down in a heap.

Florence shrieked and clawed at Penny's face. Penny wrestled with the screaming woman, getting tangled in Florence's skirts, and a hank of her hair was pulled nearly out.

John was on Edmond. With those same wicked punches he'd used on Luther, John knocked Edmond out cold. Then he had Edmond facedown and tied up.

Penny wrenched away from Florence and fought her way out of the woman's billowing skirts.

Edmond was bound tight. John turned to truss up Florence but stopped.

Penny got to her knees and her eyes followed the line of his gaze to see a pool of blood forming beneath Florence.

Dropping beside her, John lay his hand flat on her chest. "She's dead." John rose to stand beside Penny. "Edmond shot her."

Penny turned away from the sickening sight, her head spinning. She spent a few seconds letting her belly settle and her narrowing vision clear. Then she stood on unsteady feet . . . to look right into the evil eyes of Luther Payne, standing with a gun leveled on them.

"You might've gotten the better of me once, but that's not enough to make me miss either of you."

Penny saw blood streaming from Luther's nose and upper lip, and she felt a wave of light-headedness. She averted her eyes and saw blood from Florence. It was all too much, and she pitched straight backward.

Luther pulled the trigger, but he missed and that gave John time to leap. The gun came around, but John was too close, too low.

Luther hadn't lost one bit of his strength and wicked skill. He dodged the impact, but that wrecked his aim and the bullet went wide.

John hit with his whole body, and Luther staggered back against a table with breakables on it. The table crashed over and glass shattered. Luther heaved himself up and was on top of John. Fists like iron crashed into John's face.

He saw double from the blow. Another fist hit, then another. John struck out, but he was losing strength. He was losing the fight. And soon he'd lose his life and Penny's along with it. Cam's too. What a disaster.

He was glad he'd sent Trace away.

In the ever-narrowing tunnel of his vision, a specter appeared, pale as a ghost. Then the ghoulish figure moved, raising an arm as if summoning all the ghosts of Luther's ugly past. The arm came down with a crash on Luther's skull.

Then another thud, and another. Penny. Not a ghost, just a woman who'd gone as pale as one from her unfortunate problem with the sight of blood.

She bent over Luther with . . . something, and slammed it across his back where he lay facedown on the floor. John looked in shock at how Luth was bleeding everywhere from the glass. In fact, bleeding too much.

There was no doubt Penny saw it too, but she continued her assault until John was able to grab her and rip the piece of broken table out of her hand. She'd gotten hold of a stout leg.

"Enough, stop, he's out. He's down. You got him." John

pulled Penny into his arms and hung on tight. "Thank you. You got him."

———❧———

Penny's head cleared gradually. She was only barely aware of flailing away on Luther. She didn't know what she'd whacked him with or where it had gone.

But she knew who held her.

John. Her husband. A city man who'd be a constant nuisance, but it didn't matter because she loved him. She even liked him. She really, finally, believed she knew him.

Right away, when they'd first met and those men had attacked them in that alley, John had offered, without speaking a word, to die for her.

Now he'd done it again.

The last thing she'd seen as she toppled over was John diving into the teeth of a firing gun. For her. To draw Luther's fire, to save Penny's life.

As her thoughts steadied, she thought of Cam. She had to get to Cam.

Then in a dizzying rush she thought of Florence clawing at her while she was already dying. She remembered how Raddo had hounded them after he'd massacred Abe's wagon train and killed her brother.

Now she had someone to hang on to, and it felt wonderful.

"We're going to figure out a way to stay married, Mrs. McCall." John's voice was almost shaky. He was a brave, tough man for a city feller, but now he needed someone to hang on to, too.

Penny held him for a long time, then finally she raised her head and smiled. "Yes, we are."

"I'm going to contact Mr. Pinkerton and ask if he'd be interested in starting a Pinkerton office in Carson City. We could live close to your family. I might have to travel some, but we'd figure it out. You'd lose your homestead, though."

"Maybe we can live just outside of town, and I can homestead out there and raise some cattle."

He kissed her. "And some children, huh?"

Smiling, Penny had an unpleasant thought. "What if Mr. Pinkerton says no?"

She loved the idea of being close to her brother and all the others she'd come to love out here in the High Sierras. But she wanted to be close to her husband more, and she'd follow where he led.

"Then you'll have to train me to be a rancher, or I'll see whether the Carson City sheriff needs a deputy. We'll figure out something. I like it out west. I honestly prefer a man who'd take his gun and aim it at you, to a lying, sneaky, backstabbing weasel like Florence Chilton."

"I'm not fond of either sort." Penny gathered herself to step away from him. "I wonder how long it'll take Trace to get back here with the sheriff."

John searched Florence and found the key to the front gate. "Let's make it easy for them to get in." John handed her the key. "I'll make sure everyone's tied up tight, then go check Cam, if you want to open the gate."

"That sounds good. You handle all the blood." Penny took the key while John picked up the guns and frisked Luther for hideout weapons.

As Penny left the room she heard John say conversationally, "Luther, we found the evidence Raddo left behind incriminating you. Your arm has a big old piece of glass in it, so

I'm going to tie a tourniquet around it. You'll probably lose it. But you'll live to stand trial. But not here, where you're a feared and powerful man. There are wanted posters from years ago along with a lot of other things. Penny and I are going to collect a big reward for you. And you, Luther Payne, if you live, are going to hang."

Luther's muffled snarling followed Penny out the front door.

Trace and the posse came riding in an hour later, and Cam and John went out to meet them. Penny kept her eyes averted from their bandages.

Epilogue

They got to Cam's house an hour after dawn and found the whole family there.

As Penny and the menfolk came riding in from Carson City, Gwen came out of the cabin with little Ronnie on her hip. She smiled and waved, then her eyes went to Cam's bandaged shoulder. The doctor had stitched it up and bandaged it, but Cam's sleeve was stained with blood.

Gwen's smile vanished, and she came running.

Deb was a step behind her, holding Maddie Sue's hand. Deb's shirt was hanging loose as her baby grew under her heart. Deb looked at everyone. Penny saw Deb register Cam's wound, then John's. The dried but disheveled clothes Penny and John wore. She assessed them, or Penny figured that was what was going on, then rested one hand on her belly and smiled at Trace.

Not a scratch on him.

Utah hailed them from the corral where he was unsaddling horses. Adam waved from the yard with Cam's cattle.

Penny and her company of champions dismounted and announced that all the bad guys were dead or in jail.

Gwen hugged Ronnie tight while they talked.

Then Adam and Utah joined the group, and they all trooped into the cabin for the breakfast Gwen and Deb were preparing. More eggs were broken. More biscuits baked. There was the sizzle of frying bacon.

Penny joined John, Cam, and Trace at the table and drank coffee while the others cooked. Even Utah and Adam helped with the meal by carrying water and milk, stoking the fire, and doing any lifting Deb and Gwen wanted.

"I'm so tired I could fall asleep right on this table." Penny sipped her coffee and hoped it revived her. Everyone was talking over each other as they filled the others in on what had gone on.

"The sheriff wired back east to ask about that wanted poster," John said. "Luther killed the son of an important man, and there's a big reward for that and a few other crimes Luther committed. There was a price on Raddo's head, too. We're going to split it four ways."

Cam said casually, "I haven't mentioned Ronnie is the heir to a fortune. We'll have to figure out how to manage all that."

"What?" Gwen looked at the little toddler.

They took turns explaining about the Chiltons and their greedy reasons for wanting the little boy back.

"And they charged Edmond with murder?"

"Yep, just because he didn't shoot who he intended to is no excuse—though he tried to say it was. He'll hang for Florence's death."

The breakfast was on the table by the time they were done with their story. Platters of eggs and bacon, biscuits, and fried potatoes vanished into hungry bellies. When they'd finished eating and the kitchen was clean and the coffeepot empty, John said, "I need everyone's attention, please."

Penny turned to him, wondering what he was up to.

"I've wired to ask Mr. Pinkerton if I can be an agent in Carson City. Whatever his answer, I'm moving to Nevada."

Then he turned those blue eyes on Penny. "Mrs. McCall?"

"Yes?"

"Will you marry me?"

"Again?"

The room dissolved into laughter.

"We finally have time to talk about that," Penny said. "Raddo dead. Luther captured. No more threat to Ronnie."

John heaved a sigh of satisfaction. "It's safe out here at last."

"Except for the hungry wolves," Cam said.

"And raging blizzards." Deb shivered.

"And the Ts'emekwes," Utah chimed in.

Silence swept through the room.

"The what?" Deb asked.

Trace shook his head. "We can discuss it later."

"There are rattlesnakes." Gwen gave Utah a worried look.

"And cliffs, don't forget cliffs." Adam stood by the dry sink, wiping a pot.

"Avalanches and forest fires." Trace took a deep pull on his coffee, not sounding all that worried.

"And the usual crowd of cattle rustlers and bandits." Penny nodded. "That all seems like a normal, quiet life after these last few months." She smiled at John. "We did already get married. Surely you remember. It wasn't that long ago."

John slid an arm around her waist and dragged her close.

"We went through a farce of a marriage ceremony neither of us wanted. Now I want to make a choice."

He kissed her soundly right there in front of everyone. "I love you, Penny. You're a woman I admire, respect, and want to kiss, day and night, for the rest of my life."

He rested his strong hands on her shoulders. "I know I skirt the law."

"Oh, you outright break it. Just admit it."

He grinned, then the smile faded, and he was very serious. "Arresting Luther Payne was badly needed. The whole town of Virginia City was next thing to terrorized by him. He broke the law without fear. He killed with no concern he'd be arrested. He was evil and stopping him was the right thing to do, even if I had to tell a few tall tales."

"Lies."

"And search a building."

"Breaking in."

He smiled and waited. Not for long.

"You know what, husband? I agree. What you did brought an evil man to justice. And the laws you skirted—"

He kissed her for that.

"You did no harm. I can be the wife of a Pinkerton agent." She hesitated, then took her courage in both hands. "I think I can *be* a Pinkerton agent. Do you think I can help you with your investigations?"

"Now, Penny, what about—"

She quickly put her hand over his mouth. "Maybe just now and then, until the children come."

She felt her husband squirm beneath her hand. She lifted her fingers away to let him talk.

"I do think you have a knack and certainly the courage. I

can teach you how to wear a disguise and act the part you're playing." He kissed her again. "So, Mrs. McCall, will you marry me, by choice, with a willing heart? And do it for the best of reasons, because we are in love and want to spend our lives together? And will you do it because you believe God will bless our union and smile down on the life we build?"

"I do love you. And I absolutely do want to spend my life with you. Yes, Mr. McCall, I will marry you."

"Do we need to find a real pastor? Should we say our vows in front of a preacher?"

Penny kissed him again. "The legalities are already settled, so we count these words shared between us as our vows. We count our family here as the wedding guests, and the breakfast we just ate as a fancy party to celebrate."

"Then so be it. I'll love, honor, and cherish you all of my life. I promise you that now, before God and man."

"And I will love, honor, and cherish you, too. And I'll obey you unless you ask me to do something really half-witted, considering I know more about the West than you do."

Nodding, John said, "That seems fair."

Gwen said from by the sink, "I now pronounce you man and wife."

The whole room erupted into applause and hugs and happiness.

Utah said, "I might take off for a week or two and try to rustle me up a wife, too. All this romance is makin' me itchy."

The laughter broke out again.

Adam said, "I'm almost tempted to go find my wife and see if she's as mean as I remember."

Penny looked at Adam, then shook her head and looked back at John.

"We can keep building cabins as long as the forest holds out," Trace stated.

"We're surrounded by deep, endless woods." Penny linked arms with John and hoped for the best for Utah. "That seems like a safe promise to make."

"Well, now that we're duly married, I'm exhausted." John's arms tightened around her waist. He whispered in her ear, "And I'd say that a honeymoon might be in order."

It was definitely time to get some rest. Or not.

Arm in arm, Penny and John left Cam's cabin for Penny's tent. Her cabin was now nearly finished. A cabin they'd probably never live in.

"Things aren't settled for me, Penny. Thank you for joining your life to mine without knowing what the future holds."

"It holds joy, John. And a marriage blessed by God. We'll find our way together."

And indeed they did, two people, nearly strangers, brought together forever, in a land where everyone needed a champion. And everyone needed to be a champion.

Together they had both of those things, because they had courage, faith, and true love.

About the Author

Mary Connealy writes romantic comedies about cowboys. She's the author of the KINCAID BRIDES, TROUBLE IN TEXAS, WILD AT HEART, and CIMARRON LEGACY series, as well as several other acclaimed series. Mary has been nominated for a Christy Award, was a finalist for a RITA Award, and is a two-time winner of the Carol Award. She lives on a ranch in eastern Nebraska with her very own romantic cowboy hero. They have four grown daughters—Joslyn, married to Matt; Wendy; Shelly, married to Aaron; and Katy, married to Max—and five precious grandchildren. Learn more about Mary and her books at:

maryconnealy.com
facebook.com/maryconnealy
seekerville.blogspot.com
petticoatsandpistols.com

Sign Up for Mary's Newsletter!

Keep up to date with Mary's latest news on book releases and events by signing up for her email list at maryconnealy.com.

More from Mary Connealy!

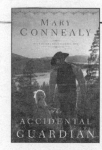

Trace Riley has been self-appointed guardian of the trail ever since his own wagon was attacked. When he finds the ruins of a wagon train, he offers shelter to survivor Deborah Harkness and the children she saved. Trace and Deborah grow close working to bring justice to the trail, but what will happen when the attackers return to silence the only witness?

The Accidental Guardian
HIGH SIERRA SWEETHEARTS #1

Also from Mary Connealy...

After Chance Boden is wounded in an avalanche, he demands that the conditions of his will go into effect: His children must either live and work at home for one year or forfeit the ranch. He trusts Heath Kincaid to see it done. But when Heath begins to suspect the accident was due to foul play, he finds his desire to protect Chance's daughter goes way beyond duty.

No Way Up
THE CIMARRON LEGACY #1

The Boden clan thought their troubles were over with the death of a dangerous enemy. But with new evidence on Cole's shooting, Justin can't deny that the plot to take their ranch was bigger than one man. While the doctor and his distractingly pretty assistant help Cole, Justin has to uncover the trail of a decades-old secret as danger closes in.

Long Time Gone
THE CIMARRON LEGACY #2

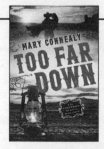

When an explosion at the mine kills workers and damages the CR Company, the Boden family is plunged deep into the heart of trouble yet again. As they try to identify the forces against them once and for all, Cole Boden finds himself caught between missing his time back in the east, and all that New Mexico offers—namely, his family and cowgirl Melanie Blake.

Too Far Down
THE CIMARRON LEGACY #3

BETHANYHOUSE

More Historical Fiction from Bethany House!

In 1900s Montana, Lizzy Brookstone's new role as manager of an all-female Wild West show is rewarding but difficult. However, trials of the heart and a mystery to be solved prove more daunting. As Lizzy and two other show members, costume maker Ella and sharpshooter Mary, try to discover how Mary's brother died, all three seek freedom in a world run by men.

When You Are Near by Tracie Peterson, BROOKSTONE BRIDES #1
traciepeterson.com

To escape an unwanted marriage, heiress Isadora Delafield flees New York. Disguising herself as a housekeeper, she finds a position at Glory Manor, the childhood home of self-made man Ian MacKenzie. Ian is unexpectedly charmed by Isadora and her unconventional ways, but when Isadora's secret is revealed, will they still have a chance at happily-ever-after?

Flights of Fancy by Jen Turano, AMERICAN HEIRESSES #1
jenturano.com

With a Mohawk mother and a French father in 1759 Montreal, Catherine Duval finds it easiest to remain neutral among warring sides. But when her British ex-fiancé, Samuel, is taken prisoner by her father, he claims to have information that could end the war. At last, she must choose whom to fight for. Is she willing to commit treason for the greater good?

Between Two Shores by Jocelyn Green
jocelyngreen.com

◆ BETHANYHOUSE